He reached out for her hand. Held it tightly. His hands were warm from holding his coffee cup. His touch was firm, yet gentle.

"You do not have to be afraid," he said. "I will not let him hurt you or Sophie or anyone else for that matter. I'm going to stop this bastard."

That scared Daisy. "He's got no moral compass, Blade. He won't fight fair."

"I had that pretty much figured out when you told us that he knocked you out of a chair."

Harsh. The words were harsh. And her body gave an involuntary flinch.

"He'll never get close enough to you again to do something like that. You have my word," he said.

Tears came to her eyes. Her grandmother hadn't been there to tell. Sophie had gotten the sanitized version, and even Jane had simply gotten bits and pieces. It was the first time she'd ever told anyone the whole ugly truth. Well, almost all the truth.

* * *

If you're on Twitter, tell us what you think of Harlequin Romantic Suspense! #harlequinromsuspense

P9-CNB-400

Dear Reader,

A Firefighter's Ultimate Duty is the first book of the three-book Heroes of the Pacific Northwest miniseries. I'm delighted to introduce you to Blade Savick, a firefighter-paramedic. Born and raised in coastal Knoware, Washington, he's a home-town kind of guy. His job gives him purpose, and when he's not working, he's either with his sixteen-year-old daughter, whom he co-parents along with his ex-wife, or hanging with his two best friends—hint: you'll meet these two again in books two and three.

But then Daisy Rambler arrives, and this newcomer and Blade suddenly have a shared purpose, both personally and professionally, which is complicated by the fact that she has her own sixteen-year-old daughter. Further complicating the situation are Daisy's past and the danger that seems to have followed her to Knoware.

First responders make really great book heroes because they're heroes in real life. I hope you enjoyed reading the book as much as I enjoyed writing it.

All my best,

Beverly

A FIREFIGHTER'S ULTIMATE DUTY

Beverly Long

HARLEQUIN®
ROMANTIC SUSPENSE™

Recycling programs
for this product may
not exist in your area.

ISBN-13: 978-1-335-75940-5

A Firefighter's Ultimate Duty

Copyright © 2021 by Beverly R. Long

This edition published by arrangement with Harlequin Books S.A.

For questions and comments about the quality of this book, please contact us at CustomerService@Harlequin.com.

Harlequin Enterprises ULC
22 Adelaide St. West, 40th Floor
Toronto, Ontario M5H 4E3, Canada
www.Harlequin.com

Printed in U.S.A.

Beverly Long enjoys the opportunity to write her own stories. She has both a bachelor's and master's degree in business and more than twenty years of experience as a human resources director. She considers her books to be a great success if they compel the reader to stay up way past their bedtime. Beverly loves to hear from readers. Visit beverlylong.com, or like her author fan page at Facebook.com/beverlylong.romance.

Books by Beverly Long

Harlequin Romantic Suspense

Heroes of the Pacific Northwest

A Firefighter's Utimate Duty

The Coltons of Roaring Springs

A Colton Target

Wingman Security

Power Play
Bodyguard Reunion
Snowbound Security
Protecting the Boss

Visit the Author Profile page at
Harlequin.com for more titles.

To all the first responders who demonstrate
such great courage.

Chapter 1

"Morning," Blade Savick said, shoving his backpack into his locker. He kept his winter jacket on. This February day, the thermometer was hovering at thirty degrees, and it didn't feel all that much warmer inside the fire station. "Heat not working?"

"Apparently not," Tony Baroque replied. His fellow firefighter-paramedic stood four lockers down, ready to end his most recent twenty-four-hour shift.

Blade heard something in his voice. "Busy night?" he asked.

"Just after midnight, there was a three-car crash at the intersection of Mill and Peyton. Six people, six transports. Two of the drivers required extrication and…it took too damn long. I really thought we might lose one or both of them."

Normally he'd have heard that on the scanner, but on

the nights that his daughter stayed, he'd agreed with his ex to turn the thing off. Everybody knew to call him on his cell if he was needed.

"Time is a tricky bastard," he said, letting Tony know that he understood. No doubt everybody at the scene would have been working as quickly as possible, but seconds turned into minutes way too fast when a victim was trapped. With that many casualties, Tony and the other paramedic on the shift would have had their hands full. The other firefighters on the team would have helped out as much as possible, but without the paramedic licensure, they were limited in offering care.

"Just after midnight? What the hell were three cars doing there all at the same time?" Blade asked, truly wondering.

His coworker looked up from buttoning his coat. "I assume one was lost, one had a death wish and the final one was late for curfew."

So one had been a teenager. That made Blade's gut twist. And whether Tony's assumptions about the drivers was correct or not, it was as good of an explanation as any as to the motivation needed to drive the outer bounds of Knoware, Washington, on a winter night.

Where's Knoware? It was their very own knock-knock joke. *No where, that's where.*

Spelled differently, pronounced the same, the joke generally got a big laugh from tourists and a small eye roll from hard-core locals. Those who were being polite, anyway.

Not that there were many tourists to be polite to right now. From April through October, they'd practically spill out of the bars and restaurants that lined Knoware's three-block business district, having consumed everything from fried pickles to freshly caught salmon. Off-season, like now in early February, the population went from 7,500 to 1,500 and locals had their pick of bar stools and restaurant tables, especially on nights like last night when the temperature uncharacteristically dropped under twenty degrees. However, stools generally stayed empty and silverware clean as most of the year-round residents needed little prompting to stay in.

Blade walked toward the door that separated the lockers and showers from the rest of the common areas. He opened it and walked into the kitchen. As he passed by the big scarred and scratched wooden table that could comfortably seat ten on mismatched wooden chairs, he snagged a doughnut from the box at the near end. He pulled a cup from the old oak cupboard that didn't hang exactly even. Might have been the cupboard's fault, or maybe the wall wasn't plumb.

The team inside the Knoware Fire Department didn't much care about things like that. Hell, they didn't even complain too much about the lack of heat.

What money they had to spend went toward equipment and training. They could make do with a building that wasn't perfect. As long as they had a working stove, refrigerator and a microwave, they were happy. A nice toaster that someone had donated was considered a real bonus.

He poured himself a cup of coffee. Drank it black. "Did you check on their conditions this morning?" he asked as Tony followed him into the kitchen. They had a good relationship with most of the folks at Bigelow Memorial, the small hospital that served Knoware and the surrounding six counties. There was generally a house supervisor who wouldn't break health privacy laws but would also provide enough information that a man might be able to sleep on his off-hours. If someone was manning the post who wasn't as forthcoming, he could always call his good friend Dr. Jamie Weathers who ran their emergency medicine program.

"I did," Tony said. "The two critical were stable enough to be airlifted onto Seattle General. The other four were admitted to Bigelow, all injuries non-life-threatening."

"Then it sounds as if you did good, man," Blade said.

"I guess." Tony pulled out a chair and reached for the doughnut box. "I should go home."

But Blade knew that he didn't really want to. Tony's mother-in-law had come to stay for a week, four weeks ago, and was still on his couch.

Blade technically no longer had a mother-in-law, not since the divorce four years earlier. But he had always liked Sheila's mom and was grateful that both she and Sheila were willing to work around his crazy schedule. He was generally on for twenty-four hours and off for forty-eight, but even that was up for grabs if somebody needed a sick day or was out on medical leave for a longer period. Sheila's flexibility made it possible that he could share custody of their sixteen-year-old daughter, Raven. Of course, his parents helped, too, but they had their own business to run so it was harder for them. "I—"

The blaring alarm interrupted him. He took another swig of coffee, feeling the burn, set his cup down and checked his watch. Five after nine. His day had begun.

In less than a minute, he had his flame-retardant pants on and was swinging his butt onto the seat of Engine 23 while he buttoned his coat. He gave Charlie, who was in charge and liked to drive, a thumbs-up. Within fifteen seconds, the remaining three of the five-person team were on board and the truck was moving.

"Male, in his sixties, fell approximately fifteen feet while attempting to climb Headstone Canyon. Unconscious but breathing." The description came through his radio. "Snagged a ledge on his way down. Approximately twenty feet up."

That last part made a bad situation even worse. He nodded at Parnell, the other paramedic on the shift, and knew the man was doing the same thing that he was. Mentally preparing for what they might encounter. Broken bones, almost certainly. Might be a severe head injury if the fall had knocked him out. And it would be a very difficult recovery for them to make. The road went only so far. They'd have to hike in the rest of the way, climb twenty feet, stabilize and immobilize the victim, and carry the man out.

"Glad I had that doughnut," he said.

He got a bark of laughter from Charlie as the man made a wide turn on Treaty Boulevard. From there, it was a one minute ride to the city limits and another eleven minutes to get to the end of the road. Now it was a half mile hike up a big sloping hill and then another mile down a narrow winding trail that would take them through the trees until they got to the base of the canyon.

There was only one other vehicle parked in the roadside lot—a make and model that might have cost close to what Blade's duplex had. So the climbers might have a few bucks. A lot of good that was doing them now.

Everybody piled out and grabbed equipment. By the time they were ready to go, one of Knoware's finest rolled up, lights flashing and siren blaring. Blade saw that it was his friend Marcus Price. The man got out of his car.

"Here, grab this," Blade said, giving him one end of an extension ladder.

"Good morning to you, too." Marcus shook his head in disgust but wasted no time, and they were off.

"You're touchy," Blade said as they humped it up the hill.

"Had a little breaking and entering at Gertie's last night."

Gertie Biscuit was the seventy-some-year-old proprietor of Gertie's Café, a thirty-seat spot where people who couldn't get a table had been known to eat their burgers standing up they were so good. "Gertie wasn't hurt?" Blade asked, concerned.

"Nope. Everybody had gone home. It happened sometime between midnight when they locked the door and five when they opened it again. Idiot must have used a damn sledgehammer to knock the doorjamb loose. They got away with some food and a little money."

"You'll get them." Knoware was a small community with limited police resources, but they weren't rinky-dink cops. Nobody was going to screw with Gertie and get away with it.

"Damn right," Marcus said.

They were at the top of the hill. It was a strenuous walk under any circumstances, and even more wearing his fifty-pound jump bag. Plus he had his end of the extension ladder. But he prepared every day for events like this, by putting in some serious cardio time and finishing off with weights.

Unfortunately, this was not the first time somebody had fallen while trying to climb Headstone Canyon. People left their ropes and picks at home and free soloed there frequently. And while it was only a hundred feet up, the hand- or footholds weren't plentiful. One had to know what one was doing. The place's real name wasn't even Headstone Canyon. It was Myrtle Canyon, named after a ring of trees at the far side. Rumor had it that in the late 1800s, a gang of thugs had hidden out in the canyon, and when they'd been pinned down, they'd tried to escape by climbing the wall. All of them had died and forever after that, the canyon had been known as Headstone.

At least their victim hadn't been alone. There had been somebody there to make the 911 call.

Blade looked over his shoulder at the rest of his team. Charlie, who was pushing fifty, and had put on an extra twenty pounds in his middle section, was red-faced and breathing heavily. "Okay?" he asked.

"Great," the man said, his eyes not meeting his teammate's.

Blade didn't push it. Charlie was his senior in the chain of command. But it concerned him that the physical aspects of the job might be getting to him. Right now, the team was able to make up for any shortcomings, but, unfortunately, they wouldn't be able to do that forever. Every person had to pull their own weight. Lives depended on it.

He started down through the swath of trees whose straggly branches reached at least ten feet over his head. Almost all were bare of leaves. But there were so many trees, it was difficult to see beyond them. Finally, the team came to the end. They were at the far side of the canyon. "There," Blade said, pointing across the way. About twenty feet in the air, on what appeared to be a narrow ledge, he could see a woman kneeling over a man's body. Her dark shoulder-length hair swirled around her face in the twenty mile an hour winds.

Maybe she heard them. Maybe sensed their arrival. But for whatever reason, she raised her face and turned to stare in their direction, and as crazy as it seemed, across the two hundred yards that still separated them, he swore he felt a pull. He motioned to Marcus to pick up the speed, and they reached the space under the pair yards ahead of the rest of his team.

"My name is Blade," he yelled. "I'm a paramedic-firefighter and we're going to help you. Are you injured?" he added, as the rest of the team arrived.

"No."

That was good. If they didn't need to devote too many resources to helping her to the ground, all the better for her injured climbing partner.

He and Marcus set up the ladder, extending it to a length that reached the ledge with about a foot extra. Once it felt secure, Marcus stepped back to make room for Blade and Parnell to start climbing.

Blade went first. When his head got over the top, he heard the woman sigh, as if in relief. He ignored that, choosing instead to look at the man on the ground.

Pale skin. Brown eyes that were open. He was conscious. Blade hadn't expected that. "Was he out for a while?" he asked without looking up. They would need to document the facts in their report.

There was no answer. He looked up at the woman. She was nodding.

She was strikingly pretty. The hair that had been blowing around was not just brown, but a rich chestnut with some lighter streaks of caramel. Her skin was very fair, her eyes very blue and her face was almost a perfect oval. The only thing not exactly right was the tip of her nose, which was red, evidence that she'd been out here in the wind for a bit. It was a stark contrast to the paleness of her lips, pressed so tightly that all color had been erased.

Worried. Likely for good reason. A fall was never a good thing. Losing consciousness could mean a concussion. Maybe a fractured skull. All kinds of bad possibilities.

"It's going to be fine," he said, feeling compelled to reassure her. He hoped it would be, anyway. Right now, his immediate concern was shifting her to make room for him and Parnell to work. The ledge was less than three feet wide and maybe seven to eight feet in length. This wasn't going to be easy. He would give Parnell the inside, next to the rock, and he'd take the outer edge.

Still holding the ladder, he motioned toward the man's feet. "I'm going to need you to move right there," he said. "Carefully."

She stood. Tall and lean, she moved easily. She got to the spot and stood.

"Take a seat," he said. Once she did that and he wasn't worried about another fall, he finished the climb, got off the ladder and quickly knelt next to the man, aware that his feet were now hanging off the ledge. He could hear Parnell moving, and soon his coworker was opposite him.

He gently ran his hands across the man's thinning gray hair. Yep, he already had a hell of a lump, just above his ear, on his left side.

"How long was he out? How long ago did he regain consciousness?" Blade asked.

"Out about five minutes. Came to about three minutes ago," she said.

Didn't mean the fall hadn't done some damage. He spared her one more look.

She didn't sound like a native of the northwest. Which

perhaps explained her clothing choices. She was dressed absolutely inappropriately for the day, and for climbing, in a light jacket and dress pants with some kind of silk scarf around her neck. She did have on some good-looking hiking boots and some leather gloves; both items looked brand-new.

What were these two doing out here on this miserable day? But that wasn't important now. What mattered now was assessing, treating and transporting to a higher level of care. He made eye contact with the man and repeated what he'd said to the woman just minutes before. "My name is Blade, and my partner Parnell and I are both licensed paramedics. We're going to take good care of you, sir. Can you tell me your name?" While he was talking, he reached for his jump bag. Equipment in hand, he started checking the man's vitals.

"Hosea Pratt. Pratt Sports Spot," he added.

Blade knew of the man and the company. Most everybody in this part of the state would. Pratt Sports Spot was one of the most successful sporting goods chains in the region. Outdoor enthusiasts flocked to Washington, and once here, they most certainly made their way to a Pratt Sports Spot. Hosea Pratt was more than an entrepreneur. He was a well-known philanthropist, and more than one recreational center had been built with his dollars. Blade was pretty sure that he'd also made some hefty contributions to Bigelow Memorial over the years.

That might pay off in spades right now. Get him a private room, maybe.

Blood pressure was a little high. No surprise. Pupils were responsive to light. Pulse was steady. Speech was not slurred. "You've got a bump on your head, sir. Can you tell me the day of the week and the month?"

"Friday. And February." The man's voice was terse. "My hip. You need to check my hip."

"We'll do that sir," Blade said calmly. "Tell me about your hip."

"I can't move my leg or get up. I'm in a hell of a lot of pain."

"On a scale of ten, with ten being the most pain you've ever had, what number are you at?" Blade asked.

"A damn twelve," Hosea said.

He could give him something to take the edge off. They were allowed to dispense certain narcotics under standing orders from Dr. Jamie Weathers. "Can't have that," he said. Again, he reached into his jump bag. "Any allergies to medicine?" he asked.

"No. Just hurry."

"Yes, sir." He quickly unzipped the man's coat, pulled his right arm out, rolled up his sleeve and stuck him with the prepared syringe.

Parnell had already fastened a cervical collar. Whatever damage was done, they didn't want to add to it by moving him without it. "We're going to strap you onto a stretcher, Mr. Pratt. And get you off this ledge. And then you'll be transported to Bigelow Memorial."

Parnell relayed the information to those on the ground and moved so that he could reach the stretcher that was being handed up.

"Daisy, you'll need to take the car back," Hosea said. "And tell Tom."

Their son, Blade thought. In all these years, you'd have thought that he'd have heard that Pratt was married to a knockout.

"Tom?" the woman asked, clearly puzzled.

Blade turned to look at her. Huh? Had she also hit her head?

"Tom Howards. COO," Hosea said. He was sounding a bit more relaxed, as if the pain medication was already doing its job.

"Of course," Daisy said. She pulled out her phone.

"Let's wait for notifications until we get to the ground, Mrs. Pratt," Blade said.

She jerked back so fast that for a second, he was concerned that she might tumble off the ledge.

"Careful," he said.

"We're not…um…married. He's my boss. My new boss. It's my first day."

"My real wife is going to be mad as a vegan alligator," Hosea said. "You're going to need to handle her, too. Get her number from my assistant."

The woman nodded, looking slightly ill.

Blade felt oddly satisfied that the two of them weren't married. But first day? That sucked. He really wanted the story about how they'd come to be here, but he and Parnell were gently rolling Mr. Pratt onto his noninjured side so they could slip the stretcher under him. Then rolling him back. Centering him as best they could without tugging or jerking.

"On my count," he said. "One, two, three." They lifted.

"Miss," he said, "you'll go down the ladder ahead of us. Feel steady enough to do that?"

She stared at him. Her eyes were so freakin' blue.

"If the alternative is spending the day here, I'm plenty steady," she said.

He suspected Hosea Pratt had made a good hire. She'd stayed calm, had summoned help quickly and had willingly accepted the tasks that Hosea had thrown in her direction. "What's your last name, Daisy?" he asked. He'd need it for the report, he told himself.

"Rambler. I'm Daisy Rambler."

He motioned for her to move toward the ladder. Which meant that she had to pass very close. At just the right time, he leaned forward and said softly, in a voice that only she could hear, "Hell of a new employee orientation. But you did good, Daisy. Don't forget about this when you ask for your first raise."

Chapter 2

Don't forget about this. Not much chance of that, Daisy thought as she negotiated the ladder on legs that were shakier than she wanted to admit. It might take a lifetime to forget the sight of her new boss falling and landing hard. At Hosea's insistence as they began their climb, she'd taken the lead and thus, had been above him. Had heard his trouble first, the scramble to find purchase on the craggy cliff, and by the time she'd been able to turn her head, he'd already been half sliding, half falling.

It had happened so fast. She'd quickly reversed directions and, upon reaching him, had thought he might be dead. It was surprising her own heart hadn't stopped at that point. But then she had realized that he was still breathing. Her medical expertise was limited to bandaging skinned knees and temperature taking. She'd called 911 and prayed help would come quickly.

And seeing the team emerge from the trees and race across the canyon floor had been one of the sweetest sights she'd ever seen. She'd…well, it sounded crazy, but her cold body had simply become infused with heat.

And when the paramedic had said that it was going to be fine, she'd believed him.

He'd been amazing. Calm. Polite. Efficient. From her inexperienced perspective, he'd gotten a whole lot done in a short amount of time without anybody feeling as if he might have been hurrying.

She needed to channel that now. Her to-do list was growing by the minute. Contact the COO. Contact Hosea's wife. Should she reverse the order? Hosea's first thought had been of his company, but didn't the wife deserve better than that? Then create an announcement for the employees. At least the company was privately held. No shareholders to reassure. Some sort of press release would have to be given to the media, however, because Hosea Pratt and Pratt Sports Spot were fixtures in this part of the country.

Even the new kid knew that.

Years from now, would she look back on this and laugh and say, *yeah, I really hit the ground running*? And then someone in the corner of the room, after hearing the story, would feel compelled to say, *great, your boss simply hit the ground*.

Oh, God. She was losing it.

Now, standing with the other firefighters and the police officer, she turned to watch Blade and the other paramedic carry Hosea down the ladder, making sure not to jostle the stretcher. It made her think that she felt rather jostled. With good reason. This morning's events aside, she'd been chasing a truck for two days. One that contained everything from her old life that she thought she was going to need in her new life.

And most everything that Sophie had, whether it was going to be needed or not, because her sixteen-year-old daughter hadn't been able to bear to leave anything behind. They'd moved grade school notebooks and soccer trophies from first grade. It had been ridiculous but hadn't been the fight she wanted to take on. Once the truck was packed, she and Sophie had cleaned their house in Denver before locking the door for the final time. Well, Daisy had cleaned. Sophie had mostly moved from room to room, wallowing in self-pity, wanting the world to know that she wasn't happy about moving.

Daisy hadn't been all that happy about moving, either. She'd loved living in Denver. But she also loved just plain living, and when she wasn't 100 percent sure that she could keep herself and Sophie safe, then it was time to do something.

The twenty-hour drive from Denver to Knoware had been accomplished over two grueling days. She and Sophie had arrived at a hotel outside of Knoware last night, and the moving van had already been parked in the lot. No sign of the movers; they were off the clock at that time of day.

The plan had been for Daisy and Sophie to meet them this morning and they would proceed to her new house, a rental that Jane, her friend of more than ten years, had assured her would be perfect. It was Jane, who'd moved to Knoware more than seven years ago, who'd told her about the job at Pratt Sports Spot.

Now, it was going to have to be Jane and Sophie who let the movers in because last night, an hour from

Knoware, her new boss had texted her indicating that he wanted to meet with her in the morning.

In her experience, one didn't say no to the CEO, especially if one wanted to keep one's new job. And she desperately needed this.

And while it was inconvenient and involved cajoling Sophie into getting up early, she hadn't been worried. After all, how could she have expected this? In the meetings she was used to, the most physical activity anyone expended was reaching for the coffee decanter in the middle of the table.

But then again, this was also her first time working as the marketing and public relations director for a sporting goods company. In that light, once she heard that Hosea intended for her to join him on his weekly climb, she'd tried to respond positively. Had walked down to the employee store and graciously accepted her new boots and gloves.

It had gone well for the first twenty minutes as they'd hiked in and started their climb. Hosea had waxed on about the need to understand and appreciate nature like their customers did. The need to live the brand.

That had been about the moment that Humpty Dumpty had fallen off his wall.

And while she'd sat beside his unconscious body, she'd envisioned the horrific conversation she'd have with Sophie that night.

How's was your day, Mom?

Great, honey. I met with my boss, the CEO, and now he's dead.

And she reasoned that her imagination really was going wild because in real life it would never happen that way. Yes, Hosea could have died. But no, Sophie would not have asked about Daisy's day. Sophie had stopped talking to her after Daisy had broken the news that they were moving. Well, mostly stopped talking. Every once in a while she'd stand at the top of the stairs and yell down.

"I'm going to hate it!"

In no particular order, Daisy had offered the following hollow platitudes.

"Perhaps you could give it a chance before you make up your mind. Jane says it's quiet in the off-season but that there's lots to do when the weather gets warmer. You've always loved visiting the coast. Maybe you can learn to surf. And Jane said the high school is small but has a great drama department."

Sophie had had some snarky response to everything but the very last one. Daisy knew that her kid loved plays. In Denver at her large high school, the competition for a speaking role was intense, and they'd both celebrated the two lines of dialogue in the role that Sophie snagged.

"Mr. Jones, thank you for waiting. Your table is ready." She'd said it with enthusiasm, likely more enthusiasm than any real hostess.

Definitely with more enthusiasm than she'd approached anything in real life in the three weeks between decision and execution of the move. Daisy had given up trying to convince Sophie that the new job would be good for both of them. She resorted to simply telling her that there was no choice. She'd not given her every detail but hopefully enough that Sophie understood the threat. Getting her to appreciate it and understand what they were doing was simply asking too much of a teenager who was scared to be the new kid.

Every day of silence and dirty looks, Daisy had told

herself that they'd get through this. Just like they'd gotten through everything else.

"What happens next?" she asked the man that others were calling Charlie.

"There's an ambulance already waiting for us in the parking lot. They'll be responsible for transporting him to Bigelow Memorial. You have transportation, miss?"

She held up the key fob that had been passed to her. The paramedics were off the ladder and already moving quickly toward the trees and the path that would take them up to where the ambulance waited.

She resisted the urge to run and catch up. Resisted the urge to stop the one who'd said his name was Blade. What was she going to tell him? It would all sound crazy. *Hey, I really appreciate the confidence that practically pours off you. It reminded me that I, too, am a pretty competent person and I can do this. I can start over. I can make a life for my daughter and myself. I can keep us safe.*

Yeah. He'd think she was an idiot.

She started walking toward her car at a much slower pace.

It wasn't yet noon, but Daisy had accomplished far more than she'd expected to on her first day. First she'd called Mrs. Pratt who'd taken the news pretty well, considering. Her exact words had been, "Oh, my God. He's such an old fool."

Then she notified Tom Howards, and the COO had hastily pulled together a leadership meeting. It had given Daisy the opportunity to meet the members of the senior team who had not been part of her interview process.

Everyone seemed very nice and they'd been particular eager to hear the details, with special attention to how

Hosea had acted postfall. Evidently, he'd been critical of others who hadn't taken adversity in stride. *Chin up.* That was generally the best you could expect from him.

By the time the meeting was concluding, they'd gotten their first update. Hosea had been examined. There was limited concern about his head injury, but he had fractured his hip. Surgery was already scheduled for that afternoon. There'd been agreement that she would write a memo to update employees, and a press release. To be reviewed by the COO prior to distribution because, after all, one can only trust the new person so much.

That had gone well enough. The COO had said both were good to go with nary an edit and finally, she had a spare minute to send two separate but identical texts. How did the morning go?

One to Jane, who could be counted on to provide details and some assurance that Daisy's personal life was not truly hanging in shambles while she dealt with the Hosea crisis. And the woman did just that with her return text that said, Furniture and boxes are all off the truck. Everything looks great in the house. I think you're going to be really happy with your choice.

The second text was to Sophie. The response came fast. The paint in my bathroom is disgusting.

Would it kill her kid to say one nice thing about the move?

Thanks for being there with Jane. We'll look at the paint tonight, she responded. She was the adult in the relationship. She had to take the high road.

After grabbing a tuna salad sandwich in the company cafeteria, she met with her team. Two copywriters, two graphic designers and one assistant. They reviewed the projects currently in play or anticipated within the next month or two. It was an impressive list ranging from product advertisements to philanthropic fundraisers to supporting a political lobbying effort in support of a local referendum to increase park funding.

Hosea Pratt had his fingers in lots of pies. That had been one of the things that had interested her when she interviewed for the job.

By the time she left for the afternoon, word had spread that Hosea was out of surgery. It had gone well. He was expected to be in the hospital for several days and then home recovering for four to eight weeks.

Now, driving home, she checked the map on her phone, which rested on the console. She'd gotten Jane's assurance that the house was in a nice neighborhood. Actually, Jane had laughed when Daisy had asked the question. Had responded that Knoware really wasn't big enough to have neighborhoods per se, not like Daisy was used to, but rather, there was a good and not-so-good side of town, defined by the railroad tracks that split them. Their new house was a Cape Cod on the good side. Two bedrooms, two baths, it would be perfect for her and Sophie.

She made the last turn and realized that she was holding her breath. She let it out. Jane hadn't steered her wrong. The houses were small but appeared well-maintained. The kind of houses and yards where there would be daffodils and tulips and newly potted plants on the porch in the spring. The kind of house where Sophie could have a friend over.

If she ever stopped scowling long enough to make a friend. *Sour attracts sour.* Her grandmother's words flashed in her head. She'd been full of goodies like that. But Daisy fervently hoped there was no truth in it. The idea of several Sophie-types lounging around her living room was very scary.

It had been her grandmother's death that had left her bereft but yet free to leave Denver and all its trappings behind. Her mother had been her grandmother's only child just as Daisy had been her mother's only child. And it would have been a nicer story had it been the three of them against the world. But her mother and her grandmother had been estranged at her mom's insistence.

Daisy and her mom had not been a formidable force. Alcohol and pills and an assortment of male friends who sometimes stayed a short time and sometimes as long as a few years made that impossible. Daisy had lived with few rules and limited attention and might well have been headed down the same path.

But then, it seemed as if everything changed in an instant when she saw the positive reading on the pregnancy test one September morning. It was her senior year in high school. And she was having a baby.

She needed to get her act together.

And she'd been doing her best ever since.

There'd been rocky patches. Her mother's death when she was just four months along. Losing the only home, such as it was, that she'd ever known.

But there'd been great gifts, too. Her grandmother had swooped in and given Daisy a new home. One filled with love. She'd taught Daisy how to care for a newborn. Then had pitched in with free babysitting so that Daisy could get her GED and attend college. Her grandmother and five-year-old Sophie had been in the audience the day she'd walked across the stage to get her bachelor's degree.

Denver had been Nana Jo's home for her entire life. There had been no way that she was leaving it. And no way that Daisy was leaving her when the tables turned and Nana Jo had no longer been able to live alone.

But now, everything was different.

"Home sweet home," she whispered, pulling into the driveway. It did look rather sweet.

The very best part was that Jacob Posse was far, far away. And hopefully, if she was out of sight, she'd be out of mind. There'd be no more unsigned cards or gifts in the mail. No more random postings on social media that made it seem as if they were still together. No more insistence to anyone who would listen that the wedding was *in the works*.

She'd escaped a bullet or worse when she'd broken her engagement to Jacob. She wouldn't make that mistake again.

Chapter 3

Blade had a silk scarf in his pants pocket, and he wasn't at all sure what to do about it.

It belonged to her, to Daisy Rambler. When he and Parnell had carried Hosea Pratt out of the canyon, the ambulance from Bigelow Memorial Hospital had been waiting for them. They'd transferred Mr. Pratt from the stretcher into the ambulance, and there'd been a few minutes of information exchange between Blade and Parnell and the paramedics who were taking over responsibility while Mr. Pratt was in transit.

When that had finished, he'd turned around, expecting to see her. He realized that she'd reached her vehicle, started it, and he hadn't noticed. But there, on the ground, was her silk scarf. Marcus had been there, too, and had reached for it, as well. Blade had lunged over him, picked it up as casually as he could, put it in his pocket and hadn't said a word. Marcus had given him a funny look, and Blade had been sure that he'd been about to say something. But he'd checked himself for some reason, and Blade considered that a small miracle.

There was a procedure for turning in property to the Lost and Found.

But he wasn't following it.

And for most of the day and night, in between a kitchen fire, a cardiac arrest, a fall off a curb and a domestic disturbance where the husband ended up with a bottle cut to the head, he'd ignored it. But now that it was morning and he was almost done with his shift, he was facing it squarely. He hadn't turned the scarf in because he had a hankering to track down Daisy Rambler and return her scarf in person.

It was the neighborly thing to do. She was obviously new to Knoware.

His cell phone rang. "Hey, Marcus," he said.

"What's going on?"

"Not much. Getting ready to leave."

"Hey, what did you ever do with that woman's scarf?"

It had been unrealistic to hope he'd forget. The man had a memory like an elephant. Blade considered lying to him, but unfortunately that was a no-go. They'd been friends for too long. "I'm going to return it to her."

"How? Do you know where she lives?"

"It's Knoware. How hard can it be?"

"Still a hassle," Marcus said. "Just turn it in. Or better yet, give it to Sheila for a Christmas gift next year."

Marcus was never going to understand how he could still be friendly toward his ex after what she'd done. "I have to go," Blade said.

"You're into her," Marcus said.

"Of course not," Blade denied. "She's obviously new to town. Maybe I can…hell, I don't know. Maybe she'd like to know the best place to buy a loaf of bread or a carton of milk."

Marcus laughed so loud and so long that Blade truly did consider hanging up on him.

"You want…you want to help her with her grocery shopping?" Marcus asked, once he had his breath back. "I saw her. I was there, remember. I know I wasn't thinking about whether beef tips were on sale at Merritt's Market."

"Goodbye, Marcus."

"No, wait. What was her name?"

He could pretend he didn't know, but it wouldn't take Marcus long to track down the report from the 911 call. "Daisy Rambler."

"Okay. Meet me for breakfast at Gertie's."

He could say no. But he was hungry, he liked supporting Gertie's during the off-season when sales were down and there was no place else he had to be on that particular Saturday morning. It was Raven's weekend with her mom. "Twenty minutes," he said and hung up.

Eighteen minutes later, he walked into Gertie's. Greeted folks he knew, which was almost everybody, and slid into the booth opposite Marcus, who was not in uniform. Instead, he had on dark blue jeans that looked brand-new and a blue-and-white button-down. He was dipping a tea bag into a stainless-steel pot.

There were two other cups on the table, already filled with coffee. "I assume one is mine," he said.

Marcus nodded. "And the other is his," he said, pointing over Blade's shoulder.

Jamie Weathers walked in, wearing a faded blue knee-length lab coat over an old polo shirt and worn jeans. He sat down and immediately reached for the creamers at the end of the table.

"Can I see it?" Jamie asked, after his first sip. "The magic scarf."

Blade rolled his eyes and continued to drink his coffee. That answered the question of whether Marcus had filled Jamie in. He was grateful when Cheryl came up to take their order. Everybody greeted her warmly. The four of them had all been in the same graduating class. Now she had four kids and said her shifts at Gertie's saved her sanity.

"Got it," she said, once they'd all ordered.

Alone again, Marcus slid a piece of paper across the table. Blade picked it up. It was an address.

"That's her," Marcus said.

"How did you get this?"

It was his turn to roll his eyes. "I have resources at my disposal that you don't. And I used to date a woman who works at the electric company. Service was started in her name yesterday. No other name on the account."

"Probably not married, then," Jamie said.

"Could be living with someone," Marcus countered.

"Shut up, both of you," Blade said. "The woman dropped her scarf. It seems like a nice scarf. I think she'd like to have it back."

"Of course," Marcus said. "When you're telling her where to buy her bread and milk, you might want to mention blue jeans. What she was wearing yesterday was not cool. Although, to be fair, she did look damn good in it."

She had. And maybe that was all this was. Physical attraction. With his daughter at his house on most of his off days, his romances were few and far between. But since his divorce four years ago, he'd been mostly okay with that.

"I think it is unfair that the two of you have a head start on me with this," Jamie said.

"It *was* terribly inconsiderate of Mr. Pratt to not be more injured so that you could have been summoned," Blade said. "I think he's still in the hospital. Perhaps you could sneak in and put air in an IV line just to get your revenge."

Jamie shook his head. "Air in an IV. So pedestrian. I'd—"

Marcus held up a hand. "Stop. I'm an officer of the law. I cannot hear these things."

Cheryl picked that moment to deliver food, and they all dug in. As he chewed, Blade reflected on the likelihood that Marcus, Jamie and him, friends since first grade at Knoware Elementary, would end up back here. He'd been the only one who'd never left. The only one who'd married. Only one with a child. Only one divorced after his wife had found someone with a bigger bank account.

Jamie had left right after high school. Brilliant, he'd sailed through college, medical school and residency. And he wasn't just book smart. He was good at everything. Kicking a soccer ball. Playing the sax. Flying his own small plane. Everybody assumed he'd end up at some prestigious teaching hospital. But he'd surprised them all when he'd enlisted and did a stint as an army doc. He'd been back in Knoware for only a year and was already running the Bigelow Emergency Department.

Postcollege, Marcus had participated in a domestic version of war, doing more than ten years with the Los Angeles Police Department. He'd been shot, knifed and once, during a domestic dispute, almost run over by a car. He'd always had catlike reflexes, which had probably saved his life on several occasions. He also had nerves of steel and significant brute strength, and Blade generally pitied the idiots who were fooled by his good manners and nice clothes.

"How's the party planning coming?" Jamie asked, reaching for the jelly at the end of the table.

"Not that great," Blade said, not looking up from his plate. Five weeks ago, he'd been told that he was the cochair of the Spring Spectacular, a dance to benefit the fire department. He'd managed to avoid that bullet in previous years, so now there was no getting out of it. Unfortunately, he was a cochair without a co. "We still don't have a corporate sponsor, so I've pretty much just been winging it." For years, one of the tech companies had stepped up, and there had been a thought that they would again. But at the last minute, new leadership had pulled the plug. "It's getting pretty late in the game. The event is in three weeks."

"I can put some pressure on the hospital," Jamie said.

The hospital had its own fundraising events. It wasn't likely.

"The woman I'm dating is a director at the bank," Marcus said.

Blade shook his head. "You'll have broken up with her by the event and that will be awkward."

Marcus shrugged. "True. But we'll still be friends."

That was also probably true. "People above my pay grade are working on it. I've been told not to worry."

"But you are," Marcus said, not sounding a bit sympathetic.

There weren't a lot of social events in Knoware during the off-season. As a result, the event was usually well-attended. If it was a mess, it would not reflect well on him but, more importantly, donations would be down and damn it, they needed that money. "Tickets are on sale, but I just heard that sales are slow."

Jamie pushed his finished plate away. "Chin up, old man."

He'd turned thirty-six three weeks ago. Jamie and Marcus were four months younger.

Jamie took one last sip of coffee and threw money down to cover his meal. "I've got paperwork calling my name."

"I'm on nights," Marcus said. "My bed is calling."

That left just Blade.

His two friends looked at him expectantly. He held up the slip of paper that Marcus had given him. "I'm going to work on my scout badges and return some lost property."

Marcus and Jamie gave each other a high five. "We'll be expecting a full report," Marcus said.

Blade tossed money down. He was trying to tamp his own expectations. But he couldn't help being a little excited about the idea of seeing pretty Daisy Rambler again. There was no way that he was letting Marcus or Jamie know that.

"I'll get that report in the mail," Blade said. "You should get it…yeah, I'd say right about as hell is freezing over."

Daisy woke up in her new house on Saturday morning when she heard a noise in her kitchen. A clang, perhaps. She listened. A knock. She was pretty sure that was a cupboard door. She sniffed. She was confident that was coffee. She reached for her phone to check the time. Eight thirty. Much later than she usually slept, even on the weekend. Much earlier than Sophie ever voluntarily got up.

Daisy swung her legs over the side of the bed. The wood floor was cold. She'd need to buy a rug. But other than a few touches here and there, the Cape Cod was really perfect for them. It had a living room and eat-in kitchen on the first floor, as well as her bedroom and a bath. There was a big two-story deck on the back side on the house, accessible by the back door in the kitchen and the slider in Sophie's upstairs bedroom. Sophie also had a bath upstairs.

It was nine steps to the kitchen. Daisy smiled when she saw her friend Jane frowning at a mixing bowl. There was an open carton of eggs and a gallon of milk next to her.

"I lost count," Jane said. The woman had spent the night on the couch after she and Daisy had finished the last of the wine they'd drunk to celebrate Daisy's new digs.

Daisy hugged her. "What are you doing?"

"Making breakfast. But I'm warning you. I'm just not that good of a cook."

"I don't care. It's about the nicest thing anyone has done for me in a long time," Daisy said. She poured a cup of coffee. "What are we having?"

Jane looked at the clock and shook her head. "You and Sophie are having French toast and sausage, and I…well, I'm going to have to run. We're prepping witnesses for this huge trial that's starting on Monday. Biggest trial of my career." She picked up a fork and started furiously mixing whatever was in the bowl.

The noise echoed in Daisy's already throbbing head. She wasn't much of drinker, and last night she'd been way over her limit. "Have you seen Sophie yet?"

Jane shook her head. "Today will be a better day," she said. She'd been a witness to Sophie's silent treatment the night before. The slam of the door after Daisy had made her once again surrender her cell phone. It was one of the many privileges that Sophie had lost recently. She'd gotten it back just temporarily yesterday in case there was an emergency during the move. "I hope so. The quiet is excruciating." She stopped. "You know, when she was four and talked nonstop, I could never picture myself saying that."

"Things will be good for you here. For both of you. Maybe you'll even meet…"

"I'm not looking," Daisy said.

"You made a mistake with Jacob Posse. You can't swear off men forever."

"Yes, actually I—" Daisy stopped when her doorbell rang. She was not expecting anybody. But perhaps it was her new landlord, stopping by to say hello. She went to the door and looked through the peephole.

"Who is it?" Jane asked.

Daisy whirled around. "It's…it's the paramedic from yesterday." Over her third glass of wine, she'd given Jane the bare bones version of the story. When she mentioned the name Blade, Jane had jumped in. And fanned herself with a dirty paper plate, saying, "That would be Blade Savick. He is *so* hot."

And maybe it had been the wine. "Married?" she had asked.

"Divorced, several years ago."

And then maybe it had been the comfort of knowing

that there was more than a thousand miles between her and Jacob. Whatever it was, for just a minute, Daisy had enjoyed a moment of wondering *what if.*

But now that it was morning and she was mostly sober, the whole idea scared the hell out of her. "What's he doing here?" she whispered.

"I don't know," Jane said, smiling. "But why don't you open the door and find out."

The doorbell rang again. She hadn't even brushed her teeth yet or combed her hair. But she couldn't just keep standing here. She opened the door.

"Hey," he said.

"Hey."

"Uh... Blade Savick. We...uh...met yesterday. I mean, I don't have any of my gear on. I wanted to make sure you recognized me."

He was talking fast and she realized that he might be nervous. "I recognize you." He looked very handsome in his brown bomber jacket, blue jeans and boots.

"I found this," he said, pulling something from his pocket.

It was her scarf. She'd realized at some point during the day before that she no longer had it. "I thought it was just one more casualty of the day," she said. "It's...very thoughtful of you to bring it by."

He was staring over her shoulder. "Hi," he said to Jane.

"Good morning. I'm Jane. Your friend Marcus Price used to date a paralegal in my office."

"Kelsie?" he asked.

Jane nodded.

"Nice woman. And really good in fantasy football. She kicked my...behind."

"I'll make sure she knows her reputation lives on.

Anyway," she said, looking at Daisy now, "I'm just leaving. I'll run up and say good morning to Sophie before I go."

Daisy nodded at her friend and turned to look at Blade. He was still standing on her porch. "Would you like to come in?"

"Sure. Who's Sophie?"

"My sixteen-year-old daughter."

He jerked back. "I have a sixteen-year-old daughter."

What were the chances of that? "Is yours talking to you?" she asked, then immediately regretted her impulsiveness. "Mine hasn't since I told her we were moving to Knoware," she said, knowing she needed to offer some explanation.

He shrugged. "Change is hard. Especially on kids. They—"

"Daisy."

Jane was halfway down the stairs. And the look on her friend's face scared her. "What?"

"Sophie isn't here."

That was crazy. Of course her daughter was upstairs. Where else could she be? There was no basement. She ran upstairs. Bed had been slept in, but it was now empty with the covers tossed carelessly aside. She ran across the hall to check the bathroom. Not even a dirty towel on the floor. Sink was dry.

Back in the bedroom, she tore open the closet door. At least half of Sophie's clothes were gone as was her red suitcase.

Her legs feeling heavy, as if she was dragging weights, she walked over to the sliding glass door. Last night it had been locked. She'd checked it when she'd looked in on Sophie just before finally going to bed.

She reached for the handle, knowing what she was going to find. Sure enough. It slid open without a sound.

Daisy ran outside onto the wooden deck and down the steps. Heedless that she was barefoot, she then ran across the cold brittle grass in her backyard and opened the door of the one-car garage behind their house.

Her car was gone.

And she felt as if she might faint. And maybe she swayed. But then there was a strong arm cupping her elbow.

"Steady," Blade said.

"She's gone," she said. "She took the car and she's... oh, God, my daughter has run away."

Chapter 4

"Where would she go? Does she have friends who would help her? Access to money? If not, where could—"

"Stop," Daisy yelled, putting her hands over her ears. She could not think. Could not breathe. Certainly couldn't answer Blade Savick's rapid questioning.

"Okay," he said, both palms in the air. "I'm sorry."

She put a hand to her forehead. "No, I'm sorry." He was a firefighter, no doubt trained to spring into action immediately. "I just need a minute," she added. For her head to catch up to her heart, which was racing in her chest.

He'd asked where Sophie would go. That answer was maybe the easiest. "She's on her way back to Denver. She was unhappy about the move."

"Okay, good," he said. "You can probably trace her cell phone."

She shook her head. "Long story but no cell phone right now."

"GPS in your vehicle?" he asked.

She nodded.

"You think she could find her way back to Denver with just that?" Blade asked.

"She can also read a paper map." Daisy had made sure of that years ago. "There's one in the car. And we just made the drive a couple days ago."

"Oh, honey," Jane said, putting an arm around Daisy and squeezing her tight. "Let's go back inside."

She let her friend lead her back to the warm kitchen where minutes ago everything had seemed wonderful. When Jane pulled out a chair for her, she sank into it.

"Would she have much money on her?" Jane asked.

"No. Probably less than a hundred dollars. Most of what she earned working part-time at the bakery was spent at the mall down the block."

"Credit card?" Blade asked.

He might give his sixteen-year-old daughter a credit card, but that wasn't her mode of parenting. "No."

"You may want to check your cards," he said.

No way. Sophie would never take her credit card without permission. But then again, she'd never have thought that she'd have taken the car and stolen away in the middle of the night, either. She grabbed her purse off the kitchen counter, and it took her just seconds to verify what Blade had seemed to know.

"My Visa is gone," she said. "I can't believe this."

"It's good news," he said. "Something to track."

He was right. Her laptop was at the other end of the table. She reached for it and within seconds had the website pulled up. She entered her password and went to pending transactions. There were three. Two for gas: $63.21 in Olympia, Washington, and $65.09 in Spokane, Washington. One for $6.19 at McDonald's in Ellensburg, Washington. She stared at the information. Then suddenly grabbed for her purse a second time and dug for her receipts. Spread them out on the table. "The first stop was in Olympia for gas. The second stop at McDonald's was in Ellensburg, Washington. The third stop was for gas in Spokane, Washington. We stopped at all those places coming here. I think she's doing our trip, just in reverse order."

"How would she remember that?" Blade asked, his tone questioning.

"She doesn't have to," Daisy said. "It's all written down. I keep a trip log. I track all my stops. I've been doing it since I was a kid, traveling with my mom. It's always in the console of my vehicle. Sophie never seemed to be paying attention to what I was doing," she added dully.

Her kid had fooled her. It wasn't a good feeling.

"She has your trip log and you have your receipts. You both know her next stop," Jane said, her lawyer mind working fast.

She guessed that was right. She lined up her receipts in order. Picked up the right one. "Her next stop will be just east of Missoula, Montana."

"What time do you think she got on the road?" Blade asked.

Daisy looked at her computer. "She got gas in Olympia just after four this morning. That means she probably left here around three."

"We were up until one," Jane said.

Daisy could just imagine how frustrated Sophie must

have been. She'd been planning her escape and it had likely seemed to her that her mother and Jane were never going to go to sleep. "She probably waited to make sure we were going to stay asleep," she said.

"Maybe she slept some herself," Blade said.

"I hope so." Otherwise, her daughter was going to be a very tired driver. And tired drivers made mistakes.

"I should call the police," she said. "Right? That's what I should do?" They could intercept Sophie. "They can be waiting for her at the gas station."

"Maybe," Jane said. "I'm not certain how that's going to go," she added, her voice tentative.

Daisy sighed. She knew what her friend was trying to tell her. The police could intervene without incident. Sophie was just five-three and 110 pounds. But what about afterward when Sophie was back here and they both had to live with the fact that their relationship had deteriorated to the point where police intervention was required?

Jane held up her keys. "Let's you and I go. We can do this."

"We'll be chasing her all the way to Denver," Daisy said, verbalizing her earlier realization. "If she left at three, she's already almost six hours ahead of us."

"I'll drive fast. She'll still get there a few hours ahead of us. But we'll find her and we'll figure out a way to fix this and then come back here," Jane said.

Daisy really loved her friend. "You can't do that. You're prepping witnesses for a big trial. The biggest of your career."

"I don't care about that," Jane said.

"I do. I'll rent a car and go myself."

"And be back to your new job by Monday?" Jane asked. "There's no way."

And new employees who worked one day but unexpectedly couldn't come back to work generally didn't keep those new jobs very long. She felt a pain in her stomach. She'd worked really hard to get this job. To get this new chance for her and Sophie. But finding her daughter was the most important thing.

"Maybe I can help," Blade said. He'd been quietly listening to her and Jane. But she hadn't forgotten that he was there. His physical presence loomed large in her small kitchen.

"My friend has a plane. If he's available, I think he'd be happy to help us. We identify the airport closest to Missoula, Montana. Once we land, we rent a car. Then we're in position to intercept your daughter when she stops for gas."

"But…" Daisy stopped. It could work. The police would not need to be involved. She wouldn't have to chase her daughter all the way back to Denver. Sophie would be safe. "I can't ask you to do that."

"You didn't ask. I offered."

"Why?" she asked. She wasn't used to getting a whole lot of help.

"I've got a sixteen-year-old daughter. I think I've got some idea of how you're feeling right now."

Daisy hated owing anybody anything. But Sophie's safety was on the line. She was a good driver but inexperienced.

"It's a good idea," Jane said.

Jane had known of this man. She wouldn't say it was a good idea if she didn't think he was trustworthy. "If you're sure," Daisy said, looking at him.

He pulled his cell phone from his shirt pocket. "I'm calling my friend now." He walked into the living room.

"Oh, honey," Jane said. "I wish I could make this better."

"We'll get through it," Daisy said. How many times had she said that over the past few weeks?

Blade was back. "I got us a ride. He's going to meet us at Rainbow Field."

She picked up her purse. Took four steps toward the door. Stopped when he held up a hand. "You might want to get a coat. It's cold outside."

Her daughter was out there, somewhere, in the cold. But maybe she could take a minute to put on jeans and a sweater and brush her teeth and hair.

She did all that in less than five minutes. Then she put on her coat and a pair of short flat-heeled boots.

"I'll lock up your house," Jane said. "Call me *when* you find her."

Daisy appreciated Jane's attempt to stay positive. She needed to do the same. "When," she repeated.

He'd returned a scarf, albeit with an ulterior motive, and ended up in the middle of a family drama. But the look in Daisy's pretty blue eyes when she'd realized that her daughter had booted it out of town had scared him. He'd seriously been worried that he was going to be picking her up off the ground. But she'd rallied. Even the realization that her kid had stolen her credit card had been taken in stride.

It was a stroke of luck that the kid was following their previous route. Without cell phone navigation to guide her, Blade figured that likely made the kid feel safe and on target.

He'd been supergrateful when Jamie had confirmed that he could leave the paperwork behind. Knowing his killer schedule, Blade had drilled him on whether he truly had the time. His friend had brushed off the concern. *Are you kidding, this is my chance to meet the elusive Scarf Woman.* And for just a second, Blade had hesitated. But the need to help Daisy, and his inherent belief that Jamie would never step over a friend, had him quickly accepting the help. Now they were less than ten minutes from the airfield.

"Our pilot is Jamie Weathers," Blade said. "He's been my friend since grade school."

"Is he a firefighter?" she asked.

"No. Physician. Intellectually superior to most of us and a born fixer. Wants to fix everything. Bodies. Situations. Relationships. If your boss had been more seriously injured from his fall yesterday, you might have met him. He's a flight doc, does emergency medicine in the field."

"I'm so grateful that we didn't need him," she said. "It was—"

Her cell phone buzzed and she snatched it up. Studied the screen. Let out a sigh.

"Not your daughter?" he guessed.

"No," she said, shaking her head. "My boss, actually. Maybe we conjured him up with our conversation. Anyway, he's awake and apparently ready for some work."

"It's Saturday," he said.

"I'm not sure that makes a difference to him. He wants a follow-up note sent to all employees."

"Just tell him what is going on. I'm sure he'll give you a pass."

She gave him a look. "That's the last thing I need is for people at my new job to realize that my home life is falling apart. No pun intended. You know, falling." She closed her eyes. "Can't believe I'm making jokes at a time like this."

"Stress relief," he said. "But unless you pushed your boss, I don't see how any part of yesterday was your fault."

She smiled, maybe for the first time that morning. "I didn't push him, but for the few minutes that I was alone with him on that ledge, I wanted to clobber him. Which isn't that nice considering he was unconscious for part of the time."

"Is this something that Hosea Pratt does with all new employees?" He turned into the airfield gate and drove down the long lane surrounded by green grass on both sides. There was no control tower at Rainbow Field. Just one large hangar filled with small planes and one runway to take off and land on.

"I don't know." She looked around. "It's pretty quiet out here."

"It's quiet everywhere in Knoware this time of year. Wait until tourist season."

"Maybe we'll still be here," she said, her voice heavy with contemplation.

"Why wouldn't you be?" he asked.

"I need to work. I need to get Sophie settled down and settled in somewhere. If I can't manage both of those things, I'll need to do…" Her voice trailed off.

"What?" he asked.

"Something," she finished. "Is that your friend?" she asked, pointing to the left.

"Yeah, that's him." Jamie was walking around his small plane, doing a visual inspection.

Blade turned into the parking lot. There were seven other vehicles already there. He parked, and Daisy had her door open before he shut the vehicle off. He understood. There was no time to waste.

Jamie looked up as they approached. He was wearing sunglasses so Blade was not able to see his eyes. And he was doing a great job of keeping his face expression free.

"Jamie Weathers, this is Daisy Rambler. Daisy, Jamie." In his line of work, one learned to be quick with the introductions.

"Thank you for taking us," Daisy said. She extended her hand toward Jamie.

"My pleasure," Jamie said. "I'm sorry for the bad circumstances and all that."

"I appreciate that," Daisy said.

"I'm ready if you are," Jamie said. He opened the door of the plane and then stepped back, allowing Blade to assist Daisy into the four-seater. While she was getting settled into a seat in the second row, he turned to Blade.

"Nice," he said quietly. "I'm surprised Marcus gave up so easily."

Blade was simply grateful that he had. They hadn't fought over a girl since they were fifteen, and he didn't want to start now. "What's the flight plan?" he asked.

"Straight east, 468 miles, give or take a couple," Jamie said. "Winds are light, weather is clear." He looked at his watch. "It's 9:40. Trip will take a little more than two hours. I think you could be on the ground and close to the gas station you're going to by noon."

"By noon?" Daisy asked. She'd gotten settled in her seat and had evidently heard at least the last portion of their conversation.

"Will that work?" Jamie asked.

She picked up her smartphone. "The stop is roughly ten hours from our new house. If she left at three this morning, that means that she'll be there about one. We should be in plenty of time."

"Remember, you lose an hour. We're Pacific time, Missoula is Mountain time," Jamie said.

Daisy's face fell. "It's going to be tight."

"We'll make it," Blade said. "Let's go."

"So, you're from Denver," Jamie said, once they were airborne.

"Yes," she said.

"And you're working for Pratt Sports Spot?" he asked.

She appreciated the effort, she really did. But there was no way that she could make casual conversation. Not when her head was so full of worry. She was just about to say that when she saw Blade turn slightly, catch his friend's attention and shake his head.

The questions stopped. And no one talked. Jamie flew the plane. Blade sat erect and watchful in the seat next to him, and she used her phone to compose a draft of the email that Hosea wanted sent. She kept it short and positive and when she was finished, she sent it to Tom Howard for review.

Then she tried to shut her mind down. But it was a mostly futile effort. Her daughter was a runaway. And a thief.

Ugly words. Words that she'd have sworn would never describe her kid.

Was it possible that she really didn't know her daughter at all? That was a sobering and sickening thought. She knew the last few weeks had been rough, but had she been oblivious to other signs that she and Sophie were living in separate universes? Connected by blood but little else?

No. She rejected that. She knew her daughter. And while this was certainly a bad thing, she was still a good kid. Maybe even brave. It took some guts to steal away from the house in the middle of the night and start a thousand-mile trip. And she was smart enough to remember that Daisy would have recorded all the stops in her travel log.

She tried to hang on to the idea that Sophie was smart. A teenager traveling by herself was vulnerable. Another driver might pass her on the road and realize that she was alone. When she stopped for gas, others could see the same thing. Was she smart enough to be watching for that?

And it didn't matter how smart she was if she had car trouble. Or if she simply got too tired and fell asleep.

Daisy closed her eyes and leaned her head against the small window. She was weary. Had been pushing herself for weeks to pack, move and start a new job. Had thought last night as she'd sipped her wine in her new home, with her longtime friend at her side, that maybe she was over the worst of it.

She was a damn fool.

Blade turned to look at her. "How you doing?" he asked.

"I'm okay," she said. It was easier to lie than to admit that she was barely hanging on.

He nodded. "We'll find her. We won't stop until we do. I promise."

"If I haven't said it, I'm very grateful for what you're doing."

"Like I said, I've got a daughter. I know how I'd be feeling in your shoes."

"Does she go to Knoware High?" Daisy asked.

"Yeah. She's a junior this year."

"Same as Sophie."

"We'll make sure and get the two of them introduced," he said.

She let out a sigh. "Brave to offer that," she said. "I mean, Sophie hasn't exactly put her best foot forward."

"No need for anybody to know what's going on here," he said. "Jamie and I are very good at keeping a secret."

"Landing in five," Jamie interjected. "And I've been telling people all over town that you cry at dog movies."

Blade shrugged. "Everybody cries at dog movies."

Daisy forced a smile, appreciating their efforts to lighten the mood. She looked out her small window and could see the airport in the distance. While not as small and isolated as the Knoware airfield, it was still relatively modest with just a couple runways and several planes already on the ground.

"Will we be able to rent a car here?" she asked, concerned at the likelihood.

"No need," Jamie said. "I've got a friend in the area. He's meeting us and he'll take you to the gas station. Once you meet up with your daughter, he can bring Blade back here and we'll fly home. You and your daughter will be okay driving back to Knoware?"

"We did it once," she said.

He smoothly landed the plane and they taxied closer to the airport. Once they were stopped, Jamie pulled out his cell phone. "He's at the West Gate. His name is Tony and he's driving a black Explorer."

"Let's go," Blade said. "No time to waste."

She had to run to keep up with Blade's long legs. The air temperature was much colder here than it had been in

Knoware. She bet it was close to zero. If she'd have left her house without a coat, she'd have looked like an idiot.

Within minutes they were at the gate and a big man standing next to a black Explorer was waving. "Hey, I'm Tony," he said as they approached.

"Blade Savick. Daisy Rambler," Blade said, doing the quick introductions. "Thanks for your help."

"Dr. Weathers saved my wife's life. There's not much I wouldn't do for him."

Daisy got into the warm back seat, marveling at her luck. If she hadn't dropped her scarf, if Blade hadn't brought it back this morning at just the right moment, she'd have had none of these resources at her disposal. Maybe she ought to be thanking Hosea Pratt for taking her on the ridiculous outing.

"We're about fifteen minutes out from your destination. Sit tight and I'll have you there in no time," Tony said.

Daisy saw Blade take a quick look at his watch. She didn't need to. It was one minute since she'd last checked it. Twenty-seven minutes to one. *Go. Go. Go.* Now that she was close, her anxiety was off the charts. If they weren't successful in intercepting Sophie, the next logical step would be to call the police. She hated that idea.

Tony had his dashboard GPS already set and Daisy watched their progress. Fourteen minutes later, he pulled into the combination gas/convenience store/fast food restaurant. Blade turned to her. "What kind of car is she driving?"

"A Toyota Camry," she said. "Gray."

"Do you see it?" Blade asked.

She finished scanning the cars that were gassing up and those parked in spaces near the front of the convenience store. "No," she said. "Oh, God. We're too late."

Chapter 5

"Don't jump to that conclusion. We could just as easily be too early. It would have been a little too serendipitous for her to be standing outside the front door when we pulled in," Blade said.

"I know, I know," Daisy said, willing her heart to slow down. She felt physical ill. What he said made sense, but she was afraid. She pulled her phone from her purse. "I want to go inside. Show her picture to whoever is working. I'm sure she would have gone in to use the restroom and probably to buy a drink or a snack."

"I'll go with you," Blade said. "Tony, can you park over there?"

"Sure thing," he said. "Take your time. She'll show. I got a feeling about this."

Daisy hoped like hell that Tony's gut was solid. When she opened the door, the warm air hit her. The cash register was just inside the door. There were three people in line. When it was Daisy's turn, she held out her phone. "I'm looking for my daughter. I believe she was intending to stop here. Have you seen this girl?"

The young man behind the counter looked at the picture. "I don't think so. I mean, I've been here for a couple hours and it's been kind of busy, but I think I'd have noticed her."

Daisy understood. Sophie was a pretty blue-eyed blonde. "It would have probably been in the last half hour or so."

The man shook his head.

Blade tossed a couple candy bars onto the counter and a ten-dollar bill. As they walked away, he handed her one. "Maybe a little sugar would help," he said.

She hadn't even eaten breakfast. The drama had unfolded before the food was on the table. "It's rarely a bad idea," she said, ripping the packaging open.

They wandered off to the side of the small convenience store, finding a spot between a rack of sunglasses and an equally tall rack of refrigerator magnets of everything to do or see in the great state of Montana.

She wanted to see one thing. Her daughter driving into the lot.

"It's good news that he hasn't seen her," Blade said, eating his own candy bar.

"Right," she said. "Assuming that she's sticking to the plan and stopping everywhere we stopped. Or, maybe she got confident enough of the way that she decided that wasn't necessary. Or maybe she simply missed the exit and she's already fifteen miles farther down the road." She closed the wrapping of her half-eaten candy bar. "There are a lot of possible scenarios."

"It *would* be easier if she had a cell phone on her," he said.

"I know that," she said. In retrospect, she was sorry that she'd taken her daughter's phone. But Sophie had been repeatedly rude to her, had refused to help with the packing and had come home late one too many times. Daisy had warned her twice that she was about to lose her phone privileges. And when the bad behavior hadn't improved, she'd had to follow through on the threat. Parenting 101.

"She might have been feeling really cut off from her friends back in Denver," he said. "Teens sometimes have trouble seeing that some situations are temporary."

Maybe it was lack of sleep or food. Maybe it was because she'd had more wine the previous night than she'd had in the last six months and this wasn't the type of situation that one should deal with hungover. Maybe it was simply that single parenting was so damn hard sometimes, and she'd had the extra burden of trying to protect them both from Jacob Posse. Whatever the reason, his remarks grated on her.

"I don't recall asking for your advice," she said, her tone icy. "I realize you have a daughter, but that doesn't make you an expert on parenting. So I guess I'd really appreciate it if you kept your opinions to yourself."

She turned her back to him and inspected the wall of chips and crackers to her left.

"Daisy?" he said, his tone questioning.

Her head was killing her. "I'm going to get some coffee." She walked away from him toward the area occupied by the fast food restaurant. She pushed her way through heavy double doors.

She stood five back in line, thinking she was the

world's biggest bitch. He'd been a nice guy. Had enlisted the help of his friends, who'd called in their own backup resources. She needed to apologize. She should buy him coffee at the very least. She dug in her purse for money.

"Daisy."

She looked up. Blade was standing at the double doors. "She's here," he said. "She's putting gas in her tank right now."

Her feet felt rooted to the spot. She'd been so focused on finding her daughter she'd given very little thought to what she was going to say to her. But she needed to move. She couldn't lose her now.

Daisy ran through the store, out the door, and slowed down only when she got within ten feet of her daughter. She did not want to rush up to her. Even if she was *this close* to unraveling, Sophie was never going to know that. She took a breath

At a steady pace, she approached the car. Got close enough to touch the trunk before her daughter looked up from her task.

"Mom," Sophie said, her voice a mere squeak.

She was safe and whole and the beautiful girl that Daisy had raised. "Hi, honey. You've had yourself quite a morning haven't you?"

"How did… How did you get here before me?" Sophie asked. She'd paid for the gas with Daisy's credit card, and she still held it in her hand. She glanced at it then looked at Daisy. "This is yours," she said.

"I know. We'll have plenty of time to sort all that out on our drive back," Daisy said. She wanted to pull her daughter into her arms, to hug her tight and never let her go. But she could tell that Sophie was strung tight, and that made Daisy hesitate.

"Are you okay?" Daisy asked.

"Kind of hungry," Sophie admitted.

"Yeah, me, too," Daisy said. The gas pump kicked off, indicating the tank was full. While Sophie dealt with that, Daisy turned to find Blade standing about five feet away.

"Thank you," she said. She had her daughter back. "I'm grateful for your help." There was more she should say. But she felt awkward and off-kilter. There'd been too much activity this morning, too many lows and now this high, and it was hard to keep it all in balance. Her focus had to be on Sophie.

"Yeah, no problem," he said, his voice tight. "I'm glad she's okay."

"Blade, I—"

"Can we just go, Mom?" Sophie asked.

Daisy turned. Her daughter looked exhausted and cold in her lightweight jacket. "Okay. Get in the car. I'm driving."

Daisy took one last look at Blade. "Truly, thank you. She's my life. I simply couldn't bear to lose her."

Blade managed to make some small talk with Tony on his way back to the plane. Talked about his job, about Knoware, about the fly-fishing that he'd done two summers ago in Montana. He was grateful when the drive ended and he could drop the presence of being okay.

He'd texted Jamie the salient details on the way back to the plane. When he opened the plane door to get in, his friend was all smiles. He took one look at Blade and said, "I don't get it. You should be stoked. Mother and daughter reunited. Mother, really hot mother, likely really grateful."

"I made a mistake," Blade said. "I didn't think it was

a mistake at the time. I thought I was offering some helpful feedback about the issue that her daughter didn't have
a cell phone. She took it that I was poking my nose into
business that wasn't mine and said nose was unwelcome."

Jamie got into position for takeoff. "Do you like it
when people give you parenting advice?"

"Not generally." As a divorced dad of a teenage girl,
he often felt a little inadequate as a parent. "I screwed
up. Didn't I?"

They were in the air before Jamie answered. "Maybe.
But on the whole, you did a nice thing for somebody
who was in a bad situation. And your text said that it
appeared that the daughter had been running on her last
legs. She was probably going to push herself until she
hurt herself or others. You and I know what that would
have looked like."

"Guess I'm going to need to be satisfied with that,"
Blade said.

"If you're giving up, you might want to let Marcus
know. He might want to take a run at it," Jamie said.

Blade felt his chest tighten, and it seemed difficult to
breathe deep. "I didn't say I was giving up."

Jamie smiled. "That's what I thought. Just a little setback."

Blade looked out his small window. Jamie hadn't seen
Daisy's face. If he had, setback wouldn't have been the
word that came to mind.

Daisy and Sophie did not talk for the first three hours
of their trip. Not because Daisy was unwilling to try. Sophie was asleep. Practically before Daisy had steered the
car back onto the interstate.

If she'd been hungry before, she was really going to

be starving when she woke up. It spoke to the level of exhaustion her baby girl had felt. It was a miracle that she'd somehow made it to that service station and they'd been in place to intercept her. She owed a debt of gratitude to both Blade Savick and Jamie Weathers that would be hard to repay.

She regretted the tenseness that had developed between her and Blade. She'd likely been too sensitive about his commentary on her parenting, but it was for the best, really. He wouldn't be knocking on her door any more early in the morning. Which would allow her to keep her focus on where it needed to be—finishing the job of raising Sophie. Once this school year was over, her daughter would have one more and then be off to college.

Maybe then Daisy could think about dating.

She could go online. Swipe right. Or left? She wasn't sure, but if everybody else was doing it, she'd figure it out. And since marketing and promotions was her life's work, she could probably write a killer ad: thirty-four-year old woman, woefully intolerant of bullies and shysters. Narcissists need not apply.

Hopefully she'd make a better choice than the last time. She couldn't do much worse. Jacob had fooled her. It would have been worse if she'd actually married him. Maybe she'd never have been able to get away.

He doesn't know where you're going. He won't find you. That had fueled her forward on her and Daisy's initial drive west.

You can disappear in Knoware. It really is nowhere.

That last sentiment had been the one Jane had shared when she'd convinced Daisy that coming to Knoware was her best alternative. Hard to judge whether it was the best alternative or even a good alternative yet. About the only thing she could say for it was that it had been eventful.

When Sophie woke up twenty minutes later, it was with a start. She jerked, blinked and then quickly turned her face toward her window. Evidently she needed a minute before getting into the nitty-gritty of the situation. Finally, she turned back toward her mother. "So, I didn't dream it," she said.

Daisy couldn't help it. She laughed. And felt the terror of the morning dissipate. She had her daughter next to her. Not much else really mattered. "We're almost back into the state of Washington," she said. "There's a few places to eat at the next exit."

"Okay."

There was silence in the car. Daisy didn't rush to fill it.

"I'm sorry, Mom," Sophie said finally. "I don't know what else to say. I screwed up."

Daisy knew all about being a teenage screwup. And she knew that she could beat this horse to death, and elaborate on all the reasons why she was appalled by Sophie's actions. Instead, she let her heart speak. "I love you, Sophie. And I desperately want to keep you safe and whole, and if there was a way to steer the world's troubles away from you, I would grab that wheel. Any day. Any time. But unfortunately, troubles will find you. I can't protect you. And the other thing I can't do is make you happy. Because happiness is a choice."

"I didn't *choose* to move," Sophie said.

"No, you didn't. I did. And because you're sixteen, you go where I go. That won't always be the case. I know that you're unhappy about the move, but you aren't giving Knoware and our new life there a chance. You've closed your mind to the possibilities before you even understand what they are."

"I miss my friends. I don't have any friends here."

"Yet. You start school on Monday. You'll make friends."

"It's horrible to be the new kid," Sophie said. "Who am I going to eat lunch with?"

"Maybe nobody. For a few days. But not forever."

Sophie lapsed into silence. Another three miles went by before she spoke. "Am I getting punished for this?"

"Well, when you get your summer job this year, I'll expect to be paid back all the charges on my credit card. But other than that, no. And I'm giving you your phone back."

Sophie looked surprised. "Why?"

"Because I understand the need for you to communicate with your old friends. Especially now. But don't pull another stunt like this one. You scared me and Jane. And I had to inconvenience multiple people to be at that gas station, waiting for you. I don't want to have to do that again."

"How *did* you manage that?"

"Long story. Like I said earlier, I'd do most anything to keep you safe and whole." There was no need to tell her everything. Always better to let her think that her mother had some kind of superpowers when it came to anticipating her next move.

"Who was the guy at the gas station?" Sophie asked.

"His name is Blade Savick."

"How did he get involved?"

"He was the firefighter-paramedic who rescued my boss. I'd dropped a scarf and he'd stopped by to return it."

"A Good Samaritan?"

"Yeah." There was no need to say more. Sophie wasn't likely to ever run into Blade Savick again.

The exit was approaching. Daisy put on her turn signal and took the curve. "Breakfast, lunch or dinner," she said, looking at the options.

"Pancakes," Sophie said, pointing to a place that advertised breakfast twenty-four hours a day.

It was five in the afternoon. Pancakes sounded absolutely wonderful.

"Done," Daisy said.

Chapter 6

It was just before noon when she got an email from Tom Howards, the COO. Come to my office at one for a conference call with Hosea.

She sent a response that she'd be there. She wasn't worried. Earlier, Tom had approved the Hosea update that she'd drafted to send employees and she'd distributed it company-wide minutes later. Hosea only had to check his email to know it had gone out.

She went to the small break room on the second floor where she'd stowed her lunch earlier. While she was there, she poured herself another cup of coffee. She was usually done with caffeine by midmorning, but she felt that she needed the extra jolt today.

It had been almost midnight on Saturday night when she and Sophie had finally pulled into the driveway. Daisy had had a headache that three ibuprofen hadn't touched. She was hungry again but, quite frankly, too tired to eat. After hiding her car keys, she'd gone to bed, intending to sleep late.

Instead, she'd woken up twice in the middle of the night and had only been able to go back to sleep once she'd verified that Sophie was still asleep in her bed. Daisy had been exhausted when she'd gotten up at nine and had hoped for an afternoon nap. That hadn't happened because there'd been groceries to buy, school supplies to obtain, and she and Sophie had looked for new paint for Sophie's bathroom. A *return to normalcy*, she'd told herself as she'd literally dragged herself from store to store.

Sleep on Sunday night had been much the same as sleep on Saturday night, proving that a *return to normalcy* was ridiculously easy to say but terribly hard to achieve when emotions were still raw. When the alarm clock had rung this morning, she'd desperately wanted to hide in bed, but she'd had to get both herself and Sophie out of the house.

The first stop had been Sophie's new school. Daisy had done most of the required paperwork online, but she still needed to stop in the office and sign a few forms. There, they'd met Sophie's counselor who looked barely old enough to drink, let alone advise her child on anything important. But Daisy had had no choice but to leave a sullen Sophie in the young woman's care.

She'd left the building feeling depressed and had to really work on summoning up her energy in order to walk into the Pratt Sports Spot offices with a smile on her face. Now, as she chewed her slightly dry turkey sandwich, because she'd forgotten to buy mayonnaise, her jaw hurt from the effort of keeping said smile in place.

At five minutes to one, she knocked on Tom Howards's door. She heard a *come in* and turned the knob. His office, like hers, was on the fourth floor of a four-story building and offered a wall of windows, letting the inhabitant have a full view of the Washington coast. Even in February, when the trees were bare and the ground more brownish-gray than green, the ocean lapping up against the rocky coast was stunning. And when she'd interviewed, it had been one of the appealing aspects of the job.

Tom was on the phone and motioned for her to have a seat in one of the two leather chairs in front of his desk. She sat and opened her notebook. Clicked her pen, ready to write. It took several minutes for him to finish his call. It was something concerning distribution that she thankfully was not involved in.

When he hung up, he smiled at her. "How's your day going?"

"Great. Getting settled," she said.

"Excellent. Thanks for coming here on short notice. I've already talked to Hosea twice this morning. Being in the hospital with a broken hip doesn't appear to have slowed him down any."

Before she could answer, his phone rang again. "It's him," Tom said.

She didn't even have time to inquire about his health before Hosea jumped in. "Daisy, this morning I agreed to be the Gold sponsor for the Spring Spectacular. It's the firefighters' annual dance. I want you to head up the effort. To be a cochair, working in conjunction with somebody from the fire department."

"Certainly," she said. This was in her wheelhouse.

"We're a little late getting into the game because, quite frankly, I'd already turned down the request. But after what happened to us on our climb, I had a sudden change of heart," he said.

A near-death experience could do that, she supposed. "How late?" she asked.

"The dance is in three weeks."

There was no way to pull an event together from scratch. The best she could hope for was that the other cochair had done some good work. "Do you have a contact name?" she asked.

"The fire chief's office was going to fax over some pertinent details to my assistant. You can get them from her. They gave me the name of your cochair. I didn't expect to know him but, as it turns out, I'm intimately acquainted with him."

Daisy looked at Tom. He shrugged, offering no help.

"You actually know him, too," Hosea said. He sounded amused, as if enjoying the tease.

It took her a full ten seconds to realize what he was saying. Later, Daisy would blame her slowness on lack of sleep. Or on optimism, that the world really wasn't that small or vindictive.

She placed her leather portfolio on the edge of Tom's desk. Carefully set her pen down. Took a breath. "Blade Savick, right?" she asked, hoping that her voice betrayed none of her thoughts.

"You've got it," he said. "You can reach him at the Treaty Boulevard fire station. If we're going to do this, we're going to do it right. It's going to be the biggest and best fundraising event that this community has ever seen. Just develop an in-depth understanding of his world and then figure out a way to convey that to donors. That shouldn't be any problem. I've arranged for you to shadow him at work for the next week."

Shadow Blade Savick. She swallowed hard, thinking the turkey rumbling in her stomach might make a reappearance on Tom's desk.

"Any questions?" Hosea asked.

"Uh…no. Got it. I'll give Mr. Savick a call today. Does he know that we'll be cochairs?"

"No idea. Now look, I've got to run. Metaphorically speaking," Hosea added with a chuckle. "No running here or dancing, but my therapist has assured me that I should be able to briefly attend the Spring Spectacular if I'm a good patient. Let's make sure it's an event we can be proud to have the Pratt Sports Spot name associated with."

"Of course," she said.

Tom ended the call. He looked at her. "I've been to these events in past years. It's a big deal."

She stood on legs that felt shaky. "Best get on it, then," she said. Hosea's office was right down the hall from Tom's. Sandra Brogen, Hosea's assistant, was at her desk. She held up a piece of paper in Daisy's direction. "I assume you talked with Hosea."

Daisy nodded. "Very exciting," she said. She didn't want it getting back to the boss that she was anything but enthusiastic about the new assignment. Daisy looked at the information.

It wasn't much. Basically just a quick email that summarized that a few of the main tasks had been done. A date had been established. A location had been reserved—the Knoware Community Center. A caterer had been hired—Gertie Biscuit. And a DJ was under contract—Knoware Tunes.

"This is all they sent?" she asked.

"That's it," Sandra said.

This project was going to have to go to the top of the pile. "Thank you," she said. She walked back to her own office and closed the door behind her. Then she sat at her desk for a few minutes.

There's no time to waste. Call him. Just call him.

She turned to her computer and within a minute had found the number for the fire station. She picked up her phone, then put it down. Did that twice more before she finally dialed.

"Knoware Fire," a man answered.

"Blade Savick, please," she said, then swallowed hard. Her throat was dry.

"Hang on," he said. "Savick," she heard him yell. She waited.

"Hello."

"Blade?" she asked stupidly.

"Yeah."

"This is Daisy Rambler."

No response.

"I spoke with Hosea Pratt earlier about the Spring Spectacular."

Still no response.

"Are you there?" she asked, feeling more than a little peevish.

"I am."

"Well, anyway, Pratt Sports Spot has agreed to be the corporate sponsor of the event. I'm your cochair," she added, plunging ahead fast. "Hosea has arranged for me to shadow you. I'm calling to inquire as to where I should show up." She finished with a flourish.

"Slow down," he said. "You're my cochair? And you're going to shadow me?"

"I just said that."

He paused. "How's your daughter?"

"Fine. Thanks for asking," she added. "But I think we should keep this just business." She needed to get this assignment behind her.

"Whatever works, Daisy. I'm on duty until nine tomorrow if you want to get started today."

She wanted to avoid it forever. There was something about Blade that made her feel off balance. "I'll be there in an hour," she said. The clock was ticking.

"Looking forward to it." He hung up.

She wasn't sure if he'd been teasing her. She figured it didn't matter. This was a shared responsibility, something they both had a vested interest in going well. That should be enough.

Blade went to find Charlie. Nothing happened at the station without him knowing about it. "I just got a call from Daisy Rambler," he said.

"Yep," Charlie said. He sat at the table with the newspaper spread around him. It was a rare minute of downtime, and Charlie was a great believer in not squandering those opportunities.

Also he apparently believed in holding his cards close.

"She's the woman who was with Hosea Pratt in Headstone Canyon," Blade said. "Apparently, Pratt Sports Spot is the corporate sponsor of the annual fundraiser. She's coming to shadow us. Know anything about that?"

"Just got off the phone with the brass. Orders are to make her feel welcome and let her hang out as long as she wants to. Evidently, the sponsorship is for even more than we asked for. Pratt Sports Spot is really stepping up. Guess Hosea *stepped off* at a very convenient time for us," he added, smiling. "And as I recall, looking at Ms. Rambler was no hardship."

Hardly.

Charlie folded his newspaper. "You got concerns, Savick?"

"Always complicates things when civilians get in the way," he hedged. It wouldn't be helpful to have Charlie know that he had an interest in Daisy.

"I guess your job, then, is to keep her from getting in the way. Can you do that?"

"I'll do my best," he said.

"I suppose it would be too lucky that she cooks," Charlie mused. "Perry can't get back too soon."

Perry Lindell had been part of the team for more than four years. Prior to becoming a firefighter, he'd been a chef in Minneapolis. "We don't want to let those skills get rusty." That was what Charlie had told him as he'd handed him an apron and knife shortly after he'd arrived.

Perry had ruptured his Achilles tendon two weeks ago. Their stomachs missed him.

"I don't think that's the first question I'm going to ask her," Blade said. He'd already put his foot in his mouth with Daisy once.

"Your choice. She'll be in your hands," Charlie said, folding his paper. He tossed it in the middle of the table and walked out of the kitchen, leaving Blade alone with his thoughts.

He'd spent most of the previous night contemplating ways he might engineer another meeting with Daisy Rambler. Had even seriously considered enlisting the help of his daughter by asking her to befriend Sophie. But had been able to pull back from that foolishness, with the sure knowledge that past decisions to keep his love life and his parenting in separate quadrants still made good sense.

And now she'd dropped into his lap.

Serendipity.

He hoped he didn't screw it up.

"You're shadowing Blade Savick," Jane said, sounding amused. She'd called just as Daisy was walking to her car.

"I'm shadowing the fire department. For work. Blade just happens to be my contact. My cochair," she amended.

"It's weird how the two of you keep getting thrown together," Jane said.

Weird. Daisy guessed that was one word for it. "It's business."

"Uh-huh." Her friend did not sound convinced.

"I just wish I'd attended one of these fundraisers before," Daisy said. "I'd know what to expect."

"I imagine that a whole lot of pictures and video exist."

She could ask around at work. Or do one better, she thought, as the germ of an idea started sprouting. Maybe there was a way to work up some interest and enthusiasm in the community.

She could...

With some effort, she pulled herself back. She couldn't forge ahead without giving Blade a chance to have input on the idea. Which was a slightly bitter tasting pill considering that it hadn't been that many hours ago that she'd told him to keep his opinions to himself.

"How's Sophie?" Jane asked.

"I haven't gotten a call from school yet that she's disappeared."

"Good girl, looking at the positive."

"There's a positive?" Daisy asked.

Jane laughed. "Of course. But sometimes it's buried under a bunch of sh…turf. You just got to be willing to pitch the *turf* aside."

"Lots of turf in my life lately," Daisy admitted. Her grandmother dying; Jacob refusing to go away; her decision that the only real alternative was for her and Sophie to leave Denver.

"Turf decomposes over time," Jane said. "Fertilizes and nourishes."

"I suppose people at work won't think it's odd that the next time something goes wrong at work, I exclaim *oh, turf*!"

Jane laughed. "Look, I've got to scoot. More reluctant witnesses to talk to. Good luck on the new assignment."

"Thanks," Daisy said. She hung up. Luck. Skill. Whatever it took, she was not going to blow her first big project. With that in mind, she took the time to send Tom Howards a quick email. She and Blade needed to hit the ground running, and she hoped that Tom responded quickly.

She opened her car door and climbed inside. When she punched in the address, she realized it was only seven minutes away.

There was something wonderful about small towns. In Denver, it had sometimes taken her seven minutes to get through a traffic light.

When she arrived, she parked on the street in front of the fire station. It was a large brick building, with three big garage-type doors. They were all closed, likely in deference to the cold biting wind that had settled in, keeping the outside temperature in the low twenties. There was a side entrance, a regular door. She debated knocking but that seemed odd so she turned the knob and walked in.

It was a small office area. She recognized the man at the desk. He'd been on the ground when Blade and the other paramedic had climbed up to assist Hosea. He was substantially older than Blade, and she thought perhaps he might be in charge.

"Hello," she said. "I'm Daisy Rambler from Pratt Sports Spot."

"I'm Charlie Smith. Nice to see you again," he said. "With two feet on firm ground," he added, with a smile.

"Thank you for everything that you and the rest of the responders did. I can't imagine how different it might have been if all of you hadn't been so competent."

"Flattery will get you everywhere," he said. "I heard that you're going to be spending some time here shadowing Blade Savick, getting to see how things work."

"We're excited about making this the best annual fundraiser that the community has ever seen."

"We're all in for that. We could use the funding. Come on, I'll take you to find Savick."

He opened the door and she felt an immediate chill. The big doors might be closed, but that didn't mean that the inside was warm and toasty. It might have been sixty degrees, but she wasn't even sure about that.

Three people, two men and one woman, were working in the large area. It appeared that they were polishing one of the three large fire trucks that were parked inside.

"I'll let Savick do the introductions," Charlie said. He pointed to a door at the rear of the building. "That way."

He opened the door for her, and when she stepped inside, it wasn't warm but warmer than where the trucks were parked. It was empty with the exception of somebody who was bent over, their head and shoulders inside an open refrigerator. She had an excellent view of their butt.

She was pretty sure she knew who it belonged to.

Not too hard on the eyes. That was what her grandmother would have said about Blade Savick's rear end.

He straightened, turned, caught sight of them, and bobbled the peppers and onions in his hands. "Hello," he said. "Didn't realize you were there."

"Just got here," she said.

"I'll leave you two to it," Charlie said. "If you've got a kind heart," he added, looking at her, "you'll help him with that chili."

Once Charlie left, she stood awkwardly by the door. She watched Blade drop the onions and peppers near a cutting board that was on the counter.

"Here, let me take your coat," he said, walking toward her.

"In a minute, maybe," she said.

He stopped six feet away from her. "Yeah, sorry about that. The heat in the building isn't great."

She walked over to the stove. There was a big package of raw hamburger next to a pan. "Paramedic. Firefighter. Cook. You wear a lot of hats."

"Only the hats for paramedic and firefighter fit," he said with a roll of his eyes.

She reluctantly started to unbutton her coat. The light blue wool would look bad with a chili stain. Once off, she laid the coat over the back of one of the chairs gathered around the table. Then washed her hands at the big sink.

Finally she turned to face him. "Ready to work," she said. "Although I have to admit, this isn't quite what I expected."

"Part of a well-functioning firehouse is that everybody eats regularly, or as regularly as possible. We've got a teammate who generally covers the cooking. Unfortunately, he's out on medical leave, which leaves the rest of us taking turns. I try not to let anybody else here know how much this terrifies me," he said.

"Charlie must have some idea," she said.

"For sure. But he won't talk. And he likely thinks this is character development for me."

"Character development and torture can look a lot alike sometimes," she said.

"You are definitely a parent," he said easily.

"It'll give us a chance to talk about the Spring Spectacular," she said. She unwrapped the hamburger and slid it into the deep skillet. "Where are your spices?" she asked.

He pointed to a cupboard. She opened it, eyed the possibilities and started selecting.

He stared at her. "How do you know which ones?"

She smiled. "You have a daughter. Don't you have to cook for her?"

"We go out a lot. And my ex-wife's mother generally takes pity on us when she knows that Raven is staying with me. She swings by with food."

"What do you eat when your daughter isn't with you?"

"Sandwiches. Cereal. I can make oatmeal."

"Congratulations," she said, offering up a quick smile.

"You think I should take that off my online profile?" he asked with a perfectly straight face.

Now she laughed. "No. Definitely not. I'm in marketing, remember. So trust me on this. Go with what you've got."

"What *I've got* is a recipe for the chili on my phone," he said, picking it up from the counter.

"I don't need that," she said.

"Really?"

His *really* sounded very similar to how a five-year-old Sophie had sounded when she'd been told she could have an extra dessert. Like life was really too good to be true. And right then and there, she decided that any conversation they might have about the Spring Spectacular could wait. She wanted him to have a chance to talk about his real work, work that he clearly excelled at. "Tell me about your days here," she said.

He cut the ends off the onion and pulled the outer skin off. Then picked up the big knife. "Well, no two are the same. But the time passes fast because we're generally pretty busy. I guess that's one of the things I love."

"I guess I wouldn't have anticipated there would be that many fire emergencies," she said.

"There aren't. But we respond to every 911 call. Most of them are medical. At least 80 percent. As serious as heart attacks and strokes. As minor as somebody being a little banged up in a fender bender."

"Where does falling in Myrtle Canyon fit?" she asked.

"Hosea was lucky. He could have had a closed head injury or a spinal fracture and things might have been a lot worse. And, by the way, don't call it Myrtle Canyon. That's the official name," he said. "But everybody knows it as Headstone Canyon."

And as he proceeded to tell her the story of why, she felt a little nauseated. What the hell had Hosea been thinking taking a brand-new employee there on her first day? "Maybe I should get a T-shirt?" she said. She walked over and picked up the cutting board of chopped onions. She tilted it and used her knife to slide them into her simmering ground beef. Gave the cutting board back to Bryce so that he could do the peppers. "You know, something like I Survived Headstone Canyon."

"I'd say that Hosea Pratt definitely doesn't embrace a slow start. Headstone Canyon on your first day. The Spring Spectacular on your second. Bet you just can't wait for tomorrow."

"I did remind myself on the way over here how grateful I am to have a job," she admitted. She stirred her ground beef and onions. He chopped his pepper. She figured now was as good a time as any to attempt to clear the air. "Blade, I thought this—" she motioned between herself and him "—might be awkward after how we left things on Saturday."

"You said that your daughter was doing okay?" he asked.

"She is. I think. But then again, I was pretty surprised on Saturday morning so maybe I'm not the best judge." She tapped her spoon on the counter. "I'm sorry. I was rude to you, and I should have apologized right away."

"You had your hands full. I overstepped. I should learn to keep my opinions to myself."

She appreciated him saying that. "It's probably not a good excuse that I was slightly hung over, dehydrated and very tired."

"Are you kidding? That makes it all better," he said with a perfectly straight face.

"Can we start fresh?" she asked. "I really want us to be friendly cochairs."

That wasn't quite what he'd been going for when he'd decided to return her scarf in person. But there was some water under the bridge now. "I'd like that," he said. He cocked his head and narrowed his eyes. "Assuming you haven't exaggerated your chili making abilities."

She picked up the large can of tomatoes that was on the counter. "Show me where the can opener is, and you can judge for yourself."

Twenty minutes later, the pot was simmering away. He'd offered her coffee and a muffin from a tray on the counter. She'd accepted both, and they'd taken chairs at the table.

"Hosea's assistant gave me an email that she got from your chief's office." She pulled the memo out of her purse and gave it to him.

He looked at it quickly. "I saw this a couple weeks ago. I guess it's good we're not starting from scratch. I mean, a few things are in place. And I was excited to see that Gertie Biscuit handles the catering. At least the food will be good."

"You know her?" she asked.

"Everybody knows her. She owns Gertie's Café. Delicious food served to standing room only during the season."

"Has she always been the caterer?"

"I don't know. The one thing I do know is that ticket sales are slow. That's not too encouraging."

"I have a couple thoughts about creating interest in the event," she said.

"I'm all ears," he said. "But in full disclosure mode, you need to know that I've attended the Spring Spectacular, but I never paid much attention to how it all came together. I don't really know what I'm doing."

"We'll figure it out together. I've had some involvement with these types of events at past jobs. The great thing is that there is typically a portion of the community that supports these kinds of events regularly. Probably come to the Spring Spectacular, and similar events in the community, every year. We want these *regulars* to definitely come this year, but if our goal is to make this a very successful fundraising event, I think we really want to find a way to grow that group. We want to add new people, allowing them, if you will, to become part of the cool regular gang."

He smiled. "This is why I floundered in my marketing class."

She waved a hand. "This will be your master's thesis. In fact, we can probably get you an honorary doctorate."

"Now you're talking," he said.

"Let me just check my phone for a second." She perused the emails that had come in during the last half hour and saw that Tom had responded. With a yes. "My idea is to use my newcomer status as a reason for people to share experiences with me about the Spring Spectacular via social media. I'll ask people to *educate* me on the Spring Spectacular by sharing pictures and anecdotes about the event. In exchange, you and I will share with them pictures and anecdotes about this fire station, the people who work here, the work that is getting done in the community. We'll be careful to protect people's privacy, but I think past donors and potential future donors might positively respond to an insider look."

He was quiet for a minute. It made her nervous.

"Pratt Sports Spot already has a huge list of email addresses of both customers and employees that we can use to push the information out. I cleared it with the COO that we could offer a promotion. Every customer who shares the link to the Spring Spectacular social media with five other people can get 30 percent off their next purchase."

She stopped. It was an information download. She'd

had time to think about this. She needed to give him more than a minute.

Finally, he leaned forward. "I like it. I've lived here my whole life, and it's different from anything else I've seen done in the community."

She felt the anxiety in her body ease up. She really wanted her first big project at Pratt Sports Spot to be a big success. "I thought the tag line might be Remember This. As in I need the community to share with me what they remember about the Spring Spectacular, and we all need to remember what the Knoware Fire Department does because we might be the next person who needs their help."

"Remember This." He repeated the phrase. "It's good. I have to admit, I hadn't even thought of a slogan, or what did you call it, a tag line."

"That's what cochairs are for," she said. "So that neither one of us has to think of everything." She was more relieved than he could possibly know. By the end of business today, she'd have one of her graphic artists setting up the framework for their social media campaign. There was really no time to waste. "The reason I asked whether Gertie Biscuit had catered before is that I thought it might also be good to get the various other people who are involved in putting this event together involved in the Remember This campaign."

"We can ask her." He settled back in his chair. "Suddenly I'm feeling a lot better about an event that, quite frankly, I've been dreading."

That made two of them. She flipped the latch on her purse and pulled out her phone. "I should take some photos of the chili making. To share."

"That's not very exciting work."

"It's real, though. Firefighters have to eat. And this is how they manage that."

"Maybe there will be a stuck cat in a tree later today," he said. "Really tug on their emotions."

"Have you really rescued cats?"

"Cats. Dogs. Small aircraft."

"What?"

"Remote controlled plane. Very upset five-year-old boy. Grateful grandmother. I should probably remind her about the Spring Spectacular."

She nodded. "Absolutely. And ask her to remind all her friends."

"My Uncle Frank used to sell cars. He never came to a family dinner that he didn't bring along some cards for us to pass out to our friends. I suddenly feel a real kinship for the man."

"It's for a good cause," she said.

"And only for a limited time. Perhaps my friends will allow me to be obnoxious for a brief period."

"I only have one friend here. Jane. She's already done so much for me that I think she's officially off the hook."

"Is she the reason you came to Knoware?" he asked.

"Not the reason." That was the need to get away from Jacob, but there was no sense bringing all that baggage up. "But the impetus. We've been friends for many years. She told me about the job at Pratt Sports Spot. Helped me find a house."

"A good friend," he said. "They're rare. I've lived here my whole life and while I've got a ton of acquaintances, I've really only got two best friends."

"Jamie, the pilot," she said.

"And Marcus, the cop. You would have seen him the day we scooped you and Mr. Pratt off the ledge."

"I remember him."

"Of course," he said, somewhat oddly she thought. He was quiet for a minute. "You know, I've got a good feeling about us working together. We both have daughters. I like to eat chili. You like to make it," he added with a smile.

Jacob had also started out wanting to be her friend, her very good friend. "Definitely friendly cochairs," she said breezily. "Do Marcus and Jamie also have kids?" she asked, changing the topic.

Blade shook his head. "No kids. Neither have been married."

"Jane mentioned that you're divorced."

"Yep. Four years ago. My ex lives in Knoware. We share custody of Raven."

"That can't always be easy."

"Nope. But worth it," he said.

"I'm betting you have excellent negotiation skills," she said. "That's good. They may come in handy when we move forward with the silent auction."

"Silent auction?" he repeated, not sounding all that excited.

She waved a hand. "It'll be great. You'll see."

Chapter 7

"How was school?" Daisy asked that night.

Sophie shrugged.

Daisy counted to ten. "Most interesting class?"

"Seventh period."

This was progress. "Why?"

"Because it meant the day was almost over."

Dead end ahead. Anybody with a brain could see the flashing sign. Even so, maybe she should try again. But damn it, she was tired. Chasing after Sophie had taken a toll, and while the few hours she'd spent with Blade Savick had been surprisingly pleasant, it had left her feeling off balance. He was smart and charming and funny.

But then again, Jacob had also been those things. And such a liar.

It was going to be very hard to trust her own judgment ever again. Right now, the best thing she could do was be cautious. That was why it had been so important for Blade to understand that their relationship was professional.

She appreciated that Blade had immediately asked about Sophie, as if understanding that her health and well-being were more important than everything else. And he had apologized, as he'd said, for overstepping.

It had been refreshing, yet somewhat unsettling. Could he be just as uncomplicated as he seemed? Just a real nice guy?

She hoped so. It would make this assignment go so much more smoothly. But right now, her focus needed to be on getting the night to go smoothly. "Dinner in thirty minutes. Chicken quesadillas with rice."

She expected Sophie to bolt for her room, but she remained in the kitchen. She sat at the table, her phone next to her, but she wasn't looking at it. Daisy pulled a package of chicken breasts from the refrigerator. She cut the meat into strips. Added some oil and spices and set it aside so that it could marinate for a few minutes while she got the rest of dinner ready.

"There was a notice on the office window that auditions for the spring play are on Thursday," Sophie said. "*Our Town* by Thornton Wilder."

Daisy could feel her heart speed up. But she kept the excitement out of her voice. "That's a classic. Think you'll try for it?"

"Maybe."

Daisy looked up from the avocados that she was peeling. She was afraid to encourage too much because Sophie might not go forward just to spite her. But she needed her daughter to know the truth. "I hope you do, Sophie. You're very talented."

There was no response. But still, Sophie stayed at the table.

She sat for the full thirty-three minutes it took for Daisy to get dinner ready. Quietly. She didn't say another word until they were both sitting at the table, food on their plates. "How's your boss doing?" she asked.

"Okay. Still in the hospital but working. He gave me a new assignment. Pratt Sports Spot is sponsoring the Spring Spectacular. It's a fundraiser for the local fire department."

Sophie looked up from her plate. "Wasn't that guy… the one with you…a fireman?"

"Yes. His name is Blade Savick."

"Savick," Sophie repeated. "I met a girl today and her last name is Savick."

"Raven?" Daisy asked, remembering what Blade had said.

"Yeah. I think so. She was picking up information about the play at the same time that I was."

"That's his daughter. And oddly enough, that's who my boss arranged for me to shadow. I actually started this afternoon."

"Was it cool? Did you see blood?"

"Yes, it was dark red and thick," she said, her voice quavering.

"Ugh," Sophie said, clearly sorry she'd asked.

"Oh, wait," Daisy said brightly. "That was chili. He was on kitchen duty."

Sophie rolled her eyes. "Lame. You're lame and that's lame."

Not really, thought Daisy. It had been fun. And the chili had been good. He'd offered her some to take home, but she'd declined. "You know I don't do well at the sight of blood," she said. "So any day I can avoid that is a good day."

Sophie chewed and swallowed. "Did he say anything about me?"

"He asked how you were doing."

"What did you tell him?" Sophie asked.

"I said that you were doing fine. Because you are. It's hard to be the new kid, Sophie. But you went to school today and as tough as it might have been, you did it. And tomorrow will be better. I just know it. Ultimately, you're going to do great."

Sophie pushed her mostly eaten plate of food to the side. "I hope you're right, Mom. I really do."

Daisy woke up late on Tuesday morning, which meant that she had to hurry through her shower, and her hair was barely dry before she and Sophie walked out the door. She dropped Sophie off at school. She wanted to encourage her to try out for the play, but she kept her thoughts to herself, settling on just a wish for a good day.

Then she drove to her office where she answered emails for twenty minutes and spent a little time with each of her staff members, making sure she knew what they were working on. Then she drove to the firehouse.

It was a chilly damp February day, but the big doors were open and she saw Blade rolling out a flat hose. She parked and waved. When she walked up, he smiled at her.

"Your chili was a big hit," he said. "The corn bread you made put it over the top."

"Our chili," she said, feeling oddly warm at the compliment. It was *just* chili. But it seemed as if lately she couldn't do anything right. Knowing that she'd done a good job on the food and that it had been enjoyed made her feel as if maybe she hadn't lost all her abilities.

"I'm a little worried that I've set some expectations that I won't be able to meet the next time it's my turn," he said.

She almost told him not to worry, that she'd help. But realized that it was unlikely she would still be shadowing him. It wasn't going to take that long to get a feel for what he and the other firefighters did. Based on yesterday afternoon, it didn't seem that complex.

"I thought I might get some photos of the fire trucks today," she said.

"Sure. Let's go."

"They're so clean," she said.

"We take pride in that," he said. "Everybody has a hand in making sure the equipment we use is clean and in good working order."

"It's got lots of nooks and crannies," she said, pointing to a door on the side of the fire truck.

Blade opened it. Inside was a bunch of tools and a couple axes of different sizes. Off to the side were what appeared to be air tanks. "Tell me about those," she said after getting a couple good photos.

"Those are SCBA or self-contained breathing apparatus. Smoke kills, you know."

"Right. So it's oxygen."

"Compressed air. About thirty minutes' worth, but that really depends on the individual firefighter and level of exertion. Bigger person, more exertion, faster depletion. I know that mine generally won't last the full thirty. I've got more like twenty-three minutes."

"Have you ever run out?" she asked. The idea of suddenly not being able to breathe was terrifying.

"I've come close," he said with a smile. "But that's not the ideal. There's a low-air alarm that rings at six minutes, and department protocol requires that we exit."

When they finished the inspection of the truck, he motioned for her to follow him. "I got you some bunker gear," he said. "Not that you'll be fighting any fires."

"Then why will I need it?"

"If you're going to ride along, I want you to be safe. Fire is predictable, yet unpredictable. We attempt to park the trucks a safe distance from the fire. But even so, I want you to be protected in the event that something goes bad quickly. Also, I think it will give you a much better feel for the role if you're actually wearing the gear. Come on, I'll show you."

He led her inside. Along one wall was a series of open-style lockers. In each hung a heavy yellow coat, the kind she'd seen a hundred times on firefighters in movies. There was also a pair of pants in what she assumed was a flame-retardant material. She looked a little closer. There were suspenders.

He smiled. "We don't want our pants to be falling down at an inappropriate time."

"Absolutely not." Tucked into the pants were the tops of a pair of heavy boots. She pointed to them. "You were afraid I would forget my boots?" she asked, amused.

He shook his head. "Everybody's gear is stored the same way."

She looked and could see that he was telling the truth. She took a photo.

"It saves time," he said. "We pull on the pants and slip our feet into the boots, all in one motion. Minutes, hell, seconds, can be the difference between saving a building or losing it to the fire. Or more importantly, saving a person. The first week of training, we practice getting into our clothes. Over and over. We're timed. If we can't get that right, they don't even bother trying to teach us the rest of the stuff."

"Can I try it?" she asked, very grateful that she'd chosen to wear pants to work. A dress would have made this very difficult. She handed him her phone. "Your turn to take photos."

"I'll do my best. Now pants and boots first. Get your suspenders up and then the coat." He pulled out his own cell phone. "I'll use this to time you. On your mark, get set, go."

She lifted the pants from the hook. They were heavier than she'd expected, but then again, there were big heavy boots at the bottom. She stepped into the pants, got her feet into the boots and pulled the heavy material up. She quickly fastened the pants and then pulled up the suspenders. They were too loose, but she ignored that. She grabbed the coat and shrugged it on. It had Velcro latches. She snapped the last one shut and looked up, pretty proud of herself.

"Not bad," he said. "But you need to cut about ninety seconds or you're never going to make the truck."

Ninety seconds. "Good grief," she muttered.

He smiled and took a photo of her. "And there's also a helmet that you have to get on," he said, pointing to the shelf above where her bunker gear had been hanging.

"I'll try it again." She took off the coat. Hung it back up. "It's all much heavier than I expected."

"It's a synthetic material that is fireproof, protects us against intense heat and provides a barrier between us and nasty chemicals."

She was just about to shrug out of her suspenders

when she realized she should try to adjust them for a better fit. Otherwise, her pants might just fall down. She worked at the metal clasp but couldn't get it to budge.

"Let me help you," he said, stepping forward.

He was close enough that she could smell the soap he'd used in the shower. It was a nice smell, reminding her that it had been a long time since she'd had the pleasure of smelling anything other than the lavender shower gel she favored.

She took a deep breath just as he reached for her right shoulder, realizing too late that as her chest expanded, it made it appear as if her breasts were just about to leap into his hands.

She let out a puff of air. And like a nice guy, he pretended that he hadn't noticed. But he was close enough that she could see his neck get red.

With one quick tug, he got the right suspender tightened. All business, he moved to her left side and made quick work of that one. For her part, she didn't breathe at all. It was a relief when he finally stepped back so that she could suck in some much-needed air.

She unfastened her pants and stepped out of them. Got everything hung back up and gave him a nod to start the clock again.

She got everything on, even the heavy, hard-sided helmet. She flipped down the visor and threw her hands in the air. "Ta-da!" she said. She took a selfie.

"You cut forty seconds off your time."

It was progress. Not much, but still. She sucked a breath in and started taking it all off. She was halfway through the fourth try when bells started ringing. And suddenly there was motion everywhere. "What now?" she asked.

"Keep going. You can ride in the truck," he answered as he and everyone else in the firehouse started pulling on their clothes. Because she'd had a head start, she was pulling on her coat just as they finished.

"Button that in the truck," he said. He grabbed her helmet from the shelf and tossed it in her direction. "Let's go."

And before she could really process any of it, they were in the truck, pulling out of the garage. She had a thousand questions, but was smart enough to keep her mouth shut. And she didn't have long to wait because within minutes, they were pulling up to a small house at the edge of Knoware. She did not see smoke or flames.

"What's going on?" she asked.

"Medical call. Chest pains," Blade said, barely giving her a look before springing from the truck. "Come on. And no photos inside."

He did not wait for her. She trailed him into the small house by at least five seconds. He was already squatted in front of the sixty-something woman, who sat on her couch, one hand pressed against her chest.

He was calm; the woman was not. Understandable. But in less than a minute, she could see the woman's demeanor start to change. For Daisy, it was a repeat of the performance she'd seen at Headstone Canyon. Blade was confident, moving fast, but appearing unhurried, and there was no doubt to anyone in the room that he was in charge. He was checking vitals, asking about medications, her pain.

When the ambulance arrived, Blade conferred with the crew and then helped to transfer the woman from her couch to the vehicle. It was over in fifteen minutes, and they were back in the fire truck and returning to the fire station.

When they were there and out of earshot of others, she said, "That was impressive."

"Nah," he said, waving a hand. "I'm pretty sure it was a panic attack, not a heart attack."

"Did you always want to do this?"

He glanced toward the bay where his coworkers milled around. "Ride around in a truck?" he asked, deliberately misunderstanding her.

"Save lives," she said.

"I wanted to be a rock star," he said. "This was my fallback. How about you?" he asked, efficiently redirecting the attention away from himself. "Did you dream of being a marketing and public relations pro?"

"Who wouldn't?" she asked.

He laughed. "Come on. Secret little ambition."

"Astronaut," she said.

"I think those space suits weigh even more than our clothes. What changed your mind?"

A pregnancy at seventeen. "I don't really know," she lied. "You?"

"I was in a band and we were playing small venues. But then I got married and we had a baby. I needed to be home." He smiled. "Bon Jovi doesn't know how lucky he is. I could have been some real competition."

"I'm sure he—"

The shrill siren interrupted her.

He waved a hand in her direction. "Let's go."

Within a minute, everybody was back in the truck and they were pulling out of the driveway. Like before, details drifted back. *Fire. 520 Willow Street.* That meant nothing to her, but she could tell by the way Blade and Charlie exchanged glances that there was more to the story.

Halfway there, it got relayed to the team that there might be people trapped inside the building. "That's what I was afraid of," he said, almost under his breath.

"Why?"

"The building is a former orphanage. Hasn't been used for that for at least fifty years. The city is trying to get the property condemned so that they can tear it town. Unfortunately, the homeless hang out there, sometimes managing to pry off a boarded-up window to get inside, especially when the weather gets nasty like the last few days."

Her throat felt tight. "What will you do?"

He didn't answer, and she didn't press. And two minutes later, they were parked.

The building was bigger than she'd expected. Two stories with—she counted fast—twelve windows across the front. Some of said windows on the first level had been blown out, and fire and smoke were visible.

The fire truck door opened, steps descended and she got ready to move.

"No, stay here," he said. "Where it's safe."

He didn't give her time to argue. He and the other firefighters were out of the truck and moving fast, unraveling hoses. One got hooked up to the truck and water started to pour onto the structure. The other was getting dragged toward a hydrant that was a couple hundred feet down the block. She got out her phone and snapped some photos.

Charlie motioned to Blade to hand off the hose. He was issuing orders, and she didn't need to guess what they were when she saw Blade and a coworker strap on air tanks and breathing apparatus and run into the burning house.

She looked at her watch. He'd said that in his experience his air lasted about twenty-three minutes. No need to worry yet.

Seconds ticked by. Minutes stretched on.

And on. It was getting so hot in the truck.

It had to be much, much hotter inside the building. And darker. And smokier.

She felt nauseous.

He'd made jokes about rescuing cats in trees. Hadn't mentioned this.

At minute thirteen, she saw a figure emerge from the doorway. It was Blade, with somebody slung over his shoulder. Just in time, she remembered her phone and got the photo. Then he transferred the person to the ground and Charlie came to assist.

Blade was walking, appeared to be okay. She started to breathe normally again.

And then he turned around and ran back inside the burning building.

Chapter 8

Even with the light on his helmet, Blade couldn't see a damn thing. The smoke was too black, too heavy. But he knew where he was headed. Sort of.

The man he'd removed from the second floor had said his friend was still inside, on the first floor. That he had a bad leg. And the last thing he'd said before Blade had slapped an oxygen mask on him was *please save him*.

Blade was going to do his best. But it wasn't looking good.

He felt his way down the hallway. The first three doors were closed, and when he quickly twisted the knob, he discovered they were locked. This gave him good reason to believe that nobody was inside. The fourth door was…hell…he'd thought it was open, but it was simply gone. He went inside and searched the room by walking back and forth. He didn't fall over anything, human or otherwise, so he quickly exited and resumed his path down the hall.

At best, he had three minutes until his low-air alarm sounded and he'd have to leave.

The fifth door was locked. The sixth door was shut but the handle turned. He knew from his search of the second floor that this was the last room. If the man he'd carried out had been right, then somebody should be inside. Unless, of course, he was in the last room going the other direction.

He quickly searched the room, getting more and more discouraged. And when his low-air alarm sounded, he knew he wasn't going to have time to search the other end of the hallway.

He'd failed.

"Exiting the building," he said. He turned to do just that, and through the smoke caught sight of a door in the far corner. None of the other rooms had one, he was fairly certain. He found the doorknob, pulled open the door and almost tripped over a rolled-up mat that had been pushed up against the door, likely to block the smoke from entering the room. Inside, his light caught the shape of a body on the floor and his heart sank. He was too late.

But when he reached to check the man's carotid pulse, he felt life. And realized that the man's face had been pressed up against a small vent, maybe a foot square, that had provided him with air to breathe. He'd done everything he could to save himself.

Blade was going to do everything *he* could to save both of them.

His headset crackled. "Where are you?"

It was Charlie, who was no doubt watching the door, making sure his team got out.

"I've got a victim. Unconscious. Steady pulse. I'm bringing him out."

"Get out of the building," Charlie said. "Now."

"I'm trying," Blade said. He knelt and managed to get the man off the ground and over his shoulder. Then he was out of the room and halfway down the hall. He thought he was home free.

And then the second floor caved in and debris rained down upon him and his passenger. There was no going forward. He turned and ran back toward the closet. His heart was drumming in his chest, and he knew that he was using his precious air at an even faster rate. To make matters worse, now he was going to need to share it.

"No path to the door," he said, trying to keep his voice calm. "There's a vent to the outside, around the back of the building. I'm headed in that direction. The opening is too small. You're going to need to widen it for us."

There was no immediate response. But then Charlie said, "Affirmative. I've got a visual." There was a pause. "Get back. We're coming in."

And Blade knew what was happening outside. Other firefighters were running for tools. It was a concrete block wall. A battering ram, with two guys working in tandem, would be the most efficient. They'd practiced it as recently as a month ago.

But practice and real life were two different things. And they were running out of time.

Regrets flashed through his mind. He could have been a better father, son, friend, ex-husband.

Unfinished business, that's what it was. And while he had always accepted the risks that came with his job, he wanted, desperately wanted, more time. And he thought of Daisy, with her infectious laugh and her pretty eyes.

She wanted to be *friendly cochairs*. He wanted something more.

The man groaned, shifted. Blade put a hand on his back. "Stay calm. Help is coming."

"Didn't want to die alone," the man said.

"Nobody is dying today," Blade said, hoping that he wasn't making false promises. He lowered the man to the floor, positioning him so that the two of them could take turns breathing from the SCBA. They were far enough away from the wall that when it came tumbling down, they wouldn't get caught with debris.

"Almost there," he heard Charlie in his headset.

Hurry, he thought.

The man reached out and gripped his gloved hand. "Thank you," he said. "For not—" his body shuddered "—leaving me," he finished, closing his eyes.

"Stay with—"

A chunk of the wall came crashing in. He could see sunlight, glorious sunlight. Then he saw Tony coming through the hole.

Together, they transferred the man to Charlie who waited on the other side. Then Blade climbed out, followed by Tony.

A cold cloudy day had never looked so perfect.

Oxygen was pressed upon him. Before he accepted it, he said one word. "Daisy."

"To the right," Charlie said.

He looked and finally located her some thirty feet away, just in time to see her collapse onto the ground.

Daisy woke up with her head in Blade's lap. "Hey," he said, his voice raspy.

"Hey," she answered. She scrambled to sit up. She

was so not good in these high stress situations. Just not wired for it. "I'm sorry."

"No worries," he said. "Are you okay?"

"Embarrassed," she admitted. "You're the one who was in danger. And you're…fine. You're fine, right?"

"Yes."

"The fire?" she asked, turning to look at the building.

"Out. We'll watch it for a while, make sure it doesn't reignite. Reinforcements have arrived."

She looked over his shoulder. There were at least another four firefighters on the scene. "Here comes Charlie," she said, watching the man walk toward them. "He doesn't look happy."

"Yeah, probably not," Blade said.

"Everything okay here?" Charlie asked.

"She's good," Blade said. "I'm good."

"There's a truck going back. Why don't the two of you get in it?"

It was technically a suggestion, but didn't sound like one. Blade stood up and held out a hand for Daisy. She took it and stood. She still felt a little nauseous and tense.

What a day. When she'd seen firefighters running for equipment, she'd gotten out of the truck and followed them. They were trying to break through a concrete block wall, and the only reasonable conclusion was that Blade was trapped. It had probably taken them less than two minutes to bust through, but the seconds had dragged on.

She'd seen the first person transferred out through the hole and her heart had almost stopped. When she'd realized it wasn't Blade, she'd gotten even more frightened. Was he in some other part of the building? Was he already dead? And then she'd seen him crawl out, and well, for first time in her life, she truly understood the phrase *my knees buckled* because hers surely had. She'd gone down like a deflated balloon.

She and Blade got in the truck. She had a thousand questions, but wasn't sure where to start or what was appropriate to ask. And she was fairly confident her voice was no longer steady. So, she kept her mouth shut on the drive back to the fire station.

"I should go," she said once they were out of the truck.

"Are you sure you're okay to drive?"

"I am. Is the man you saved going to be okay?"

"I think so. I saw them getting him into an ambulance as we were leaving."

She turned to go. Then turned back to him. "I just have to tell you that your time inside that burning building was the most difficult minutes of my life. Well, maybe the minutes of active labor were more difficult, but that was sixteen years ago and my memory isn't what it used to be."

He laughed. A big laugh. "Thank you, Daisy. After today, I needed that. And I'm sorry if I in any way made you remember childbirth."

She felt drained. Yet oddly exhilarated. She'd watched a man save two other men, literally carry them out of the fire. It was the most courageous act she'd ever witnessed. Compared to that, her life contributions certainly paled. In all fairness, most peoples' life contributions wouldn't stack up all that well. She didn't know how to tell him that. So she segued into what she could more easily discuss. "I took some photos. I'll work on them tonight."

She would never have been able to do what he did today. But the one thing she could do right now was create an amazing Spring Spectacular campaign to make sure that others got to *see* the Knoware Fire Department, see their commitment, their bravery. That could open a spigot of money that might help them for many years to come.

"You're off tomorrow, right?" she asked.

"I am."

"You should probably get some rest."

"I'm fine," he assured her.

She wasn't sure if she believed him, but there was no use arguing. "I'll see you later."

There were about ten things he wanted to tell Daisy but now wasn't the time. It had been a tough call. He was trained to respond to emergencies and to stressful situations; she was not. She was undoubtedly shook. Right now was not the best time for her to deal with him trying to take their relationship to another place.

But he intended to have that conversation. He liked Daisy Rambler. A lot.

A truck rolled into the third bay, and he saw Charlie get out. He mentally prepared himself for what he knew was coming. He hadn't done anything that Charlie wouldn't have done, but that probably wasn't going to make a difference.

"Ms. Rambler leave?" Charlie asked.

Before she'd been Daisy. Suddenly she was Ms. Rambler. "Yes."

"Good. Grab a glass of water for both of us, and then why don't you come to my office for a minute."

Blade did as instructed. Once he'd handed Charlie his water and closed the door behind him, Charlie sat back in his chair. "I checked your tank. You were almost out of air."

"I know." It had been really close.

"You said you were exiting the building. That's what we expected."

"I know, Charlie. But then I saw a door and I just couldn't go until I'd cleared the space. Once I found the man, I moved as quickly as I could, but then the second floor came through."

"You were smart to get back to the outside vent. It made it easy for us to find you," Charlie said, somewhat grudgingly. "Only had to punch one hole through."

"You did a good job with that."

"Don't try to butter me up. You were lucky today, Savick."

"I'll take luck any day," he said.

"What's going on between you and Ms. Rambler?"

Ms. Rambler again. Blade instantly felt defensive on her account. "I'm not sure I understand the question."

"The question is a two part, but I'll talk slow to make sure you're getting it," Charlie said sarcastically. He knew that Blade knew exactly what he was asking. "My question is why was she the first person you looked for when you emerged from that hole, and why did she take a swan dive upon seeing you?"

"I...uh...felt responsible for her being at the fire. I wanted to assure myself of her safety."

"Uh-huh. Part two of my question?" Charlie prodded.

"She's a civilian. She got...overcome."

Charlie studied him. "If you were any other idiot in that chair right now, I'd be easily convinced that you might have been stupid today because you were trying to impress a woman. But I think more of you than that. I'm right, aren't I?"

"You're right," he said. He knew where Charlie was

going. Firefighters without the right motivation were dangerous. To themselves and others.

"Okay. Then we're done talking about it. Drink your water. You're probably dehydrated."

"Thank you, Charlie."

The man nodded. "You saved lives today," he said, his voice gruff. "Count that as a win."

Chapter 9

Daisy woke up the next morning when Sophie barged into her bedroom. "I can't find my shoes," her daughter said. "And I need fifteen dollars for a Knoware High T-shirt and please, please, don't pack carrots in my lunch."

Before she could answer, her phone buzzed. It was a text from Hosea. Call me in ten. I want to talk about the new product brochures.

What new products? What brochures? Oh, God, where was her coffee?

"Mom," Sophie said, her voice impatient.

Daisy sighed and crawled out of bed. She found Sophie's shoe under the couch cushion, dug up some cash in her purse and replaced the carrots she'd packed the night before with slices of yellow pepper. That took nine minutes and she called Hosea back right on time. He launched into the topic, and it took her at least half of the conversation to figure out that they were talking about brochures that were in development for a new line of women's athletic wear that the stores would be carrying.

By the time the conversation ended, her coffee was ready. She poured a cup and looked at her watch. Once she got to work, she'd figure out which one of the graphic artists had been assigned the project and make sure that her team was on the same page as Hosea, who really shouldn't be thinking about things like this when he had a new hip to contend with.

For now, she could sit for five minutes, maybe add a few lines to her gratitude journal. She pulled the journal from her leather bag. She'd started this a few months ago, when she'd still been in Denver and hadn't made the decision yet to move. Those had been dark days, and she'd been determined that it wouldn't pull her under. She'd started the journal as a way to fight back.

She opened it to a clean page. She began writing.

I am grateful that the two men were successfully pulled from the fire. I am grateful that they will see more sunrises and sunsets. I am grateful for the brave firefighters who risked their lives. I am grateful for Blade Savick. I am grateful that he's made me think that there really are good men.

There it was. In black and white. Not that anybody else would ever see it. She was careful to protect her journal, was careful that Sophie never saw her writing in it.

She put her pen down and thumbed through the photos on her cell phone. She'd thought about doing it the night before but, quite frankly, hadn't quite been up to the task.

Now she smiled when she came to the ones he'd taken of her trying to get on her bunker gear. Felt her heart start to beat fast when she got to the ones of the fire.

The one of Blade carrying the man from the burning building was spectacular. Like a movie shot. Certainly the photo that they should use to kick off the campaign.

She had a couple photos of them busting a hole through the concrete blocks. But after that, nothing. Taking pictures had been the last thing on her mind.

Feeling inspired, she turned to her computer and started working on the email that would go to customers and employees.

When Blade got off at nine the next morning, he met Marcus and Jamie for breakfast at Gertie's. He'd heard from both of the men within hours of the fire at the old orphanage. Word traveled fast in this town. Both had busted his balls for being a hero, but he'd heard the genuine concern in their voices.

After breakfast, he'd buy some groceries because Raven would be at his house that night. He might not cook a lot for her, but he always tried to keep fresh fruit and vegetables in the fridge for her to snack on, as well as staples like milk, bread, cereal and eggs.

When Blade walked into the restaurant, he saw Jamie. On his way back to the booth, he caught Cheryl's eye and she quickly brought a cup of coffee to the table. "Bless you," he said.

She smiled. "Waiting for Marcus?"

"Yeah."

"I'll watch for him."

Blade and Jamie exchanged a smile. No need for close observation. Marcus had a presence about him that caused people to sit up and take notice. One of Marcus's former girlfriends had said it was *like the air changed when Marcus was in the room.* Which might have sounded pretty outrageous if one hadn't experienced it firsthand.

And sure enough, when Marcus in full police uniform stepped into the room, almost every head turned. He greeted people as he made his way to the booth.

"Sorry I'm a little late," Marcus said, pushing his menu to the end of the table. None of them needed that.

"Fighting crime?" Jamie asked.

"I had to take Chief Ralley to the Urgent Care. Chest discomfort."

"That's why we have 911," Blade said.

Marcus smiled. "I've got lights and a siren."

"What did they say?" Jamie asked.

"They told him to stop eating salsa on his eggs in the morning," Marcus said.

"You think that's it?" Jamie asked.

Marcus shrugged. "You two have the medical knowledge. Not me. He seemed okay with the explanation. He's back at his desk."

Cheryl walked up to the table. She had a hot tea for Marcus in one hand and a coffeepot in the other to top off Blade's and Jamie's coffees. She filled Blade's to the brim but left plenty of space for Jamie to add cream. All three men ordered breakfast.

"Any more chasing runaways?" Marcus asked, looking at Blade. "I got the rundown from Jamie," he added. "Returning lost property. Finding missing teenagers. Those Boy Scout badges are piling up fast. Better find a seamstress or a hot glue gun so you can get them attached to your vest."

"Funny," Blade said. "I…uh…have seen Daisy Rambler."

"Tell me you're not stalking her," Marcus said.

"Almost the other way around. She's been assigned to shadow me at the fire station."

"Why? What?" Marcus and Jamie spoke in unison.

"Pratt Sports Spot is sponsoring the Spring Spectacular. She's my cochair."

Marcus sat back in the booth. "You lucky dog."

"She was at the fire yesterday."

"Oh, boy," Marcus said.

"Having her there…" His voice trailed off.

"What?" Jamie demanded.

"Having her there made a difference. When I was inside the building, waiting for them to push a hole through the damn building, I was doing a bit of soul-searching."

None of them made fun of that. They'd all been in situations where it wasn't always clear that they were going to come out the other side both mentally and physically whole.

"I want a…relationship with her. And I'm out of practice," he admitted. "I don't want to screw this up."

Now that made them smile. "Tell us how we can help," Marcus said.

"I told her that I wanted to be friends, and she very quickly clarified that we could be friendly cochairs." He did air quotes around the last two words.

Cheryl delivered their food and they dug in. Finally, Jamie looked up from his pancakes. "Friendly cochairs isn't a terrible place to start from."

"It's like settling for fast food when you could have a burger at Gertie's. Fine but really not what I want," Blade said. These were his two best friends. He could tell them the truth.

Marcus shrugged. "She sounds as if she might have

low expectations. You have to overdeliver, reliably. You need to be the best friendly cochair she could ever have imagined. You'll establish trust. The relationship can build from there."

"For now, just be a pal," added Jamie unhelpfully.

"I don't want to be her pal," Blade said, pushing his plate aside. "But I get the point."

"You were the one who was interested in showing her where to buy her milk and bread," Marcus said, taking his last bite. "That sounds friendly."

Blade said nothing. Hard to talk when one's teeth were clenched.

"Definitely don't kiss her," Marcus said.

"Goes without saying," Jamie said, pulling money from his pocket.

"Both of you *were* my pals," Blade said, emphasizing the past tense. "And I never kissed either one of you."

Marcus stood. Looked at Jamie. "I think our work here is done."

Blade watched them leave. He was pretty sure both of their shoulders were shaking with suppressed laughter.

He was still trying to find the humor when he was unpacking his groceries thirty minutes later. But his priority now had to be catching a few hours of sleep. During the night, he'd slept for a few hours before the alarm had sounded and they'd been en route to an accident scene. It had been a young woman, early twenties, close enough in age to Raven that his stomach had churned the entire time they were extracting her from the vehicle. Not drunk but admitted to being tired, and Blade thought it was likely she'd fallen asleep at the wheel and veered off the road, running smack-dab into a tree. She hadn't been able to get out of the car, but had been able to reach her phone and call 911.

The incident had taken the better part of two hours, and once he'd been back at the fire station, there was no way he was sleeping again. Every time he closed his eyes, he'd seen Raven in that driver's seat. It had made him also think about how tired Daisy's daughter had been when he'd seen her at the gas station. Kids were dumb, and generally thought they were invincible, not realizing that at a certain point their bodies would simply give out.

Now he lay in his bed, determined to think about something besides teenage drivers. Thinking about Daisy Rambler was a very good alternative. *Be a pal.* That was the best advice his friends had been able to come up with.

They were useless.

Or, maybe not.

After all, he'd jumped into a sexual relationship with Sheila. And when she'd gotten pregnant just two months later, he'd been determined that they would handle it. And both of them had tried. But it had never really been right. Perhaps if they'd have slowly developed a friendship first, it might have worked out differently.

It felt odd that he wouldn't see Daisy today. In just two days, he'd gotten used to having her around, to seeing his work through fresh eyes. When he'd seen her fall down at the scene, he'd been scared that she hadn't listened to his instructions to stay in the truck and had somehow breathed in too much smoke. He'd reached her and made sure she was breathing. By that time, she'd been coming around. He hated seeing her head on the hard ground, and it had seemed the most natural thing in the world to gather her up and rest her head in his lap.

He hadn't been thinking about what Charlie or anyone

else would think. Hadn't been thinking about anything but Daisy. Had he been too forward? Had he jumped the bounds of friendly cochair?

There'd been no time to talk about it afterward because she'd hightailed it out of the fire station. At that point, he'd had little time to dwell on it because he'd had to talk with Charlie and then finish his shift.

But now, in his own home, in his bed that he'd not shared with anyone for quite some time, it seemed as if all he could do was think about Daisy and how she'd felt in his arms. Soft, feminine. Delicious.

He looked down. Well, now. No way for his boxers to hide *that*.

He was a damn fourteen-year-old.

Ridiculous. He closed his eyes and did a mental inventory of the medical supplies currently in storage at the fire station. He finished that and did it again, just for good measure. Looked down. Let out a breath.

All quiet on the southern front.

Daisy pulled into her garage, shut the door and sat for a minute in her car. It had been a busy day. A productive one. She'd made a ton of progress on various Remember This social media posts. She'd been right about the emotional impact of the photo of Blade carrying out the first victim. It had gotten a lot of attention. But then again, so had the photo of the chili on the stove. People were interested in the firefighters' world.

In return, there had already been five photos posted by others. All had featured previous Spring Spectacular settings, and people had done a good job of sharing a short story about the photos. One of the more mundane things she'd quickly realized was that she was going to need a new dress. People had been really dressed up.

She heard voices when she opened the door to the house. Thought, at first, it was the television. But when she walked into the living room, she saw that it was Sophie, on the couch, and another teenage girl, on the floor nearby.

"Hi," Daisy said. She smiled at her daughter. Then turned to the other girl. "I'm Daisy Rambler, Sophie's mom."

"Hi. I'm Raven. Raven Savick."

Blade's daughter. In her house. Wow. She was a pretty girl with brown silky hair that hung down to the middle of her back. She was tall. Got that from her dad. "Nice to meet you. Are you two studying together?"

"Running lines," Raven said. "We're both trying out for the school play." The girl stood up and stretched. "My dad is on his way to pick me up."

Blade was coming to her house. Daisy resisted the urge to find a mirror. "This is a rather odd coincidence, but I actually know your dad. We're cochairs of the Spring Spectacular."

"They made chili together," Sophie said dismissively.

Daisy said nothing. Adding *And I almost saw him die yesterday* probably wasn't appropriate.

"He doesn't like to cook," Raven said, not meanly, just matter-of-fact. "He's also…well he's not the best dancer I've ever seen. Isn't there dancing at the Spring Spectacular?"

"There is, but he'll be busy running around, keeping things organized. Probably won't even have a chance to dance."

"Better for everyone," Raven said. She looked at Sophie. "I'm glad we could do this. I feel a lot better about the auditions."

"Yeah, me, too," Sophie said. "Maybe we could do—"

The doorbell rang, interrupting her.

"—it again," she finished as she headed for the door.

"Check first," Daisy called out.

"I know," Sophie said.

She did, no doubt, thought Daisy. She'd drummed it in her child's head to always check before opening a door. And in the more recent months, she'd known to keep the door closed and immediately get her mother if it was Jacob or one of his friends.

It was Blade, and he was holding a big gift basket. "Hi, Sophie," he said. He did not remind her where they'd met.

"Hello," Sophie said. She was looking at the basket.

He held it out. "This was on your front step."

Daisy moved fast. "Hi. Hey, let me take that," she said. She'd pulled into the garage and come in through the utility room. She hadn't even looked at the front door.

She set the basket on the hallway table. It was lovely. Beautifully wrapped in lavender-colored cellophane and coordinating ribbon, it was filled with a huge box of chocolates, multiple boxes of gourmet teas and coffees, shortbread cookies, cashews and more.

"Who's it from?" Sophie asked.

"I don't see a card," Daisy said, trying not to get alarmed. Maybe Jane had sent it. Or someone from Pratt Sports Spot. That was it. Maybe Hosea's assistant, Sandra Brogen, as a welcome gift.

"Let's open it," Sophie said.

"Um…" Daisy said. She again checked to make sure there was no card on the outside of the packaging, then opened the ribbon and peeled away the cellophane. Then she shifted items in the basket to make sure a card hadn't fallen in somewhere. "Let me just take a quick look outside," she said.

She opened the door, searched the front porch and step, but there was nothing. When she walked back inside, it was easy to see that Blade was puzzled by her behavior.

"It looks like something that might have come from Tiddle's Tidbits and Treasures," Blade said.

Daisy looked at him blankly.

"It's a gift shop, right on Main Street. They've got a lot of nice stuff. Really good chocolate," he added, looking at the box. "Morgan Tiddle owns the place, and if it came from there, she might be able to tell you who sent it."

"Good to know," Daisy said, working hard to be very casual. Maybe he thought it was odd that she wasn't opening the chocolate and offering them some. Nobody was eating anything in the basket until she knew more about it. But she couldn't tell him that because he'd either think she was crazy or he'd have questions that there was no way she intended to answer. "Did you know these two are both trying out for the play?" she asked, switching the subject.

"Raven had mentioned trying out last night. I didn't know the two of you had met," he added, looking at the girls.

"We have English and Algebra II together," Raven said.

Blade turned to Daisy. "On my way over here, I checked on ticket sales to the dance. More tickets were sold *today* than in the previous two weeks. That has to be a result of the social media you're doing."

"Good news," she said. She would think about that,

not about a stupid basket that had the ability to make her feel as if there was something heavy sitting on her chest.

"Super news," he agreed. "We should get going, Raven."

The girl swung the strap of her backpack onto her shoulder. "See you tomorrow, Sophie."

Then they were gone. Sophie walked over and looked at the basket closer. "You're freaked out about this, aren't you?" she asked. "You think it's from Jacob."

Daisy had not told her everything about Jacob, but she'd told her enough that the girl knew that Jacob Posse was not to be trusted. "I'm not *freaked out*. It's just an unexpected gift, that's all. And it's definitely not from Jacob. He doesn't know where we are." She turned her back to the basket. "Come on. I'm starving."

"What's for dinner?" Sophie asked.

She'd planned to make pasta and shrimp, but suddenly that seemed too big of a task. "Pizza. Jane told me about a good place. Get your coat. We're going now."

"That was weird," Raven said, once they were in the car. "Sophie's mom was acting all normal until you brought that basket inside."

"Yeah," he said. "What did you think of her?" he asked.

"Sophie or her mom?"

"Both of them," he said.

"Sophie seems kind of cool. And I think she'll definitely get a part in the play." She paused. "She told me about last Saturday, about trying to drive back to Denver. I was a little surprised to hear that you were involved in the apprehension. Her words, not mine," she added. "You didn't say anything."

"Yeah, I didn't think it was my story to tell. She didn't use the best judgment. A sixteen-year-old new driver has no business taking off in the middle of the night and attempting a long drive. She could have injured herself or others. She certainly caused her mom a lot of worry." He drove for another minute. "Apprehension, huh?"

"I think she was relieved that somebody stopped her. But you know, it's hard to admit something like that, especially to an adult."

He turned his head. "You are so smart sometimes." Truly, he was impressed at her emotional maturity.

"I know," she said smugly.

"And Daisy?" he prompted. "What's your impression of her?"

"I already said. She was fine, but then she acted like that box of chocolates was a bomb or something. Maybe you should tell her that there are no terrorists in Knoware. Only boring people."

He smiled. "I'm not boring. You're not boring. I have disproven your hypotheses."

She leaned her head back. "What's for dinner?"

"Lasagna. Your grandmother made it."

"Oh, thank God."

They drove in silence. When he was making the final turn, Sophie looked at him. "What do *you* think of Daisy Rambler?"

Chapter 10

"I think she's...nice. Very nice," he added quickly. "Has been very helpful with the Spring Spectacular."

She stared at him, but didn't say anything for a long minute.

"What?" he finally asked.

"I think you should take dance lessons."

He scratched his head at the change of topic. "I have a full-time job and I'm a dad. Why would I want to spend the few hours of downtime that I have taking dance lessons?"

"Because maybe you'll want to dance at the Spring Spectacular. You don't want to embarrass yourself."

"It's that bad?"

She shrugged. "What was it you used to tell me in fifth grade when I played basketball but couldn't even hit the rim with my free-throw shot? You used to say that perhaps I should shoot a few hoops on the weekends to polish my game. I think your dancing game could use some shine."

"Smart and funny. As a parent, I hit the jackpot, you know that," he said, pulling into the carport where he and his tenant, who rented the other side of the duplex, parked their vehicles.

"Wasn't trying to be funny, Dad."

They got out of his SUV. He rounded the back end and ruffled up the top of her hair. "I'm hungry. Hurry up!"

The next morning, Daisy made a point to swing by Hosea's office. Sandra was at her desk, hands busy on her keyboard. "Good morning," Daisy said.

The woman's hands stilled and she looked up, but she did not turn away from her computer. The message was clear. *I'm busy. Make it quick.*

"I…uh… I got home last night and there was a lovely gift basket on my front steps," Daisy said.

"Well, that sounds like a nice surprise," Sandra said. Her fingers lowered, back onto the keyboard.

Daisy didn't think this was looking good. But she'd come this far. "Unfortunately, there was no card. And I thought…well, I thought perhaps it came from here."

Sandra shook her head. "Not from this office. Perhaps from the staff in your department."

There was no way she was asking them. That would be even more awkward. It would probably take about three minutes for it to circulate around the entire company that the new marketing and public relations director was *hinting* to her staff that she'd enjoy and appreciate a gift from them.

"Sorry to have bothered you," Daisy said.

Sandra didn't answer, but she did start typing.

Daisy managed to keep herself busy until it was a reasonable time for an early lunch. She left the building and drove the two miles to downtown Knoware. And she found the Tiddle's Tidbits and Treasures without any trouble. It was in the middle of the block, between Gertie's Café and a bar called Feisty Pete's advertising beer for three dollars Monday through Friday.

It had two big bay windows, both beautifully decorated. One would have to be mostly blind not to realize that Morgan Tiddle had a love for the Irish. There was lots of green and white, and even though it was a miserable, cloudy and rainy day with temps in the low forties, it made Daisy realize that spring really was around the corner.

A bell tinkled when she opened the door. There was a pretty woman, maybe midthirties, behind the counter. She was tall and slim with the exception of a small pregnant belly. "Good morning," she said.

"Morning," Daisy said. "What a beautiful store." It really was. Besides the stunning selection of sweaters and blankets, there were framed photographs of the Washington shore for sale along one wall, glass cases of jewelry in the middle of the store, some blown glass on shelves, and a lovely selection of candy and teas near the cash register."

"Thank you. It's a labor of love. Mostly." The woman smiled. "Of course, in season, when every day is long, it's really just labor." She looked down at her stomach. "Soon, I'll be able to speak with some authority on labor."

"When is your baby due?"

"Late summer. It's lousy timing because it will still be our busy season when the baby is born. But I've been told that it's just the first of many times that my child will interrupt my finely tuned plans and that I should just start getting used to it."

"Sounds like good advice."

"Do you have children?"

"A daughter. She's in high school."

"Oh, my gosh. You look way too young for that," the woman said.

"I started pretty early," Daisy said, leaving it at that.

"Well, it's lovely to meet you. I'm Morgan Tiddle."

"Daisy Rambler."

"Would you like a cup of tea Daisy while you browse?"

"Um…not today. But I will come back and take you up on the offer," Daisy said. "Right now, I just have a question. I received a gift basket yesterday, and it was suggested to me that by the looks of the basket, it might have come from this store. There was no card. And I just feel terrible that I'm not able to thank the person who sent it."

"Was it chocolates and teas and nuts?"

"Yes."

"That was the only basket we did yesterday. I hope you liked it."

"I did. Do you recall who ordered it?" Now that she was close, her palms were sweating. It seemed so gauche in such a pretty place.

"It wasn't ordered in advance. Not that that is much of a problem, right now. We have time to create the baskets on the spot."

Daisy took some comfort in knowing that her panic was apparently not obvious because the woman's tone was still friendly, helpful. Cheery.

"Maybe if you could describe the person," Daisy suggested.

"It was a man. Late thirties or early forties, although sometimes it's really tough to tell."

"Hmm. Color of hair?" Daisy asked.

"Brown. Perhaps losing a bit in the front," she added, with a smile.

The age was right. The hair was right. "Tall?" Daisy asked.

"I guess. The thing I really did notice is that he had a beautiful gray overcoat. I thought it might be cashmere."

She'd never seen Jacob wear a cashmere coat. But he had worn a couple cashmere sweaters so it wasn't a stretch. "You might think this is really odd, but did he happen to pay with a credit card?"

"Well, I don't remember. Let me look at my computer. My sales are date and time stamped, and I remember it was right after I opened at ten o'clock yesterday that he came in."

"That would be so helpful." She waited while the woman clicked keys on the keyboard. When she finally looked up, Daisy's heart was beating fast.

"It was a cash sale," the woman said. "I'm sorry I can't be more helpful. I guess you'll just have to enjoy having a secret admirer. He seemed very nice."

There had been a time when she'd thought Jacob had been nice. Sane. "Thank you for looking," Daisy said. "I'll… I'll be back when I have more time to shop."

She got out of the store fast and then almost stumbled on a crack in the sidewalk because she turned her head so fast, trying to scan both directions. She ran to her car, got in, dropped her keys, snatched them up, and finally got the damn car started and in gear.

She was three blocks down the road before she took

a breath. And then it was big gulps, trying to flood her brain with oxygen.

She definitely should not jump to conclusions.

She should not hide her head in the sand, either. She was a little less emphatic about this one because, quite frankly, it sounded kind of good to her right now. She could forget about the basket, forget about this conversation with Morgan Tiddle, and pretend that her lunchtime errand had been all about getting a sub sandwich.

But while that was intoxicatingly simple, it could also prove very dangerous.

Could she go to local law enforcement? Could she trust them? Would they believe her? Even if they did, what could they really do?

After the one time, Jacob had never physically harmed her. Had been careful that his threats, or promises as he called them, were never overheard by others. The Denver police hadn't been able to help her.

She was going to have to look out for herself and for Sophie. Just like always. And one of the ways she did that was by keeping a good job, making sure she earned enough money so that there was something in the bank should the need to move on quickly become real.

She skipped lunch and went back to work. She was surprised to see fourteen Remember This emails. More early adoptors—that was what they called it in the public relations world. The first folks to jump on board. They were key to getting a new program or campaign off the ground.

Some of the early adaptors had just a single photo attached and a short story; some had written paragraphs and attached multiple photos. She started reading.

Stacy wrote that she'd met her husband Carl at the

Spring Spectacular. He'd stepped in after her original date to the event had gotten drunk in the parking lot and thrown up on her coat. Carl, who was part of the band, had witnessed the event and then helped her pour the idiot into the back seat of a friend's car. He'd then escorted her inside. Every time the band took a break, Carl had come to find her. And once he'd even ducked out of his playing responsibilities and danced with her. They'd been married six months later. That was over ten years ago. They hadn't missed a Spring Spectacular since. She'd attached a photo of the band.

It was a good story, but Daisy made a note to check on security for the parking lot.

Patrice Reynolds had sent a note that the Spring Spectacular was the only time, outside of funerals, that she remembered her father willingly put on a suit. She'd attached a picture of her mother and father. It was dated February 12, 1981. It appeared to have been taken at the event.

Daisy made a note to make sure there was a photographer booked.

She kept reading, not just because the stories were adorable, but she also wanted to make sure there was nothing offensive in either the emails or the photos. Once she did that, she copied everything over to the social media sites in hopes that it would motivate others to get in on the action. Then she made sure she sent a short personal note to everyone who'd sent something in, to let them know that their submission had been received and was appreciated.

She was halfway through her afternoon when her cell rang. She looked at it. Blade Savick. She ignored the little flip in her stomach. "Hi, Blade," she said.

"Hey," he said. "How's it going?"

"Great. We got fourteen more Remember This responses."

"That's great," he said.

"You seem surprised."

"Well, I knew it sounded like a really good idea, but I just wasn't sure about how the good people of Knoware would respond. I'll take a look online."

"At least half of them mentioned the photos I put online yesterday. One of them sent a recipe for white bean chicken chili." She paused. "Several made very specific comments about being grateful for the brave Knoware firefighters."

"Now you're making me blush," he said, trying to brush off the comment.

"It's going to be hard to top those photos," she said.

"Well, bring your camera tomorrow," he said. "That's why I was calling. We've got a training assignment set up. We're drilling on chemical spills, and Floyd Manufacturing Company has given us some space. I was going to text you the address, but thought it might be helpful for you to have some explanation, too."

"I appreciate that. I'll watch for the text."

"No problem. By the way, did you find out who sent you the gift basket?"

"Uh…no. I mean, I tried. I went to Tiddle's Tidbits and Treasures. Morgan Tiddle is a delight, and she remembered the sale because she had to make the basket up rather quickly. However, it was a cash sale."

"She couldn't tell you anything about the person who bought it?"

"It was a man."

"Well, that eliminates about half of the world's population," he said, his tone teasing. "But it was somebody she didn't know?" he asked.

She really didn't want to talk about this. Why was he so interested? "Yeah."

He was quiet for a minute. "Not that many strangers in Knoware this time of year."

Should she tell him? No. She immediately dismissed the notion. She did not want anybody in Knoware to know about Jacob Posse and what a fool she'd been. "Well, I guess it remains a big mystery," she said lightly.

"Could she describe him?" he asked, evidently not good at reading the clues that she was done with this conversation.

"Late thirties, early forties. Brown hair, cut short. Six feet. On the slim side."

"That could be me. Although clearly on a bad day since I just turned thirty-six."

Blade Savick was funny. She liked that. "Could be a lot of people," she said.

"Right," he said. He was silent for a minute. "I guess that's it, then. I'll see you tomorrow."

She hung up. A minute later, she got a text with the address. Chemical spill. Yikes. That didn't sound fun at all. A second later, her cell phone dinged again. This one was a text from Sophie, saying that she was home from school.

She would have to tell her daughter that the basket sender's identity was unknown. She didn't want to scare her, but she also wanted her alert. It was a balancing act. Tipping too far over on either side could easily do more harm than good. She didn't want her daughter to be afraid of men or relationships; she also wanted her to be very wary of Jacob Posse and his posse, no pun intended, who hung on his every word and likely wouldn't hesitate to get their hands dirty if it earned them an approving nod from Jacob.

Blade carried a tray of cheese, meat and crackers in one hand and a twelve-pack of beer in the other. He kicked the door with his foot and it swung open.

"Evening," Marcus said, reaching for the beer.

"Smells good," Blade said.

"Twice-baked potatoes in the oven," Marcus said. "T-bones on the grill."

Blade walked into his friend's house. It was a two-story, too big for a single guy, but Marcus liked to work with his hands and he was slowly remodeling the whole place. He'd done the kitchen first because he was also a good cook.

He'd be a hell of a catch for some nice woman except that he had no interest in settling down. That likely had something to do with the fact that his father had been married four times.

"Where's Jamie?" Blade asked.

"Covering for a sick ER physician."

"Good night to have an emergency," Blade said.

"Right. If I ever get shot on the job, I hope he's the one to patch me up."

Blade opened a beer. "You're more likely to get shot by a jealous husband."

"Never a husband," Marcus said. "Don't date married women."

"True," Blade said. "Although I do recall a couple of women who were very recently divorced."

"Rebound sex can be very rewarding," Marcus said. "Speaking of ladies, how's Daisy Rambler?"

"Okay, I guess. Although something kind of weird happened."

"Weirder than finding her on a ledge in Headstone Canyon or chasing her runaway daughter across the state?"

"Point made. Raven and her daughter connected at school. Both are interested in the school play. Raven went to Daisy's house after school yesterday. I picked her up."

"And Daisy answered the door dressed in plastic wrap and nothing else."

"That's your world, not mine," Blade said. "No, while I was there, she discovered a gift basket on her doorstep. A nice one. I was sure it had come from Tiddle's."

"Who sent it?"

"That was the issue. There was no card. And it freaked Daisy out. I could tell. She was trying to hide it but... well, she's not very good at it."

"She should check at Tiddle's," Marcus said. He was chopping romaine lettuce with a big knife.

"She did. Morgan remembered a guy ordering the basket, but he was a stranger. Paid cash."

Marcus put the knife down. "Did she say what the guy looked like?"

"Why?"

"We had another break-in in the business district last night. Feisty Pete's. Almost the same situation as at Gertie's. They kicked in the back door. Got away with almost a thousand bucks that the bartender hid in a coffee can in the back room."

"Camera?"

"No. But the bartender said that there was a stranger in the bar that night. A man. Brown hair. Nothing special about him. Had a beer and left. But once I heard that, I went back to Gertie's. She remembers that the morning of her break-in, there was a strange guy at her counter eating sunny-side-up eggs and rye toast. She said she remembered because hardly anybody wants their eggs sunny-side up. And when he ordered, he said *I want them looking at me.* The waitress evidently repeated the phrase about ten times that morning."

"Tiddle's is between Gertie's and Feisty Pete's," Blade mused.

"Yeah."

"I imagine all strangers in town are getting an extra special look," Blade said.

"Always good to make people feel welcome," Marcus said. "It occurs to me, however unfortunate this fact may be, that Daisy Rambler is also a stranger."

Chapter 11

"She is." Blade paused. "You think she brought trouble to our town?"

"I don't know. But because you apparently have a fondness for Ms. Rambler, I'm willing to give her the benefit of the doubt."

Have a fondness. So formal. "I saw her face. If the brown-haired man followed her here, she isn't happy about it."

"Then ask her."

"I did. Gave her an opportunity to tell me the truth. She didn't take it."

"Perhaps she just doesn't like you," Marcus said.

"I'm going with another theory," Blade said. "Brown-haired stranger is a threat. I'm not sure if he's a serious threat or just a pain in the ass. I'm going to work on getting her to trust me enough to explain it to me in better detail."

"Good plan," Marcus said, picking up the remote control. "Come on. The game's about to start."

"You'll let me know if anything else pops up on a brown-haired stranger," Blade said.

"That's what friends are for."

The next morning, Daisy plugged the address Blade had given her into her GPS. It said it was a twelve-minute drive. She glanced at her watch. She was early. She passed a bakery, slowed on impulse, and made a sharp right-hand turn to go around the block. Another couple turns and she pulled up in front of the cute little bakery. It had red-and-white gingham curtains in the windows and a lovely hand-painted sign. Knoware Bakery and Café.

The other firefighters had, thus far, been good-natured about her questions and her photo taking. She wanted to keep it that way. Plus it wouldn't hurt to placate Charlie some. He'd been downright chilly in his approach after the fire at the orphanage.

Sometimes refined sugar was exactly the right peace offering.

She opened the door and the scent made her smile. It smelled delicious, just like a bakery should. There was a scattering of tables, and most of them were full with singles and couples enjoying a cup of coffee and a morning treat. The tables all had fresh flowers in slim vases. Daisy hung back and watched a customer at the glass counter pick out a pastry and carry it to an empty table.

A woman, maybe midthirties, was behind the counter. She had short spiky blond hair that was tinted pink at the ends. She wore lots of makeup, but she knew how to put it on. Her smile was genuine when she greeted Daisy. "Good morning. What can I get you?"

"A dozen—no, make that two dozen—pastries to go," Daisy said. She had no idea how many people would be at the training this morning, and she wanted to have plenty. She had no doubt that the treats would get eaten.

"Of course." The woman grabbed a box, and Daisy started picking out a variety of scones, muffins and jelly-filled rolls. When she was finished, she pulled a credit card from her purse. "This is such a lovely place," she said. "I'm glad I stumbled upon it."

"Are you new in town?" the woman asked.

"I am. My daughter and I just moved here. She's in high school."

The woman behind the counter looked at Daisy's credit card. "Is Sophie your daughter's name?"

That surprised Daisy. "Uh…yes."

"She's all I've been hearing about. My daughter is Raven. Raven Savick."

Daisy was grateful that the pasties were still resting on the counter because if she'd have been holding them, she might have dropped them. This had to be Blade's ex-wife. Now that she knew the connection, she could easily see the resemblance between Raven and her mother.

"I'm Sheila Rice. I was Sheila Savick."

Daisy extended a hand. "Daisy Rambler. It's nice to meet you."

"You're cochairing the Spring Spectacular with Blade."

"Yes." Sheila seemed to know a great deal about Daisy. She felt at a disadvantage. And wasn't sure what to say next. She settled with, "So, have you worked here long?"

"My parents opened this bakery more than forty years ago. I grew up here. Literally. I was working behind the counter when I was thirteen. I was gone for a few years when I was married to Blade and Raven was little, but after the divorce, it just seemed like the right place to come back to."

So what prompted the divorce? That was the question she really wanted to ask. Blade seemed nice and normal as did Sheila. "It was a pleasure to meet you," she said. There was no need to know more. It wasn't as if she was interested in a relationship with Blade. She didn't want a relationship with anybody. "And especially nice to meet Raven's other parent. I know our daughters don't think it's necessary for us to know their friends' parents once they're in high school, but I have to tell you, it gives me some comfort."

"With you a hundred percent there." Sheila picked up a pen and grabbed a business card from a holder on the counter. "This card has the bakery number and you can usually reach me here, but I'll put my cell phone number on the back."

Daisy pulled out a business card and did the same. She passed it across the counter and picked up her pastries. "I guess I'll see you later," she said.

Once she was out of the bakery and back into her car, she sat for a minute before driving away. She supposed, in a town the size of Knoware, it wasn't that unusual that she might have encountered Blade's ex-wife. But it still felt as if it was an unexpected peek into Blade's life.

In ten minutes she was at the factory. Her first surprise was that she saw trucks from fire departments other than Knoware. She counted. At least eight other towns. Maybe she should have bought three dozen pastries.

"Hey," Blade said, walking quickly in her direction. "I thought that was you."

"This is like a convention of firefighters," she said.

"We generally pool our resources for hazmat training. It can be expensive to set up, and quite frankly, in a big hazmat situation, which most of them can get big in a hurry, we'll be coordinating with other fire departments. It's good if we all have had similar training. Most of the departments here are physically located within seventy-five to a hundred miles of Knoware."

She held up the boxes of pastries. "I got some treats. Maybe not enough."

He looked at the boxes. "This will be plenty. We've got a bunch of other stuff on the break table already." He started walking toward the big concrete building. "Let's go inside. I'll show you some of the equipment. Maybe you can get some photos."

"You're starting to think like a marketing person."

He smiled. "No need to be insulting me this early in the morning."

"Fighting words," she said, punching him lightly on the biceps. Why had Sheila ever let Blade Savick go?

They deposited the pasties on a long white table in a small break room. "You might want to keep your coat on."

Indeed. While it was warmer inside than out, it certainly wasn't warm. Maybe fifty degrees. She suspected that whoever owned the building kept just enough heat going so that the pipes didn't freeze.

He led her into the main part of the building. "What was this place?" she asked. There were the remnants of a few machines or partial machines. A saw. A vise.

"Furniture factory. At one time, if you had a Floyd table, you were something. They opened in the early

1900s but closed their doors over ten years ago. Couldn't compete with furniture that wasn't as nice but cost the consumer a whole lot less. They're still trying to sell the space, but in the meantime, they let us use it for lots of training when we want a big indoors space."

"How often would you do hazmat training?" she asked.

"At a minimum, every other month. Because we don't run into these situations every day, it's important to keep our skills fresh." He pointed at a corner of the building. "Today we're wearing Level A PPE." He smiled. "PPE is personal protective equipment. That's the highest level. All one piece, it protects everything from your toes to your nose. The responder wears his breathing apparatus inside the suit."

It sort of looked as if the firefighters were stepping into a big blue tent.

"It's absolutely airtight. Nothing is getting in. There is a release valve to let *out* air that is expelled as the responder breathes. Otherwise the suit would blow up."

"And they might float away like a blimp?" she asked.

"Something like that. These babies are heavy, they slow a responder down and they generally can't be worn for more than twenty to twenty-five minutes."

"This is fascinating. Is it okay if I take photos now?"

"Yeah. I already told everybody here what you'd be doing, and everybody gave permission."

The firefighter closest to them looked up. "Just get my good side, would you?"

"She doesn't have that much time," said the guy next to him.

She pulled out her phone and started snapping.

Twenty minutes later, the actual training started. By that time, Blade was in his Level A suit, looking as if he was ready for a moon walk. The scenario was a chemical spill and associated fire in an enclosed space. It included everything from the initial call to 911 from a scared secretary in the office, played quite convincingly by one of the firefighters, to the very end when the fire had been extinguished. It took hours, but she didn't get bored watching.

Afterward, after many of the firefighters had left, she and Blade sat at the break room table. The firefighters had attacked it after the training, and now there were just a few items left in a few boxes. "That was so interesting," she said, taking the second to last pastry out of the box. "I got some great photos. I don't think people understand how much time firefighters and EMS spend training."

"Probably not," he agreed, not sounding concerned. His damp-with-sweat hair was flat to his head, but he still looked very handsome. He was finishing a slice of homemade bread from a big loaf that someone had contributed. "They just expect that we'll show up knowing what we need to do. It's not that different from me going to the bank to borrow money and expecting the loan officer to be competent."

"There's a difference between getting some paperwork right and saving lives," she said.

"Sure. Of course." He took his last bite. "So today is the play tryouts."

"I know. Sophie was so nervous this morning that she was actually voluntarily talking to me."

"I don't think Raven slept much last night. I heard her moving around in her room and she was rocking some dark circles under her eyes this morning, and I'm pretty sure it wasn't makeup."

"Do you know when they find out?" Daisy asked.

"It gets posted online tonight at seven."

"Oh, this could be a very good night or a very bad one," she said.

"We could always bribe the judges," he said.

Her head jerked up. "What?"

"I'm kidding, I'm kidding."

She put down her plastic fork. "I get parents going crazy to help their kids. Because you do desperately want your children to have a good life, to do well, to have a future. I'd like to think that I wouldn't lie or cheat or take advantage in some way. But I won't deny that in the right circumstances it's possible to see myself making a bad choice."

"I doubt that. Common sense would prevail," he said.

"And the rock-solid conviction that my luck is such that I'd get caught," she said with a roll of her eyes.

He laughed. "That and you know that the best lessons in life are the times you failed."

"This is a poor segue, but I met your ex-wife this morning," she said.

"I wondered about that when I saw the pastry box."

"She seems very nice."

"She's pretty nice."

She waited, but he didn't seem inclined to say more. She wasn't going to push. If he wanted to talk about it, he would.

They each chewed for a few minutes.

"So I suppose you're wondering why we're divorced?" he said.

"It's none of my business."

"It's not a big secret. If you'd lived in Knoware longer, you'd probably already know. It didn't make the local newspaper but pretty darn close."

"What happened?"

"She had an affair and left me for the other guy."

"Wow. I… I'm not sure what to say."

"Yeah. That seemed to be most people's reaction at the time. But while I wasn't happy about it, I also wasn't that surprised. I knew she wasn't happy. She didn't like my job. So many odd hours and interrupted dinners. But I wasn't about to give it up. Oddly enough, now that we're not married, she's much more tolerant of what's required and works really hard to accommodate my schedule so that I get to see Raven. She married the guy she had the affair with. And I get along okay with him. He's good with Raven. That's all that really matters to me. I was surprised when she went back to work at the bakery. She probably doesn't need to, you know. But I guess it really does run in her blood."

"As you say, odd how things work out," she said.

"What about Sophie's dad?"

She had expected the question. "He's dead."

"I'm sorry. I didn't realize you were a widow. I assumed divorced."

She had intended for that to be it. A simple answer and certainly no need for an explanation of Jacob. But that felt kind of slimy, as if she was benefiting from a false assumption on his behalf. "I got pregnant with Sophie when I was still in high school. My mother, a single parent, died before Sophie was born. Luckily, so very luckily, my grandmother stepped in and long story short, I managed to have a child, finish high school, and subsequently college because she was in my corner the whole way. Sophie's dad and I never married. A few years after her birth, he was killed in Afghanistan." She stopped, took a breath. "But I was engaged relatively recently. It... uh...didn't work out."

"Your choice or his?" he asked.

"Definitely mine," she said. "I don't like to talk about it much."

He nodded. "Does this failed engagement have anything to do with your response to the gift basket?"

She wanted to tell him the truth, the whole ugly truth. But as nice as he'd been, she'd known him just a few days. Didn't know that she could really trust him. Didn't know whether he'd keep it in confidence. What if he shared it? What if Hosea Pratt heard the story? She'd had to leave one job because of Jacob; she didn't want to have to leave another.

She shook her head. "Oh, no. He's moved on, I'm sure." She looked at her watch. "I really should be getting back. I'm going to work another couple hours and then go home and pretend that I'm not on pins and needles until they make the play announcement at seven."

"You mentioned something before about a silent auction. I'm off the next two days. I could work on that."

"You'll have worked a twenty-four-hour shift, so I assume that you'll be sleeping tomorrow morning at least."

"Yeah. I'll leave work around nine. If I can have until noon or so, that should do me."

"I would need to sleep until five in the afternoon."

"Nah," he said, dismissing her concerns. "You get

used to it. And I may even catch a few hours during the night if there aren't any calls."

"How often does that happen?" she asked.

He shrugged. "Not that often, truthfully. But maybe we could meet for lunch."

Lunch. That sounded awfully much like a…date. "I… uh…"

"You know, to strategize the approach," he said. "You could coach me on looking pathetic so that when I go into businesses and ask for a donation, everybody will pony up."

Handsome and virile-looking Blade Savick wasn't going to be able to pull off pathetic. And he clearly wasn't seeing this as anything but a means to a successful Spring Spectacular. "We'll work on needy," she said. "If we do a good job of showing the immense need, then I don't think donations will be a problem."

"Pathetically needy. I'll work on it," he said. "Practice in the mirror."

"Maybe ask your daughter for some acting tips," she suggested.

"It'll cost me," he said. "In some way, at some time. Second gospel truth of parenting."

"What's the first?"

"Nobody sets out to do a bad job. But it's harder than it looks."

She held out her hand. "High five to that."

He lightly tapped her hand with his, but it was enough that his heat transferred to her and warmth infused her chilled body. And just that quick, the thought that she wouldn't need her electric blanket with him in her bed crossed her mind.

"I should be going," she said, standing up.

"You don't like the pastry?" he asked, eyeing her half-finished Danish.

"No. Loved it. Just full." *She* was the pathetically needy one.

Chapter 12

At six fifty that evening, Daisy was taping woodwork in Sophie's bathroom. Sophie was on her bed, her headphones on. Both of them were doing a pretty good job of pretending that they didn't have a care in the world.

But she knew her daughter. And Sophie was tense as a cat who'd done the math and eight of his nine lives had been accounted for. Or that was what her grandmother would have said if she'd been there to witness the silent, restless tapping of Sophie's fingernails on her duvet cover.

Nana Jo had a bunch of those types of saying. If she thought someone was shady, he was lower than a snake's belly. That was what she'd said about Jacob Posse. Not the first time Daisy had brought him to her home but certainly the first time Jacob had brought trouble to their lives.

She wondered what Nana Jo would say about Blade Savick. She'd appreciate his sense of humor, his humility. Would like that he was actively involved in raising his daughter even if the marriage hadn't worked out.

Would she think that Daisy had been a fool for not confiding in him, for not telling him about Jacob and the crazy way he'd acted? Or would she think Daisy had been wise to not mix her current life with her past?

Sophie sat up on her bed. "It's 7:01."

"Then you best take a look," Daisy said, holding her breath.

Ninety seconds later, Sophie was dancing around her room. Leaping on and off her bed.

"Calm down, you're going to break a leg," Daisy said. "Get it. Break a leg. Theater talk."

"The lead. The freakin' lead," Sophie said, ignoring her mother's attempt at humor.

"Language. And yes, the darn lead," Daisy said, all smiles. "You're supertalented, Sophie. I knew that you'd do well."

"And Raven, too," Sophie said. "I'm glad. I wanted both of us to make it. Me more, of course."

"Of course. I'm glad she made it, too. She seems nice."

"Oh, Mom, do you really think it's going to be okay. Here? In this place?" Her daughter was no longer laughing, but very serious.

"I think it can be, Sophie. I think it can be very okay, maybe even really good. We just have to give it a chance."

Daisy was getting ready for bed later that night when she got a text from Blade. Good news for our girls, it said.

Perhaps you heard my big sigh of relief across town, she wrote back.

He sent back a smiley face and added, See you at noon tomorrow at Gertie's. She'll be our first ask.

That made sense, she thought. Gertie Biscuit was the caterer for the event. She recalled that when Blade had looked at the scant details that had been provided to Hosea's assistant, his comment had been that the food, at least, would be good. She was anxious to get the menu decided.

She heard Sophie giggle. She'd been on the phone with Raven Savick for over an hour. Daisy knew that she should probably walk upstairs and tell her to shut it down for the night. But she didn't have the heart. There weren't that many nights like tonight—where big dreams came suddenly true. She'd didn't want to do anything to squash Sophie's joy. If the girl was tired tomorrow, well, she could catch up with her sleep on Saturday.

She sent a text to Jane, telling her Sophie's good news. Then she turned off her light and thought about meeting Blade for lunch the next day. She realized that she and Sophie had something in common—both had something to look forward to. Five days ago, when she'd been chasing Sophie across the state, she hadn't been sure that she'd feel this way again for a long time.

Blade got to Gertie's early. It allowed him to snag a booth and a cup of coffee from Cheryl.

"Waiting for Marcus and Jamie?" Cheryl asked.

He shook his head. "No. Um… Daisy Rambler."

Cheryl gave him a look. "Who is Daisy Rambler?"

"She's new to town. Works at Pratt Sports Spot, and she's my cochair for the Spring Spectacular."

"Is she nice? Or will we have to band together and run her out of town?" Cheryl asked.

"This from the woman who used to carry bugs outside to set them free versus stepping on them in high school."

"Bugs are one thing. New people, well, that's different."

"I don't think you're going to need to worry about Daisy. She's…um…she's—"

Daisy walked through the door of Gertie's looking fabulous in her pretty blue coat and knee-high black boots. Cheryl turned and looked. When she turned back to look at Blade, she was smiling.

"As I live and breathe," she said, almost under her breath.

"What?" he asked, not taking his eyes off Daisy who was crossing the small café. He stood up.

"As I live and breathe, I think I'm seeing a woman who can make Blade Savick speechless."

There was no time to answer, to deny, because Daisy was at the table. "Hi," she said, looking at Blade.

"Hi," he said, thinking maybe he wasn't speechless, but he did feel a little breathless.

"I'll give you two a minute with the menu," Cheryl said, backing away from the table. "Not that you don't know it by heart, Blade," she added. Then smiled at Daisy. "I'm Cheryl, by the way. Can I get you something to drink?"

"Coffee, please," Daisy said.

"Cream or sugar?" Cheryl asked.

"Just black."

"I knew that," Cheryl said with a quick look in Blade's direction.

"That was odd," Daisy said, once they were alone.

"Yeah, that Cheryl. She's an odd one," Blade said.

Daisy sat down. "Cute place. And pretty busy given

that it's not the busy season." She did air quotes around the last two words. "I really can hardly wait to see the difference in this place once the tourists arrive."

"Locals try to stay away," he said. "And even though the crowds might give me hives, there is something about the biscuits and gravy here that make it worth the risk."

"Breakfast served all day," she mused. "So what I think I'm hearing is that I might want to go with that over my typical tuna or turkey sandwich."

"Not telling you what to do," he said easily. "But you're going to be jealous when you see my plate."

"Fine. Convinced." She put her menu to the side.

Cheryl returned with her coffee. Daisy ordered a small biscuits and gravy with a scrambled egg on the side. Blade ordered a large with two eggs over easy.

Cheryl walked away. Daisy picked up her coffee. "Please don't take this question the wrong way. I like breakfast as much as the next person and I'm looking forward to the biscuits and gravy, but... I wasn't thinking a breakfast buffet for the Spring Spectacular."

"Don't be fooled. Before Gertie opened Gertie's Café here some twenty years ago, she was a chef in a big hotel in San Francisco. Her husband, who sadly has passed away, designed and hand built boats. My friends Marcus and Jamie and I all worked for him for several summers when we were in high school. Sometimes she would cook dinner for us. It was amazing. And she's done a lot of these events in Knoware. Always really good, regardless of whether she's cooking dinner for five or five hundred."

"You sound very fond of her."

"I am. Her husband always called her Gertrude Grace and said that he was the luckiest son of a gun ever to have married her and somehow managed to keep her. She's cooked for lots of famous people, but she never brags about it. She won't disappoint."

That was a big relief. Food wasn't the most important part of a successful event, but it was a pretty darn important part. "Have you given any thought to the menu for the Spring Spectacular?"

"Uh...no."

Maybe she was just going to have to take this piece and run with it.

"I imagine Gertie has a few ideas. We'll snag her once the lunch rush is over. But right now, we eat," he said, motioning at Cheryl who was carrying a tray their direction.

She set the plates down and refilled their coffee. "I'll check back," she said.

"It smells delicious," Daisy said.

"Yeah." Blade pointed to her eggs. "So you eat your eggs scrambled?"

"Mostly."

"Me, I've always been the over-easy or over-medium type. If I'm making a sandwich, I cook them over hard," Blade said.

"You know how to cook an egg sandwich?" she asked, as if she could hardly believe it.

"Funny," he said. "But I can't abide an egg straight up. Don't like them looking at me."

She dropped her fork onto the table. Jacob had eaten his eggs that way. And had described them in exactly that manner when he'd ordered.

"Something wrong?" Blade asked, his look intense.

She looked down, as if her fork was the most interesting thing she'd seen in a long time. "No. Why would it be?"

He didn't answer, and she reluctantly forced her gaze to meet his. He shrugged. "Just asking."

They both started eating and didn't talk again until they were finished. Blade pushed his dish to the side. "I think I'll see if I can get Gertie's attention."

He slid out of the booth, all long legs and easy swagger. She watched him walk to the counter. He was nothing, absolutely nothing, like Jacob. It was just a weird coincidence that he'd described sunny-side-up eggs in the same manner.

Four minutes later, he came back, laughing and smiling at something the woman at his side had said. She was probably in her early seventies, but she moved easily. Her hair was gray, her eyes were blue and military dog tags hung from a chain around her neck.

"This is Daisy Rambler," Blade said when he got close. "Daisy, this is Gertie Biscuit."

"It's a pleasure to meet you," Daisy said, scooting over in the booth to make room for Gertie on her side. She pulled a business card from her purse and slid it across the table. "Breakfast was delicious."

"Biscuit is my name, biscuits are my game," Gertie said. "And I've got the T-shirts to prove it," she added, waving her arm in the direction of a display stand of Gertie Biscuit coffee cups, T-shirts and baseball caps.

"I think you're a marketing genius," Daisy said.

Gertie laughed. "I got lucky and fell in love with Nicky Biscuit. I used to tell him that if he'd have been Nicky Smith or Nicky Jones, I wouldn't have given him a second look." She fingered the dog tags. "These are his. He served in Vietnam. We weren't sure he was going to come home. After he did, he wore them every day for fifty years. I wear them now in his honor."

Daisy could feel her throat get tight. Gertie was living proof that great loves happened to real people. It could happen to her someday. "That's a wonderful story," Daisy said.

"Speaking of great stories, I saw some of the social media that's been generated by your Remember This theme. And my employees were all talking their favorite memories from the dance."

"Encourage them to send them to me," Daisy said. "I'm excited that you're doing the food. Blade and I wanted to chat with you about the menu given that it's just a little more than two weeks away. We were hoping that we might continue on with the concept with the food but just aren't sure how to do it."

Gertie nodded. "I actually was thinking about that just this morning once I overheard my employees. I've got an idea. But don't hesitate to let me know if you're not crazy about it." She waited until they both nodded before continuing. "I've been doing the event for the last eighteen years. I've kept records of what we served every year. And I also have the records of the previous two caterers, going back another twenty-five years. So that's more than forty years of menus."

"Let me guess," Blade said with a smile. "All of them have chicken in some form or fashion."

"Well, lots of them do. But even so, it was fixed in a different way. And there were lots of years where beef, pork or fish was the main dish. I think they even went through a pasta phase. And who could ever forget the ham balls."

"Ugh," Daisy said.

Gertie chuckled. "No worries. I'll go through the menus. First pass, I'll delete any choices that I'm absolutely opposed to making. Like ham balls. Second pass, I'll pick out maybe ten to fifteen that I think would be best. We could post the choices and ask readers to vote on their favorite. And that's the one I'll cook."

"I love it," Daisy said. "I think it will drive a lot of social media participation—people really get into talking about food."

"They might even have a photo they can share of one of the choices," Gertie said. "Customers used to pick up a fork when their food arrived at the table. Now they pull out their cell phone."

"So true," Daisy said. "I'm trying to get a handle on our expenses. Can you give me an estimate of how much it would be per person?" In her experience with past events, the food costs always took a big chunk out of the proceeds.

"I donate the food," Gertie said. "And I'll provide all the table linens, table decorations and flowers. The community center has plates and silverware."

Her head was reeling. "Gertie, that's incredibly generous."

Gertie waved a hand around. "This community is, to use your words, incredibly generous to me. Has been for the last twenty years. I want it to remain strong and vibrant. Services, like fire and EMS, are a necessary part of that. I'm happy to do it."

Daisy looked at Blade. He shrugged. "I think her mind is made up," he said.

"And you know better than to argue with me," Gertie said, her tone amused. She looked at Daisy. "You better watch this one, Daisy. He's got an innocent look about him, but I remember him and his two friends when they were just kids. There was always some sort of mischief going on. They're all grown up now, but I'm not sure they've completely shed the trappings of their misspent youth."

"I don't even know what that means," Blade said. "But you know that we'd never give you any trouble."

"I do. And I know you, Marcus and Jamie always overtip my servers, as well." She stood up and extended her hand to Daisy. "I'll be in touch."

Daisy watched her greet customers as she made her way back to the kitchen. Then she leaned forward in the booth. "I love her."

Blade nodded. "Everybody does."

"I think she's a bit fond of you," Daisy said.

"Don't sound so surprised," he said.

"I'm not," she protested. "You would be easy to..." She stopped. *Like? Love?* Oh, good grief. "Easy to be fond of," she finished. "And I'll be even fonder of you if you can help me whip up some fantastic silent auction items. I was thinking that I should probably draft a letter of appeal."

He shook his head. "That will likely be best for any of the larger employers in the area. But if you want participation from smaller businesses, like the ones that line Main Street, I'd suggest we let our feet do the talking."

"I'm willing to try it," she said. "I've got a couple of free hours this afternoon. Do you have time now?"

He slid out of the booth. "I'll make you a deal. I'll even take the lead at the garage at the tail end of the business district."

He'd said it casually. Too casually. She smelled a setup. "What's special about the garage?"

He shrugged. "Nothing really. But the people who own it may be a soft touch."

"Who owns it?"

"My parents. Come on, I'll introduce you. It'll be a good place to start. We can work our way back."

On automatic, she walked out of Gertie's Café and followed his lead to turn left. The wind had picked up, and strands of her hair blew across her face.

She ran her tongue over her teeth, hoping she didn't reek of biscuits and gravy. Meeting someone's parents really required clean teeth, brushed hair and fresh lipstick. Right now, she had none of that. But then again, it wasn't as if this was personal. No, it was business. Just business.

But a stick of gum wouldn't hurt. She hurriedly reached into her purse and popped a piece into her mouth.

"Both of your parents work at the garage?" she asked.

"Yeah. My mom started working on cars when she was a teenager. Her parents owned this shop. When they got too old to run it, she and my dad bought them out. He'd always helped out here on the weekends, and now it's his full time gig, too."

His mom worked on the cars. "I feel bad admitting this, but I think I might have been really sexist and assumed your mom ran the office and did the books."

He smiled. "She does some of that. But she'd rather be working on a car."

Three blocks later, they were in front of the business. It was painted a cheerful and tasteful yellow and gray. There were three bays, and all of them had cars inside being worked on.

"They look busy," she said. "Maybe we should come back."

"They're always busy. That's a good thing. Come on." He headed toward the middle bay. "That's Mom."

Daisy could see the back of a woman with her head

under the hood of an SUV. She was wearing blue work pants and a white shirt. "Hey, Mom," Blade said as they approached.

She straightened and turned. "Oh, what a nice surprise," she said. She leaned forward to hug Blade. "Are we on fire and I didn't know it?"

"Hey, I get over here once in a while," he protested good-naturedly.

She was lovely, and if the clothes were utilitarian, the rest of her was pure feminine. Her brown hair was cut short and highlighted with streaks of blond. She wore light makeup, and her lipstick looked pretty fresh. Daisy resisted the urge to put her hand in front of her own mouth. The woman smiled when she looked at Daisy. "Hi, I'm Gemma Savick."

"Daisy Rambler," she said, shaking hands. "Blade and I are working together on the Spring Spectacular."

"Oh, I've heard all about you," Gemma said. "My granddaughter Raven said you have the coolest clothes."

"I don't know about that," Daisy said. "Raven is a lovely girl. I'm glad that she and Sophie, my daughter, have hit it off."

"And both of them got parts in the play," Gemma said. "That worked out nicely."

"Gosh, Mom, you're awfully up to-date on things to play the *I never see you* card," Blade said.

Gemma winked at Daisy. "So what do I owe this rare visit to?"

"We're looking for silent auction items for the Spring Spectacular. I know that you and Dad always attend."

"Bought tickets the first week they went on sale. Wouldn't miss it," she said. "And, of course, we'll contribute something. How about five free oil changes and a tire rotation and balance?"

"That's perfect," Daisy said.

"My work is done," Blade said. He turned to Daisy. "Good luck with everybody else."

His comment drew a stare from his mother.

Blade turned to Daisy. "At our house, we call that *the look*. It generally means that a person has stepped in it up to his waist. And I emphasize *his*, because in all cases *the look* is reserved for me or my dad." He turned back to his mom. "Relax. I'm doing my part. Equal all the way. But speaking of Dad, where is he?"

"He…uh…isn't here."

"He is not having coffee with Schrader?" Blade again looked in Daisy's direction. "This guy keeps wanting my dad to invest in diamonds. He's a nut."

"No. He's not with Schrader," Gemma said.

"So where is he?" Blade prodded.

"He had a doctor's appointment." Gemma picked up a rag and wiped at her fingers.

That made Blade cock his head. "His hip?"

"No."

She didn't know Gemma Savick well, but by the sudden inability to meet Blade's gaze, it seemed as if there might be more to the story. She sneaked a quick sideways glance at Blade, and she knew immediately that he was also concerned.

"Then what for?" he asked.

When Gemma looked at Blade, her eyes were kind. "It's your father's health, Blade. It's for him to decide what to share."

"What the hell?" Blade said.

"I will tell him you stopped by," Gemma said. "And that you were concerned."

Blade stared at his mother. "Is this something that you should be with Dad? This place can run without you. You know that, right?"

Gemma tilted her chin down. "I do know that." She didn't sound angry, but her tone was definitely cooler.

"I just think—"

"Daisy," Gemma said, interrupting her son, "it was lovely to meet you. I'll get a certificate made up for the silent auction item and make sure it gets dropped off at your office at Pratt Sports Spot. But right now, I need to get back to work." She turned back to Blade. "Goodbye. I will let your dad know that you stopped in."

She walked away from them.

Blade turned to Daisy. "I'm not sure what just happened here."

"Talk to your dad," she said.

"Oh, I will. Count on that," Blade said, sounding frustrated.

"You know what, I can take the silent auction from here," Daisy said.

"No. No way. We're cochairs."

"Yes, but—"

"I'm actually a very good multitasker and a supreme compartmentalizer. It sorts of goes with the job. One situation cannot be allowed to impact another. That could ultimately compromise care. Plus, as nice as you are, you're still a stranger. There will be more pressure to give if a local boy is standing there, doing the asking."

"If you're sure."

"Let's go. Next stop is the ice cream shop. I'm thinking an ice cream party for the lucky auction winner and twenty of his or her closest friends."

"Or a free quart of ice cream for the next twelve months," she countered.

He waved a hand. "Quart, hell no. Half gallon at the minimum. We do things big here on the West Coast."

He was right. He was big and bold and fun. This was going to all be over in just a couple weeks, after the Spring Spectacular.

She was going to miss it. A lot.

Chapter 13

Blade silently stewed about the conversation with his mother while he and Daisy worked the street. Within two hours, they'd collected auction pledges from fourteen merchants, everything from ice cream to free haircuts to complimentary year-end tax processing. Daisy was confident that Pratt Sports Spot would donate a nice gift, and Blade had volunteered to see what the Emergency Room physicians at Bigelow Memorial would pony up. As a medical team, they'd been known to be very generous. He was confident that Jamie had something to do with that.

He and Daisy had parted ways late afternoon, and it had taken him about six seconds to decide to pay another visit to his parents' business. This time he found his dad in the front office, standing behind the counter, his hands busy on a computer. As always, his dad looked up when the bell above the door tinkled, and smiled when he saw it was his son.

But Blade could see the wariness in his eyes and knew that his mom and dad had talked, and his dad had been expecting his visit. That wariness was enough to make Blade's gut tighten.

"Hey," Blade said. He took a quick look around to make sure they were alone.

"Hey, yourself," his dad said. At sixty-three, Larkin Savick was still trim. Had walked two miles a day for as long as Blade could remember. His hair was more gray than brown, and he'd given up the pretense of only needing glasses for reading several years prior.

"How's it going?" Blade asked.

"It's okay," his dad said.

Blade decided he wasn't going to dance around it. "I stopped in this morning. Mom said that you were at a doctor's appointment, but she didn't want to provide much detail."

His dad held up a hand. "Your mom was just doing what I asked of her."

"Okay. So what's the deal?"

"Three weeks ago, I was diagnosed with pancreatic cancer."

The words hit Blade like a sledgehammer. And because his mind refused to embrace pancreatic cancer, he focused on the timeline. "Three weeks ago! And I'm just hearing about this."

"Things have been moving kind of fast," his dad said. "And I didn't want to worry you until we knew more."

Worry. Pancreatic cancer. The words bounced around in Blade's head, smacking into one another. Hell yes, he was worried. This was bad. But he was a trained emergency responder. Knew to get the facts so that he could assess. "So what are the doctors saying?" he asked, hoping that his voice didn't reflect that his heart was racing.

"They said I'm lucky. That most of the time, this cancer isn't diagnosed until it's rather advanced, stage three or four. But I'm stage two. With an aggressive treatment plan, they're optimistic."

Optimistic that they could destroy the cancer? Optimistic that he would live another year, three years, five years? Blade wanted to drill into the definition but knew that now wasn't the time. He knew what that aggressive treatment plan might look like. He walked around the counter and reached for his dad. Hugged him hard. "I'm sorry, Dad," he said.

"It's a kick in the nuts, all right," his dad said. "But I'll get through it.

"We'll get through it," Blade said.

His dad shook his head. "No. That's why I didn't want your mother to say anything. You've got your own life to live, Blade. A big job and raising a teenage daughter. You don't need to be worrying about me. I don't even want your mother there. She doesn't need to see this."

With most any other person, Blade would have brushed off the comment as a poor attempt to appear stoic. But not his dad, who rarely said anything that he hadn't thought long and hard about. "That seems unnecessary," Blade said. "We want to be part of this. I want to help in any way that I can."

"Of course you do. And the best way that you can help is to go on about your life without worrying about me. I've told your mother to do the same thing."

Blade felt bad. "I sort of insinuated to her this morning that she wasn't with you because she thought the garage couldn't run without her. But you didn't want her there, did you?"

"Nope. And I think you should consider yourself fortunate that she didn't throw a wrench at your head."

"I'm an idiot," Blade said.

But then maybe his father was, too. His dad no doubt thought he was protecting his wife. And his wife was feeling rejected and left out of the process. It was a mess. But Blade was confident that his parents would sort that part out. How he was going to be of any help to his dad when he felt decidedly helpless was another issue.

"What can I do, then?" he asked, deciding it was best to be direct.

"The thing I don't want you doing is treating me like I'm half dead. We're going to go on about our lives, juggling tasks, managing priorities, having a beer now and again."

"You can't ignore this, Dad."

"I'm not. I've been busy getting a second opinion, which fortunately or unfortunately, depending on your perspective, matched the first diagnosis. I'm going to be starting a combination of radiation and chemotherapy in hopes of shrinking the tumor before surgery. I'm dealing with it. But I do not intend to talk about this 24/7. In fact, right now, I'm done talking about it. Tell me about Daisy Rambler. Your mom said she was very pretty."

He had a thousand questions, but his dad had been pretty clear. Time to change topics. And it wasn't a hardship to talk about Daisy. "She is pretty. Nice, too. We've got some things in common. She's got a sixteen-year-old daughter at Knoware High. Her name is Sophie and she and Raven have connected."

"Interesting."

"We're just working together on the Spring Spectacular."

"Of course."

"She's a marketing type so that's really great," Blade added.

"For sure."

Blade smiled. "I'm not fooling you, am I?"

His dad shrugged. "I can't take much credit here. It was your mom who picked up on something. She said, and I quote, 'I think Blade might really like this woman.'"

"We'll see how far that gets me."

"You've been alone a long time," his dad said. "So long that it might feel comfortable. But a life is meant to be shared with someone. I don't know what I'd have done without your mom these last forty years."

But yet he was deliberately cutting her out of his current battle. Blade wanted to point out the hypocrisy but held back. "I didn't say I was giving up."

His dad laughed and slapped him on the back. "That's my boy!"

When Daisy got home from her afternoon with Blade, Sophie was not there. And for just a quick second, she panicked. Had her daughter run again? But then common sense settled in and she realized that play practice had started. She started to breathe again.

Trust was a funny thing. It was just assumed until it was breached, and then it was hard to rebuild.

She would trust Sophie again. But it might take a while.

She settled down on her old sofa in her new house with a glass of white wine in hand. It had been a good day. Substantial progress had been made on the Spring

Spectacular. Meeting Gertie had been a real relief, and any concerns she'd had about the food had been abated. Obtaining donations for the silent auction had been surprisingly easy and really fun.

Blade had been spot-on when he'd said that it would go better if he was there for the ask. People knew him. Liked him. Respected him. All of that had been patently obvious. Tomorrow, she would draft an email to Hosea asking what Pratt Sports Spot might be willing to add.

Meeting Gemma Savick had been a surprise. She could not help but wonder what the big secret was that she was guarding. While Blade hadn't said anything about it, she suspected that after they'd parted, that he'd either immediately called his dad or returned to the business to find him.

She had a feeling it was something significant.

Maybe she should call Blade.

That was what she'd do if it was Jane who was potentially getting bad news about a parent's health. That was what friends did.

Before she could talk herself out of it, she dialed his number.

"Hi," he said.

"Hi. I…uh… I wanted to let you know that I already got something from Gertie on the choices for food. It's already posted and responses are coming in."

"Great, thanks for letting me know."

"Oh, sure." She paused. She needed to just ask. "I've been thinking about you. About your dad. Have you talked to him?"

"Yeah. Just left the garage."

"Everything okay?"

"Not really. Look, my dad won't want this broadcast

around, but I know you won't do that. He's got pancreatic cancer."

She, who knew little about health care, knew enough to realize that this was bad. "I'm sorry, Blade. That had to have been difficult to hear."

"Yeah. My dad was pretty clear about it, though. He doesn't want to dwell on the situation, and he doesn't want the rest of us to be concerned. It's his problem and he's dealing with it."

"Everybody copes in different ways."

"I know. But it's tough."

His voice had cracked on the last comment. "Of course it is. And this information is so new to you right now that you probably have a thousand questions that maybe he either wasn't willing to answer or able to."

"How did you know?" he asked. "I don't know what to tell Raven. It's her grandfather."

He wanted to protect his daughter. But there was no way. She would remember for the rest of her life hearing the news that Nana Jo wasn't going to recover. He was in a tough spot. And when she'd been hurting and needed help to find her daughter, he'd jumped in with both feet. "Do you have Raven tonight?"

"Yeah. She should be home from play practice soon."

"Will you tell her right away?"

"I think so."

"Will she immediately want to go see your dad?"

"Probably. But I think that may not be a good idea She'll be emotional and right now, he wants everybody to pretend that this is *not that bad*."

"If it feels right, maybe once you've talked, the two of you could meet Sophie and I at Know Your Scoop. That place had some amazing-looking ice cream."

"It's forty degrees outside."

"My interest in ice cream is not weather dependent," she said.

He laughed.

She was glad she'd been able to make that happen.

"You're right. Mine, either. That sounds…really great. And Sophie may be a big comfort to her."

"I think she could be. I'm certainly not saying this is what is going to happen, but it wasn't that long ago that Sophie and I lost my grandmother."

"I'll let you know how the conversation goes."

"Good luck."

Ten minutes later, Sophie came home, script in hand. "This play is going to be so cool." She took a breath and didn't stop talking for the next half hour. She sat at the counter while Daisy cooked angel hair pasta and shrimp. By the time they were finished, Daisy knew that the play director, who was also the honors English teacher, was hysterical; the costumes were ridiculous, and the male lead was the cutest boy in the senior class.

Daisy put their dishes in the sink. "I think it's going to be amazing."

"*I'm* going to be amazing," Sophie said loftily. "I don't know about everybody else. Well, I do think Raven is going to be pretty good."

"Speaking of Raven, I want to talk to you about something."

"You don't like her," Sophie said, jumping immediately to the wrong conclusion.

"No. That's not it at all. I wanted to tell you that tonight, Raven is going to learn from her dad that her grandfather is ill. Seriously ill."

"Ill like Nana Jo?"

"Different than Nana Jo, but still very serious. And Raven is likely to be upset and concerned. I just thought you should know. Because I thought it might be good for both Blade and Raven to have something else to think about, I invited them to join us for ice cream tonight. I found a place called Know Your Scoop. Get it. Know as in Knoware."

"This is such a weird place," Sophie said.

She said it as if weird and bad were not the same thing. That made Daisy feel good. "You're okay with going for ice cream?"

"Of course. I like Raven. And I'm sorry about her grandfather. That sucks."

"Don't say sucks. But it does. It truly does."

Blade ordered Chinese for dinner. It was Raven's favorite. She ate as if she hadn't eaten in about a year. "Hungry, huh?" he asked when she'd finished her second helping of chicken fried rice.

"I'm a growing girl," she said. She pushed her plate away. "But I think I've reached my limit." She started to get out of her chair.

"Can I talk to you for a minute?" he asked, holding up a hand.

"Sure," she said, settling back down in her chair. "Did I do something wrong?"

"No." He stopped, thought about it. "Did you?"

"Not that I know of. Hoping that my science teacher will start the school on fire with a Bunsen burner doesn't count, right?"

He thought she was kidding. "I saw your Grandpa Savick today."

She waited.

"He had some news for me that I wanted to share with you. It's…not great news."

She straightened up in her chair.

"He has cancer, Raven. Of the pancreas."

"What's the pancreas do?"

"It's part of the digestive system," he said. There was no need to get too technical.

"Can you live without it?"

"You can. But sometimes removal isn't the first course of action or the best. Your grandfather is in the process of working with his physicians to determine the best course of action. He doesn't want us to worry."

"Are you worried, Dad?"

Sometimes his little girl was very grown-up. "I'm concerned," he admitted, not wanting to lie. "But if your grandfather is staying positive and that's what he wants from all of us, I'm willing to give it my best shot."

"Am I going to freak out if I look this up on the internet?"

He nodded.

"He could die from this?"

Again he nodded. "But that's not saying he will. He may respond very well to treatment and be here to dance at your wedding." His dad had been telling Raven for years that he couldn't wait to dance at her wedding. When she was thirty, he would always add.

"Should I call him?" she asked, her eyes filling with tears.

"Maybe in a day or two, once you've had time to let this settle just a bit. Right now, I've got another suggestion. Earlier today, Daisy Rambler and I were canvassing the business district, asking for donations for the Spring

Spectacular silent auction. We got something from Know Your Scoop, and Daisy thought it would be great if we could sort of pay back their kindness with our own purchase of some ice cream." That wasn't exactly right but close enough. She didn't need to know that both he and Daisy had been concerned that she was going to be upset. "You up to meeting Daisy and Sophie there for a treat?"

She sniffed. "Yeah, I guess."

"Good. I'll give her a call. And just so you know, she was with me earlier this afternoon when I first learned something about your grandfather's situation so she's in the know. I suspect that she'll have told Sophie. So don't feel as if there's anything that you can't talk about."

Twenty-two minutes later, he and Raven were already at a table when Daisy and Sophie entered. They both had on coats and scarves, and from a distance looked more like sisters than mother and daughter.

"Hey," he said, standing.

Daisy smiled at him and the world, the whole world, seemed brighter. Damn, but she was getting in his head. "Hi." She switched her gaze to Raven. "I'm glad you could join us, Raven."

She nodded, but quickly turned to Sophie. "Want to check out their flavors?"

When the girls were at the counter, Daisy looked at him. "How is everybody?"

"I think she took the news pretty well. We'll see once she has some time to look it up on the internet. That will properly scare the crap out of her."

"Yeah. It's good to have information at your fingertips, but it's pretty easy for me to go down a rabbit hole. Once when Sophie was little, I went online and in about six seconds I went from thinking she had a sore throat to being convinced it was viral spinal meningitis. We got in the car and practically flew to the emergency room. She had a sore throat."

The girls, evidently having decided, motioned them to the counter. Everybody got a dish and returned to the table. Blade and Daisy said little. There was no need. The girls talked non-stop about the play.

Well after the ice cream had been finished, Daisy looked at her watch. "We better get going."

Blade pushed back his chair. "Where did you park?"

Daisy waved a hand to the right. "Just up the street."

"We're the other direction, but we'll walk you to your car," Blade said.

"That's not necessary," she said.

Blade didn't bother to answer. He just motioned with his hand for all three females to precede him out the door. At the car, there was an awkward moment when Raven and Sophie hugged each other and he and Daisy simply stood.

Daisy and Sophie got into her vehicle, and he and Raven turned to walk away. He was five feet away when he realized that something was wrong.

He turned and listened again as the engine on Daisy's vehicle failed to catch. It wasn't going to start.

"What's wrong?" Raven asked.

"I don't know," he admitted. He'd grown up the son of two people who knew their way around, in and under a car. Thus, they'd always solved these types of issues. In a classic example of parents wanting a different life for their child, they'd been insistent that he get a summer job anywhere besides the garage. Therefore, his own vehicle literacy was limited.

He walked around to Daisy's side and tapped on the

window. "What's the trouble?" he asked once she'd opened her door.

"I don't know," she said, somewhat distractedly. She was looking in her side mirrors. What the heck was she expecting to see? He glanced up and down the street. Empty. Not unexpected. It was a cold, damp night.

Finally, she looked back at him. "It ran fine on the way here."

"Try it again," he said, nodding toward the ignition.

Same result as before. "Pop the hood," he said.

She did and he looked around, but quite frankly, it was all pretty much a foreign language. He slammed the hood down and came back to her side. "I don't know," he admitted. "But I've got a plan. The garage has an after-hours number."

"Who answers that?"

"One of the mechanics or maybe even my parents. They take a rotation with on-call duties. Although when it's my mom's turn, Dad never lets her do a night call alone. He always goes with her."

"I don't want to bother your parents tonight. It's been kind of a day for them," she added.

"Yeah." She was right. "I'll tell you what. How about if Raven and I drive you and Sophie home? Then I'll take your keys and drop them off in the after-hours box at the garage. In the morning, somebody can come take a look, fix the problem and drop the car off. I'm not exactly sure what time that might be, however."

"That might work," she said. "It's Saturday. We don't need to go anywhere right away. I do hate inconveniencing you, however," she protested.

"No inconvenience," he said.

"I'm going to try one more time," Daisy said as if the fourth or fifth time might be a charm. It wasn't.

She and Sophie got out of her vehicle, and she locked it. They quickly walked to his SUV, which was a block in the other direction. He turned the heater on high once they were inside.

It took about five minutes to reach her house. During the drive, he sensed a tenseness about her that made him nervous. Car trouble was no fun, but she seemed to be unusually concerned about it. And Sophie was also being extraordinarily quiet, barely answering Raven. Very different from earlier in the night.

What did Daisy and Sophie know that he didn't know?

Chapter 14

When he pulled into the driveway, Daisy turned to Blade. "I really appreciate this," she said. It was true. If he'd not been insistent about walking them to the car, then he'd likely not have realized that she had trouble.

She and Sophie might have been stranded. She doubted there was a cab service in Knoware. Maybe a ride service, but the likelihood that anybody was eagerly looking for passengers on a cold winter night was slim. She'd have had to call Jane and she'd already imposed upon her enough.

"Of course," Blade said.

"For payback, I'd be happy to take the meeting with the Spring Spectacular photographer on my own."

"We have a photographer."

"We do. I booked one this morning." She opened her door. Heard Sophie do the same in the back seat.

"I'll get in the front," Raven said, also opening her

door. That made Daisy smile. No self-respecting teenager wanted to ride in the back seat when shotgun was
available. She thought the girl had done really well tonight. Raven and Sophie had had their heads together at
the ice cream store. It had been a good plan for them to
give Raven a chance to confide in her friend.

Blade opened his door. "I'll walk you to the door,"
he said.

"That's not—"

He shook his head. "You've met my mother. You do
have some kind of idea what she'd say if I wasn't a gentleman?" he asked, his tone teasing.

"She'd give you *the look*."

"Or maybe worse, which is not someplace you want
to go."

She stopped protesting. He wouldn't be dissuaded,
and the sooner she and Sophie got inside, the better she
was going to feel. She was unsettled. The surprise gift
from Tiddle's. Now car trouble. It could all be nothing.

But she couldn't shake the feeling that it wasn't.

"Don't forget, I need your car key," Blade said.

She had forgotten. Because her head was in what-if
mode. *What if* Jacob had found her? *What if* he intended
to make good on his promise that he couldn't accept that
they weren't together?

As they walked up the sidewalk with Sophie in the
lead, Daisy removed her car key from the key ring that
also included her house and office keys. She was five feet
behind her daughter when Sophie screamed.

As fast as she moved, Blade was faster, putting his
body in front of Sophie's. Daisy caught up and stood staring at her front door, which had clearly been kicked in
and was now hanging somewhat crookedly on its hinges.

"Oh, God," she said, dropping her keys on the concrete. She didn't pick them up. Instead, she pressed her hand flat against her coat, in the general area of her heart as if it was suddenly racing.

"Go back to the car," Blade said, his voice hard. "Right now. Lock the doors."

"I have to go—"

"No, not inside," Blade said, seeing where her head was going. "Please, just do what I'm asking." He looked her in the eye. "I don't want Raven alone in the car."

She knew that was maybe partly true, but she also knew that Blade was using the lever that he knew would gain her cooperation. "Fine," she muttered. Her house had been broken into. Her sweet little house that she'd lived in less than a week had been…violated. She felt sick.

She wrapped an arm around Sophie's shoulders and together they went back to the car, both getting in the back seat, because Raven was now sitting in front.

"What's wrong?" Raven asked, turning around.

"Somebody kicked our door in," Sophie said.

"Oh, my God. Who does that!" Raven exclaimed.

Who indeed, thought Daisy. She watched Blade who now had his cell phone up to his ear. Who was he talking to?

She didn't have long to wonder because it was just minutes later that a black SUV came fast around the corner, flashing lights on. It was a Knoware Police Department vehicle, and she saw the officer quickly get out.

"It's Marcus," Raven said.

Blade's friend. Had he been on duty or had Blade reached out directly to him? She was grateful for the fast response, but this was going to be awkward. He was going to ask her questions. She had a choice. Was she brave enough to answer truthfully, knowing that Blade would be there, listening, maybe judging?

If she lied, and it was Jacob, then she might be exposing herself, but more importantly, Sophie, to danger. That was unacceptable. She'd been willing to keep her counsel up to this point, but this upped the ante.

She watched the two men confer for a minute. The porch light captured the energy, the intensity of the discussion. Finally, with Marcus shaking his head, he entered her house with Blade on his heels.

Blade wasn't sure what Marcus had been thinking when he'd told him to wait outside. "Hell, no," he'd said.

"Then at least stay behind me," his friend had muttered.

He agreed to that. Marcus was the one with the gun. And if the person who had broken down Daisy's door and caused her to press her hand against her chest in immediate anguish happened to get shot, well, so be it. He'd taken an extra thirty seconds on the porch to fill Marcus in on Daisy's car trouble because it had dawned on him as Daisy and Sophie walked back to his SUV that this wasn't the first bit of trouble for them this evening.

Had somebody deliberately tried to delay them in order to have more time in their house?

He really, really wanted the son of a bitch to be inside. While he'd been waiting for Marcus to arrive, he'd stepped to the side of the house where he could see both the front door and most of the backyard. If they had spooked somebody inside by their sudden arrival, Blade was going to make damn sure they didn't get away. But he'd seen or heard nothing unusual.

Marcus and he advanced into the Cape Cod home.

Daisy had left the foyer light on. They flipped more switches as they walked. Kitchen, living room, downstairs bath, bedroom. It was the first time he'd seen Daisy's bedroom, and he thought that even if he hadn't known it was hers, he still would have easily guessed. It smelled like her. And the bedspread with brightly colored flamingoes seemed to fit her perfectly.

There was nobody downstairs. And it didn't appear that anything had been damaged.

They went upstairs. Sophie's bedroom and bath were empty. The sliding door to the back deck was locked. Marcus unlocked it, and the two of them stepped out. Marcus shone his powerful flashlight on the small backyard.

"I'm going to check the garage," Blade said. "I've got her keys. I can find the right one for the side door."

Marcus gave him a glance that would have put most people in their rightful place. "I do not attempt to insert IV lines at an accident scene. Because I know that's your job. I'll check the garage," he added. "If you want to stay a respectful distance behind, that's your business. If you get killed, I'm going to swear that I didn't know you were there."

"Okay. I get it. You're the cop, I'm the firefighter-paramedic. We all know our place."

Three minutes later, the garage had been searched. It was empty, and both the overhead door and the side entrance door had been secured.

"Let's get everybody inside," Marcus said. "Easier to chat where it's warm."

Blade walked back to his SUV. He opened the driver's door. "There's nobody inside and I don't see any damage," he said.

He heard Daisy's release of breath.

"Marcus wants everybody inside. Probably has a few questions," he added, looking at Daisy.

Everybody got out. Raven and Sophie went first. He walked next to Daisy. Halfway up the sidewalk, he leaned close. "It will be important that you tell Marcus anything that might be helpful."

"Of course."

He hoped she understood what he was saying. Because if he saw any attempt to skirt the truth, he was going to call her out. Her safety was too important.

When Daisy entered, even though she'd been assured that there was no danger, her eyes still darted from corner to corner, as if needing to see for herself. Marcus walked up and extended a hand. "I'm Marcus Price," he said. "We met briefly last Friday at Headstone Canyon."

"I remember," Daisy said.

"Great. Why don't you have a seat," he said, motioning her to the couch. "I think it would probably be best if the girls went upstairs. That okay with both of you?" he asked, looking at Daisy and Blade.

Blade was reminded of why Marcus generally got people to do what he wanted them to do. He knew how to phrase the question.

Daisy nodded. "I'll be up soon," she said, looking at Sophie.

A message passed between mother and daughter. He couldn't decipher it, but he was confident that neither one needed words right now to communicate.

"Raven," Blade said, "please lock Sophie's sliding door. We unlocked it when we went outside and checked the backyard and garage."

Once the teenagers were out of the room, Marcus

asked, "Anything look out of place or missing?" He'd taken a seat across from Daisy. Blade stood behind her.

Daisy shook her head. "I mean, I haven't looked at everything, but it looks just how we left it."

"What time was it that you left?"

"About 7:15."

"And where did you go?"

"To Know Your Scoop. To meet Blade and Raven," Daisy said.

"You went straight there? No stops for gas or groceries, maybe bread or milk?" he asked, flashing Blade a quick look.

"No," she said.

"How long were you at Know Your Scoop?"

Daisy turned her head to meet his eyes. "About forty-five minutes?" she said.

Blade nodded.

"So you all left about eight o'clock?" Marcus asked.

"Yes. I tried to start my car, but the engine wouldn't turn over. Fortunately Blade had walked me to my car, saw the trouble and offered us a ride home."

"You came straight home?" Marcus asked.

"Yes," Daisy said.

Marcus sat back in his chair. "Any idea who might have been responsible for kicking your door in?"

Blade moved from behind Daisy to a spot where he could see her face. She looked at Marcus, then at him, and finally back to Marcus. "I might have some idea," she said.

"Who?" Blade demanded.

Marcus threw him a look, but didn't tell him to shut up. "Who might that be?" he asked in a much more moderate tone.

"There's a man. His name is Jacob Posse."

"Tell me about Mr. Posse," Marcus said.

"Well, before I moved here, we had sort of a whirlwind romance. He seemed perfect. He was polite to everyone and nice to Sophie and my grandmother, although my grandmother never really liked him. She was smart. I was dumb. He told me that he was temporarily in a hotel because he'd been transferred to Denver on business. He showed me pictures of his house back in Iowa and took me with him on house-hunting trips in Denver. He was full of fun anecdotes about his job and his coworkers." She stopped. "To make a long story short, everything he told me was a lie. I know this because once we got engaged, I saw some behaviors that concerned me. Possessiveness. Angry outbursts when I worked late. Attempts to isolate me from my friends."

She drew in a breath. "When I told him that this was unacceptable, he'd always apologize and tell me that it was just because he loved me so much. When he tried to convince me to move up the wedding date by months, I got really nervous." She licked her lips.

There was something she wasn't saying.

"Was he physically abusive?" Marcus asked.

Blade felt his gut tighten and when Daisy sent him a pleading glance before answering, he mentally started disemboweling Posse.

"Once," she said. "He slapped me. Hard enough that he knocked me out of a chair."

Blade stared at the floor. Before he started work on the man's innards, he was going to break every bone in his hands. Slam his face against the floor, hard enough to break a nose, crush a cheekbone.

"I worked with somebody whose husband was a cop,

and she volunteered to have her husband check him out. He discovered that he wasn't a banker with an MBA. He drove a truck. He didn't have a great house in Iowa but rather he lived outside of Denver in an old house with at least fifteen other people. A commune of sorts. And the kicker was, he was the leader. The business trips were excuses for him to go back to Cedar Rapids, Iowa, where a similar group of people lived. He picked up work that would take him through the Midwest from various companies."

"What happened after you learned the truth?" Marcus asked.

"I broke off the engagement. He was furious. He told me that he was the chosen one and that he'd been waiting for his soul mate. I was her, and there was no way that he was ever going to let me go. I reported him to the police. I got a restraining order."

"But he continued to harass you?" Marcus asked.

"Indirectly. Anonymous letters and phone calls. Unexpected gifts. I'd look up from my grocery cart and he'd be across the store. I'd be shopping at the mall and he'd be sitting in his car in the parking lot. He'd stay the required distance away from me, but he'd make sure that I saw him. I went back to the police. They said there was nothing they could do."

She sounded so weary. Blade almost told Marcus to stop, that they had heard enough. But he stayed quiet. They needed to hear everything. Because they needed to find him.

"Does Mr. Posse know that you're in Knoware?" Marcus asked.

"I've done my very best to prevent that. When I resigned from my old job, I lied and told people that I'd inherited a little money after my grandmother's death and would be traveling for a while. The forwarding address that I had to leave with the post office is a box at the Seattle post office. I figured I could get there every so often to see if anything of importance had arrived."

"What about Sophie?" Blade asked. There was no way that she wasn't in contact with kids from Denver. The move had been difficult for her. She'd have probably wanted to complain about it to friends either in person or more likely online, where most anybody could find it if they tried hard enough.

"She knows about Jacob. I had to tell her, had to warn her to be careful. Not everything," she added quickly.

He suspected that Sophie didn't know that Daisy had been physically attacked.

"I've tried to shield her from the scarier details," Daisy said. "When we moved, I told her that she absolutely could not tell any of her friends that we were going to Knoware. She could tell them that we were moving to the Pacific Northwest but nothing more than that. We went over it a hundred times. Well, maybe that's an exaggeration, but she knew. And earlier this week, after I got the gift basket with no card, I asked her if she'd told anybody. She said that she had not."

Maybe she'd told the truth and maybe she hadn't, Blade thought. Kids lied, especially when they did something that they knew wasn't going to sit quite right with their parents. Self-preservation. The need to please. Whatever the reason, it happened.

"Describe Jacob Posse," Marcus said.

"Five-eleven. Slim build. Brown hair. Brown eyes."

The description could fit the stranger who'd been in to Gertie's Café and Feisty Pete's bar. Like he'd thought before, it could roughly fit a whole lot of people, including him.

She didn't compare him in any way to Jacob Posse, did she? The thought made him ill.

"Do you happen to have a photo of Jacob Posse?" Marcus asked.

"On my phone," she said. She reached for her purse. When she had her phone, it took her a couple minutes to find it. "Here," she said. She passed the phone to Marcus.

He studied it, then gave the phone to Blade.

It would have been so easy for him to find fault. The man's eyes were a little too close together. His nose a tad long. Maybe his ears stuck out from his head. But in truth, he was a good-looking guy wearing a nice shirt and pants. He didn't look evil. Certainly didn't look like somebody who would hit a woman and knock her out of her chair. He gave Daisy back her phone.

"Send that photo to me," Marcus said. He gave her a card. "Text it to this number."

He waited while she did it. Then he continued. "Daisy, I don't want to scare you more than necessary, but this week, there were two separate break-ins in our downtown area. One at Gertie's Café and one at Feisty Pete's bar. Both establishments reported that a man matching that general description was a customer."

She closed her eyes as if her worst fear was being realized.

"Were you aware," Marcus continued, "during your association with Jacob Posse, of him committing any similar crimes?"

She drew in a deep breath and opened her eyes. "No. But honestly, it would not surprise me. He was…pretty free with his money. He took me to nice restaurants.

To entertainment where the tickets were pricey. It fit his image of successful businessman. Where he got that money, I have no idea."

"I'll show his photo to folks at Gertie's and Feisty Pete's. We'll see if anybody recognizes him," Marcus said. "Is there anything else that you can tell us that might be helpful?"

"I don't think so."

"Okay. Your plan was to have your vehicle towed in by Savick's Garage?"

"Yes."

"I'm going to want a copy of their findings."

"You think it was tampered with?" Daisy asked.

"I don't know. But I think we need more information. For now, how do you feel about staying in this house?"

"No," Blade interjected. "Absolutely not."

Marcus didn't react to Blade's comment. He stayed focused on Daisy.

"I...uh. I'm not crazy about the idea. I guess Sophie and I could go to a motel. I'm sure there are vacancies this time of year."

"Absolutely not," Blade said again. He was a broken record. He moved closer to Daisy. "You and Sophie can stay with me, in my duplex. Sophie can bunk in Raven's room. She's got two twin beds. You can have my room and I'll take the couch."

"I... I..." Daisy stopped.

"Take a minute," Marcus said, standing up. "Blade, follow me, would you?" He didn't wait for an answer.

"Don't tell me it's a bad idea," Blade said once they were in the kitchen.

"I have no intention of telling you that. What I want to remind you is that she's had a tough night. Likely feels as if she's boxed into a corner. You demanding she take certain specific actions doesn't help her still feel independent and in control."

Blade stared at his friend. "I really hate it when you're right," he said finally.

"I've had a little bit more experience with this," he said. "Sadly, domestic issues are still one of our major crime categories."

"Posse hit her," Blade said, his voice cracking.

"I know. And I want you to remember that you'll only be hurting yourself and your family if you try to avenge that. Don't be stupid, Blade."

"I'm not a fool," he said.

"Yeah. But I don't think you've ever been in exactly this situation before, either."

"What do you mean?"

"I've known you since you were six," Marcus said. "When you look at Daisy, it's a look that I've never seen before, not even when you were married to Sheila, no matter how hard you tried to make your marriage work."

Blade let out a sigh. "You and Jamie told me to be a friend. A pal. I want more."

"Of course you do," Marcus said. "And while I don't know her nearly as well, I get the distinct impression that she's interested in more than friendship when she looks at you. I'm just telling you to be careful. She's likely feeling pretty vulnerable right now. You aren't going to want to take advantage of that."

That pissed Blade off. "You think I'd take advantage of her?"

"Not knowingly. In a hundred years, you wouldn't do that. I'm just saying be careful."

186 A Firefighter's Ultimate Duty

"This from a guy who has had more women in his bed in the last month than I have in my entire lifetime."

"Exactly. I know what I'm talking about. I didn't love any of those women. Liked, yes. Respected, always. Enjoyed, generally. Not love. The stakes are higher for you."

"I never said I loved her."

Marcus shook his head. "You didn't need to."

Before Blade could form words to respond to that, Marcus had turned and was walking back to the living room. "Come on," Marcus said, looking over his shoulder. "It's getting late. I'll take care of getting this door secured. You need to get these two settled at your place."

Two hours later, Daisy wasn't quite sure how it all happened, but she was climbing into Blade Savick's bed. His empty bed. That now had clean sheets and fresh pillowcases. He'd insisted upon stripping the linens once they'd gotten to his apartment, which was a nice two-bedroom on one side of a duplex.

Sophie was settled in Raven's room, and it was a testament to how tired they must be because both were already asleep. Sophie had had almost no reaction to the news that they were temporarily relocating to Blade's. She'd packed quickly and had been waiting, bag in hand, by the time Daisy had her own suitcase ready.

On the way to Blade's, they'd stopped at Savick's Garage and dropped off her car keys. Blade had written his phone number on the tag. Then they'd driven to his house. He had been quiet. She wanted to know what he was thinking. Was he disgusted that she'd been so stupid? Well, join the club. She was pretty disgusted with herself. Was he regretting the impulse to offer temporary lodging? Well, he didn't need to worry much about that. Because if Jacob had found them, they were going to have to move on.

Fortunately, the story that her grandmother had left her money wasn't completely false. It wasn't a lot. But enough that she and Sophie wouldn't starve. Enough that she could afford not to have a paycheck come in for a month or two. Enough for them to start over again.

It would be so hard on Sophie.

It would be hard on her. To leave Jane. To leave a promising job. To leave Blade. Funny, brave, hard-working Blade who was a good son and a good father. But she would do it. No matter how much it hurt. She would never allow Sophie to be physically harmed.

She could hear Blade moving around in his living room, probably getting his bed ready. He must be tired. She certainly was. Thank goodness tomorrow was the weekend. Raven and Sophie had play practice from ten to two. Maybe she could get a nap in.

In the morning, she intended to go back to her car. She wanted to be there when Savick's Garage arrived, and she wanted to see her car in the light of day. She knew next to nothing about vehicles, but maybe she'd simply have a sense for whether Jacob was behind her troubles. Not that she'd ever had much of a *sense* about Jacob.

He'd fooled her. Fooled Sophie, but then again, she was a kid so that wasn't a great deal of consolation. Had fooled her coworkers. That was maybe more significant. She'd taken him to a few after-hours events, and he'd been charming. That was why it had been important that no-body from her work know where she was headed. They knew the relationship had ended—she'd told them that much. But she hadn't given them the gritty details. No one really needed that. She hadn't wanted them to un-wittingly cough up information about her whereabouts.

Although now both Marcus Price and Blade Savick had it. She trusted Blade and he clearly trusted Marcus. That was good enough for her.

She'd lived in Knoware for less than a week, and her home no longer felt safe. It wasn't Knoware. It was her. She'd brought the trouble.

Not a great feeling. She closed her eyes, hoping that tomorrow would be a better day. It really had to be.

Daisy was in his apartment. More specifically, in his bed. Blade stretched out on his couch, feeling the bottoms of his feet jam up against the end. He turned on his side and bent his knees.

Blade knew it was possible that it wasn't Posse. The car thing could have been a fluke. For all he knew, maybe she didn't maintain her vehicle well. The house door, well, it could have been teenagers. Or someone home-less looking for a warm place to stay. The place had been empty for a few months up until the last week, so maybe they didn't realize that someone had moved in.

All kinds of reasonable explanations.

But none of them felt right. Not after hearing the things Posse had said and done. Tomorrow, he and Daisy were going to have to talk about how to make sure that she and Sophie stayed safe. For now, he was content that they were with him, under his care.

Chapter 15

Daisy woke up at seven thirty, more than an hour later than usual. It was a testament to the comfort of Blade's bed. She lay still, looking around. It was a simple room, just a bed and a dresser. Mission style. No chair, no shelves. Not even a rug on the hardwood floor. But there was a beautiful piece of art on one wall—it was a sleek combination of an intricately carved four-foot section of wood mounted on a five-foot slab of polished metal.

Masculine. Unique. Unforgettable.

Much like Blade himself.

She desperately wanted a cup of coffee. Did not want to wake up Blade. She could not hear any sound of movement from the living room. Nothing from upstairs, either. No surprise there. If allowed to, the girls would sleep, likely rolling out of bed just in time for play practice.

Daisy slipped from under the covers. She'd worn yoga

pants and a T-shirt to bed. No bra. She took the time to put one on now. Then ran a brush through her hair.

She stopped in the bathroom on her way to the kitchen, closing doors quietly along the way. But she needn't have worried because he was up, dressed and eating a bowl of cereal at the table.

"Good morning," she said.

"Good morning." He studied her. "How did you sleep?"

"Really well, thank you. It was a big week. I was tired."

"Stressful night," he added.

"It was." She pulled out a chair and sat down. There was no way to avoid the conversation they needed to have. "I suppose you think I'm pretty gullible or maybe even stupid."

He shook his head. "Would you like some coffee?"

Was he deliberately trying to change the subject? "Uh…yes."

"Black, right?"

She nodded. He got up and poured her a cup. He added some to his half-full cup. "Toast? Cereal? I can make eggs," he said.

"Coffee is great," she said. She waited until he sat back down. "I should have said something the night you found that gift basket on my front door. But I was trying very hard not to let my old life spill over into my new life." She took a sip of coffee. It was good. "I don't like to talk about Jacob. I'm embarrassed about how…dumb I was."

"He sounds like a con artist, somebody who works hard to cultivate an image that allows him to get what he wants at no thought to the consequences for anybody else."

It was a very succinct and accurate way to describe Jacob. "But still," she said.

"He's the bad guy here, not you," Blade said.

"Do you want to know what I was most thankful for?" she asked. She had never told anyone this.

"Yes, what?"

"That my grandmother was dead before I found out the truth about Jacob. She never cared for him, but it would have been so painful for her to know how badly I was deceived. How badly I was hurt. For her to know that he continued to threaten mine and Sophie's safety… She never had to, and for that, I will always be eternally grateful."

He reached out for her hand. Held it tightly. His hands were warm from holding his coffee cup. His touch was firm, yet gentle.

"You do not have to be afraid," he said. "I will not let him hurt you or Sophie or anyone else for that matter. I'm going to stop this bastard."

That scared her. "He's got no moral compass, Blade. He won't fight fair."

"I had that pretty much figured out when you told us that he knocked you out of a chair."

Harsh. The words were harsh. And her body gave an involuntary flinch.

"He'll never get close enough to you again to do something like that. You have my word," he said.

Tears came to her eyes. Her grandmother hadn't been there to tell. Sophie had gotten the sanitized version, and even Jane had simply gotten bits and pieces. It was the first time she'd ever told anyone the whole ugly truth. Well, almost all the truth.

"There's one more thing," she said. "Nobody knows

this. Well, that's not true. The police in Denver know this, but nobody else. After he hit me, I made the decision that I was going to leave him. But I didn't do it for a couple weeks. During the interim, I found an opportunity to look at his laptop computer."

"And you saw something that bothered you?"

"Scared the hell out of me," she corrected. "Over the past couple of years, there have been a couple stories that made headlines about women who were held captive for years. Sometimes in relatively plain site. In the basement of a house. In a shed in the backyard. Undetected while they were abused in horrible ways."

"Right," he said, encouraging her to go on.

"He had set up files in his computer. He'd downloaded articles about these poor women from newspapers. He'd scanned magazine articles. He had a document that listed a bunch of links. I clicked on some of them. They were for rope and other restraints. Even steel brackets that could be drilled into concrete."

"What did the Denver police say?"

"About what I expected. That it wasn't illegal to keep an electronic file of publicly released news articles. Or to look at odd things for purchase. I just wanted it documented somewhere what I had seen. In case."

"In case you disappeared."

"Yes." And damn it, her eyes filled with tears.

"Hey, hey! Don't cry," he said, somewhat pleadingly.

She did not want to. She sniffed and blinked and still a sob escaped.

In one smooth movement, he was out of his chair and kneeling next to her. He gathered her in his arms. And he held her, her head resting against his chest, and he rocked her gently.

"It's okay. That is not going to happen to you. I promise you that," he said.

"I know. It's a crazy thing to worry about."

"Not crazy. Not one bit crazy."

She lifted her head. "Thank you for saying that."

Their faces were close. So close.

And he leaned in and kissed her.

And holy hell, she kissed him back. And it went on and on.

A groan of pleasure. A gasp of joy. His. Hers. Sweet God in heaven, they were consuming one another.

His hands found the hem of her T-shirt and slipped under. Her back arched and she threw back her head, giving him access to her neck. "Daisy?" he whispered.

Yes, yes, her body begged in response. "Take—"

The slam of a bedroom door had them springing apart, like balls in a pinball machine, back to their respective chairs.

The girls came around the corner. "Morning," they said, almost in unison.

"Good morning," Blade said. His voice sounded so normal. "You're up early."

"We're hungry," Raven said.

"Famished," Sophie agreed.

"French toast?" Raven asked.

"Sounds good," he said. "We've got bacon, too," he added.

What the hell? she wanted to scream. Ten seconds earlier he'd been about to eat her for breakfast. Now he was reciting the menu.

"What's wrong, Mom?" Sophie asked.

All eyes turned to her. She resisted the urge to lick her lips so that she could have one more taste of Blade.

"Nothing. I'm good. Just need another cup of coffee. French toast with bacon sounds delicious."

Raven and Sophie fell upon breakfast like starving wolves. Daisy ate a half a piece of French toast and one slice of bacon. He had no idea what he ate because his mind was going about a hundred miles an hour and he wasn't thinking about his breakfast.

He'd kissed a fair number of women in his lifetime. Nowhere near as many as Marcus, but then again, he was only human. And kissing was nice.

It was, however, not generally a damn explosion that made his knees weak. His mouth had found Daisy's, and it was zero to sixty in about three seconds. Speed. Sensation.

Sex. That was where his head had gone. He wanted her. Flat on her back, in his bed, on his couch, on the damn floor. He wanted her naked with her legs wrapped around his waist. He wanted her wet and hot and...

That had been about the point that his daughter and her daughter had tumbled down the stairs. He supposed he should be thankful. If they had come down five minutes later, it might have been a whole lot more difficult to separate quickly.

"I'm going to change clothes," she said. "I'd like to be there when the garage comes to get my car."

"Uh...yeah. Sure, we can make that happen," he said without making eye contact. "I'll call it in now."

Daisy nodded and pushed back her chair. The girls followed her down the hall. He picked up his cell. His dad answered.

"Hey, Dad, I dropped off a set of keys last night," he said.

"I saw that. What's going on?"

"Daisy Rambler, my…my cochair for the Spring Spectacular, had some car trouble last night. Her vehicle is parked outside of Know Your Scoop. Can you send a truck to tow it in?"

"Of course. I have one available right now."

"Excellent. Daisy and I'll meet you there." Blade ended the conversation.

In ten minutes, Daisy returned. She was dressed in a green-and-blue-striped flannel shirt and blue jeans. It should not have been sexy, but it was. She was holding up her cell phone. "I just got a text from Marcus. He said he showed Jacob's photo to the staff at Gertie's and Feisty Pete's, and nobody thought it was the same man."

"That's a relief," he said.

"I know. Big one, right." She shook her head. "Maybe Sophie and I should—"

"No. There's still the issue of your car and your house."

"I guess you're right."

"I know I'm right. We should get going. Raven has a car. Is it okay with you if she drives Sophie to play practice? She's really a very good driver."

"That's fine," Daisy said.

Blade walked down the hall and knocked on his daughter's bedroom door. She opened it a crack. "If we're not back in time, you can drive Sophie to play practice," he said. "But straight there and you don't go anywhere afterward."

"But there's this party where there's going to be all kinds of drugs and alcohol," she whined. "I was planning to go."

"Don't be a smart-ass," he said, rolling his eyes. "I'm serious, Raven," he added.

"I get it, Dad. We both do. We're not going to be stupid."

He thought that perhaps sometime during the night Sophie might have confided in Raven what she knew about Jacob Posse. It wouldn't be everything, based on what Daisy had said, but likely enough that his daughter knew not to mess around with it.

"Thank you," he said.

He walked back to the living room. "Did you hear that?"

"I did. I trust them. And anyway, it's Saturday morning. There's no parties this early," she said optimistically.

He smiled, opened the door and looked outside. He didn't see anything that concerned him, and motioned for Daisy to come. He checked the door behind him to make sure it was locked. They walked to the carport in silence.

He really didn't know what to say.

Weren't public relations people supposed to be good communicators? Why the hell wasn't she saying something?

He started his SUV and pulled out. He drove two blocks. The silence was killing him. "I guess we got lucky earlier," he said. "Things kind of got carried away." Damn. That didn't sound right. "I didn't mean in a bad way," he added quickly. "It was good. Very good." He gripped the steering wheel. He slowed down the SUV. "You should probably get out. I'm just going to run myself into that tree over there."

She laughed. For a good long time. In fact, for a whole block. "That seems drastic," she said finally.

"I know. But it appears that I'm doing things in a big way this morning."

"Yeah," she mused.

"I'm going to have to call Marcus up and tell him that I'm a jerk."

"Why?"

"He told me not to take advantage of you."

She turned her head. "*Marcus* told you that?"

"He's got quite a bit more depth than you might imagine at first glance. I, of course, told him not to worry about it. And then…well, we both know what the *and then* was."

"I wasn't resisting," she said.

"I didn't think so," he said. He turned down Main Street. "But still, the timing might have been bad," he added.

She didn't respond.

He guessed that was his answer. He tried to ignore the pain in his chest. And focus on what was important—finding out what was wrong with her car.

He parked behind her vehicle. He could see a truck from Savick's Garage heading toward them. It was his father.

Blade and Daisy were standing by the vehicle by the time his dad got out of the truck. "Daisy, this is my dad, Larkin Savick. Dad, Daisy Rambler."

"It's a pleasure," his dad said, extending his hand. "So you had some trouble last night."

"Yes," she said. "I drove here with my daughter. The car ran fine. Like it always does. But when we went to leave about forty-five minutes later, it wouldn't start. I tried it about five times."

"Okay," his dad said. "Maybe you should try it one more time this morning."

She nodded and used her keys to unlock the door. Blade could tell that she wasn't hopeful. She turned the key and the engine immediately caught. "What!" she exclaimed.

She turned her head to look at his dad. "I'm so sorry to have had you make a wasted trip."

"That's no trouble," he said. "It does seem a bit odd that it wouldn't start last night but immediately turned over this morning."

A bit odd. The phrase pulled at Blade's gut. "Dad, here's the thing. Daisy has reason to believe that somebody might be interested in causing her some trouble. If this is odd or off in any way, I want to know if there's anything that we can do to figure that out."

His dad looked at him, as if waiting for more of an explanation. When it didn't come, he turned to Daisy. "Drive it to the garage, Daisy. We'll let Mrs. Savick take a look."

"I'll follow you," Blade said to her.

Once they were at the garage, his dad took Daisy's cell phone number and promised that he would give her a call. They did not see his mom. He assumed she was in the back, probably under some car. He and Daisy walked back to his SUV.

"Maybe we're making too big a deal out of this," she said. "It started. I should be happy."

"Let my mom take a look. She's really good."

"Your dad is very nice," she said. "I wonder what he is thinking of me."

"He's probably thinking you might have a secret, but really, he's got no room to judge."

"Now what?" she asked.

"I need to buy groceries."

"Blade, we need to talk about this, about Sophie and me staying at—"

"My apartment," he finished her sentence. "Yes, that's where you're staying. And we can talk about it. But right now, I want to stop and get some groceries. And I don't want to leave you by yourself. So will you come with me?"

"Of course," she said.

When he pulled into the grocery store lot, he found a spot near the door. They got in, grabbed a cart, and headed for the fruits and vegetables. "Pick out anything that you and Sophie like to eat," he said.

"How do you grocery shop if you don't cook?" she asked.

"I go for the basics." To prove that, he added grapes and apples and raspberries to the cart. Then bags of romaine lettuce, yellow peppers, carrots and tomatoes.

"I think you're better at this than you let on," she said.

"I'm strong here and in dairy," he said.

She smiled. "I'll make a deal with you. You buy that stuff, and I'll focus on the ingredients for a few dinners. Fair?"

"Exceedingly," he said.

They were in the checkout line fifteen minutes later. Too late he realized that Charlie was in the line next to him, paying for his groceries. That was the thing about small towns. Everybody shopped in the same place. "Savick," Charlie said. "Ms. Rambler."

"Hi, Charlie," Daisy said. If she was thrown off by his formality, she didn't show it. She was being as pleasant as usual.

"You two shopping together now?" Charlie asked.

Daisy opened her mouth but no sound came out. She clearly didn't know what to say.

"She offered cooking lessons and I couldn't turn her

down," Blade said easily. "There's a payoff here for all of us."

Charlie picked up his sacks. "Right. Well, you two have a good morning."

Blade paid for the groceries and they carried the sacks to his SUV. "Did I do something to upset Charlie?" Daisy asked once they were inside.

"I think he's concerned about having you shadow me at work if there's a personal relationship between the two of us. We've had engaged and married firefighters assigned to the same station, but they aren't allowed to work the same shift. The concern is that they might put their personal feelings ahead of their professional judgment with negative consequences."

"I wouldn't want you to do that. Or expect that," she said. "I mean, if we had a personal relationship."

"It felt rather personal to me this morning," Blade said, suddenly irritated.

"We need to talk about that," she said.

Not if she was going to tell him that it had been a mistake. "You think we could table it until we at least get the ice cream put away?"

"That's fine," she said, her own tone short.

This was just great. When they got back to the apartment, he was relieved to see that the girls had left for play practice. He didn't want to have to pretend that everything was just fine in front of them. However, the apartment seemed especially quiet. He methodically put the fruit and vegetables in the refrigerator, taking time to make sure they were arranged just right. The ice cream went in the freezer, and so did the bag of shrimp that Daisy had thrown in.

There were boxes of pasta, cans of tomatoes and artichokes, fresh herbs. Strange things on his shelves. Just one of the very little ways she was changing or had changed his life. He'd met her exactly nine days ago. How could he feel so strongly about keeping her in his life?

How could he not, was perhaps the better question.

Jamie and Marcus had told him not to kiss her. They'd been right. He shut the cupboard door too hard, and the sound echoed through the apartment. He was not particularly skilled at these types of conversations, but he was not a coward. "Maybe we should talk," he said, motioning to the living room.

She nodded. Took a seat on the couch.

He sat in the chair. She seemed like a practical person. He was going to start there. "Until we know for sure whether Jacob Posse has followed you to Knoware, you need to take steps to ensure your safety. This duplex has a security system, double-hung windows and bolt locks on every door. It is more secure than any hotel room."

"It's very nice," she said, looking around. "Your landlord keeps it very nice."

He smiled. "I'm the landlord. I own the building and rent out the other half. I sock away that check every month. It's college money for Raven."

"Good plan."

"Speaking of Raven, she and Sophie seem to be getting along quite well."

"Agree."

Now it was time to go big or go home. "Things got a little heated in the kitchen this morning. I… I don't know exactly what to say about that. You turn me on, Daisy. You are nice and smart and incredibly sexy. But I can control myself. If I made you uncomfortable in any way,

I'm sorry. It won't happen again." It would kill him, but he could do it.

She nodded. "I… I guess I appreciate you saying that."

"I'm not just saying it. It'll happen. I mean, nothing will happen. Nothing," he added, for emphasis.

She stared at him, her blue eyes so very intense. And speaking of nothing, she said nothing. For a long minute. He forced himself to wait.

"Then I reject the offer," she said.

She held her breath. And realized that her hands were curled so tight that her fingernails were digging into her palms. She forced herself to relax.

"I'm not sure I understand," he said.

"I'm not interested in nothing." For a professional communicator, it was not one of her most grammatically correct sentences.

But since the purpose of communication was to impart a message, she figured she was pretty successful when his eyes took on a gleam.

"Are you saying what I think you're saying?" he asked.

She looked at her watch. "What time does play practice end?"

"Two," he said, his voice suddenly hoarse.

She stood up. "I'd prefer a bed over the couch."

He practically vaulted out of his chair. And suddenly they were kissing again and it was as good, every bit as good as before. His tongue was in her mouth, his hands were cupping her face, and their legs were entwined.

"A gentleman would ask you if you were sure?" he said when he came up for air.

In response, she took his hand and led him down the

hall to his big comfortable bed. She sat on the bed and started to unbutton her shirt.

Standing before her, he stilled her hands. "Let me," he said.

With infinite patience he slid buttons through little holes and when done, he slipped her shirt over her shoulders and tossed it aside. He stared at her blue bra. "It matches your eyes," he said.

"So do my panties," she said.

He sucked in a breath. "So lovely," he said, gently tracing the slope of her breasts with his index finger.

She was pretty confident he wasn't talking about lingerie any longer. She reached for the hem of his long-sleeved T-shirt. In one smooth motion, she pulled it over his head. Then she ran her hands down his bare chest. He was muscle and bone and heat. She leaned forward and licked a nipple.

"Sweet God," he said. He gently pressed her back, but she shook her head.

"No." She slipped her thumbs under the waistband of his jeans. She was pretty sure he wasn't breathing. Inched her thumbs lower, caressing his skin.

Then she very quickly unbuttoned his jeans and slid the zipper down. He was hard. Deliciously hard.

"Daisy," his said, his voice hoarse.

She smiled and freed him from his boxers. Then she took him in her mouth.

Chapter 16

At one thirty, a naked Daisy slipped out of bed. "Everything okay?" he asked.

"We should get dressed," she said. "In case play practice gets over early." She was reaching for her bra and panties.

Such a shame for someone with a body like hers to ever wear clothes. He stretched, his muscles feeling loose. "What are we going to tell our daughters?"

She sat back down on the edge of the bed. The bed where he'd made her come not once but twice. He held back a smile. She'd been kind of noisy. It had been an incredible turn-on.

"I don't think we should tell them anything," she said.

He sat up straight. Was she sorry? Ashamed? "Why?" he asked, trying for casual.

"Sophie has had to absorb a lot of change lately. I can't introduce one more thing that is different."

"That's the only reason? You're not sorry?"

She smiled. Leaned down and kissed him. "It was wonderful. As wonderful as I hoped."

He relaxed. "Just the girls? How about everybody else?"

"Marcus will ask, won't he? Since he told you not to take advantage?"

"He'll be concerned," Blade admitted. "Not in an intrusive way. But he has the background information and knows that emotions have been volatile the last twenty-four hours."

"I think if we each have someone close to us we want to confide in, that's fine. But they need to understand the importance of keeping the circle close. Neither of us want our daughters to find out through gossip."

"Agreed," he said. He was generally a pretty private guy. But there was somebody who would need to be told something. "My ex-wife and I have an understanding. No big changes that impact Raven without giving the other one a heads-up. I need to tell her that you and Sophie are living here. I don't have to give her details," he added.

"Good, that might make me blush," she said with a smile. Then she looked more serious. "I get that and I respect that. Charlie?" she asked.

He shook his head. He didn't like the idea of not being forthcoming, but Charlie was acting very odd about things. "I think not."

"This could be difficult," she said. "I'm not a good liar."

"That's good," he said. "I mean, I wouldn't have wanted to have done what we just did with someone who was a very good liar."

"You are a glass half full kind of person," she said. "I

like that." She put her shirt on and reached for her pants. "Now get your ass out of bed."

He found her ten minutes later sitting at his kitchen table. She had her laptop open. "You are not going to believe this," she said. "We are getting hundreds of likes on our posts. And forty-two responses, and it looks as if most everybody is attaching a photo. You know what I think we should do?"

"No, but I think it's probably something sensational," he said. She hadn't had a bad idea yet. And her best had been taking his hand and leading him to the bedroom.

"I think we should do a video to some cool music, featuring all the photos. We'll run it in the background."

"Like they do at weddings when they show pictures of the bride and groom when they were two and naked in the bathtub," he said.

"Exactly like that, but G-rated. Maybe PG. Some of these dresses are pretty revealing. Which reminds me, I need to go shopping. It seems like a mundane task given everything else that is going on, but the dance is just two weeks from tonight."

"You want to go to Seattle tomorrow? We could take the girls. I know Raven would love that."

"It would give me a chance to check my post office box," she said. Her cell phone rang. She picked it up, looked at the number and frowned.

He glanced at her phone. "That's the garage," he said.

"This is Daisy," she answered. She put it on speaker.

"Daisy, it's Gemma Savick. How are you?"

"I'm fine, Mrs. Savick."

"Gemma, please," she said. "Listen, I think your car is fine. I didn't find anything wrong with it. You can pick it up anytime."

She shrugged in Blade's direction. "Well, thank you for checking."

"Oh, sure. I do have a question, though."

"Of course," Daisy said.

"Your car is relatively new."

That didn't sound like a question to Blade. His mom was going somewhere.

"Yes, just a couple years old," Daisy said.

"I noticed something on two of your spark plugs that I thought was odd. There were signs that they'd been removed."

"What?" Blade said. "Sorry, Mom. I'm listening in."

"I didn't realize the two of you were still together," his mom said,

He probably didn't want his parents surprised by the news that Daisy and Sophie were staying with him. "Yeah, well, in addition to Daisy having some car trouble, somebody broke into her house. I offered her and her daughter a place to stay."

"Oh."

Such a tiny word. That said so much. His mom wouldn't ask more questions now given that Daisy was on the line, but later, he better be prepared. "Tell me more about these spark plugs," he said.

"Right. Well, spark plugs don't usually need to be replaced for several years. And generally, if two were getting replaced, the others would also be replaced, under the assumption that they would likely all go bad around the same time. But it's pretty clear that just two have been monkeyed with."

Blade didn't know much about cars, but he knew this. "A car won't start without properly connecting spark plugs."

"Start. Run. You've got it. It's a pretty good way to temporarily disable a vehicle if you know what you're doing. Sometimes the spark plugs are hard to reach. In your vehicle, they're relatively easy to get to."

Blade wanted to kick his own ass. If he'd known what to look for the night before, maybe he'd have seen it. "Mom, just so I'm clear. You're saying that if Daisy drove to the ice cream store and her car was working fine, then somebody tampered with her car while she was inside. And then sometime after she left her car on the street for the night, they came back and replaced the plugs."

"I suspect that's exactly what happened. I think your bigger question might be how they easily got access. Would whoever might be responsible have been able to get inside the vehicle in order to pop the hood release lever?"

Blade looked at Daisy. "I don't know," she said. "I use a fob to unlock my doors. Can it be… I'm searching for the right word…can it be copied?"

"Definitely. I could give you the complicated explanation, but perhaps the easiest way to understand this is to picture Person A who has her fob and Person B who has a clone remote. Both are near the vehicle when Person A unlocks it. Person B takes a series of relatively simple actions allowing him to intercept the signal. Person B now has a fully functional remote to Person A's car."

Daisy got so pale that he was afraid she might slip out of her chair. She didn't have to respond to his mother's explanation. He could see by the look on her face that she believed it was entirely possible that Jacob Posse now had access to her car.

She was scared.

He understood the feeling. He was pretty damn spooked himself.

"Okay, Mom. I think we've got it. We'll be by in a day or two to pick up Daisy's car. Can you keep it parked inside until then?"

"Of course."

"Great, thanks. Goodbye." He reached over and disconnected Daisy's phone.

Daisy looked at him, her blue eyes wide. "This is a nightmare."

"It's okay," he reassured her. "We can handle it."

She stood up fast. "It's not your problem, Blade. This is my problem." She put her hands to her head. "I have to think. Oh, my God, I can't think." She started to pace around the room. "I need my car. I have to drive to work. I have to drive Sophie to school. I have…a life, damn it. That I need to take care of."

"Calm down," he said gently. "You can rent a car. We'll leave your car at the garage."

"I don't want your parents sucked in to my troubles."

"Okay. We'll ask Marcus if we can park it in his garage. He's got a three-car garage and only his city-issued SUV and his personal vehicle. He has an extra space."

"This is not a good long-term solution," she said, frustration evident.

"It's not meant to be. That's not going to be necessary."

"How can you be so sure?" she asked.

"Because we're going to find Posse, and Marcus will either arrest him if he can successfully connect him to the crimes, or I will convince the bastard to leave and not come back."

He heard a car slowing and looked outside. "The girls are back."

"Don't tell them what's going on," she said quickly. "I don't want Sophie to know."

She can handle it, he wanted to protest. But what if she didn't? Daisy would never forgive him. She wasn't asking to hide it forever. "We'll tell them you're getting a rental because the garage is still working on your car. They won't be that curious as long as there are wheels."

Raven and Sophie came in, talking a mile a minute. It was a half hour later before he or Daisy got a word in edgewise. "Sounds like the two of you had a lot of fun," he said. "And speaking of fun, we're thinking about a trip to Seattle tomorrow. Daisy has to do some dress shopping. You two in?"

Sophie and Raven exchanged look. "For sure," Raven said.

"Then homework gets done tonight," Daisy said, looking at her daughter. "No arguments."

"Fine," Sophie said.

"You, too," Blade said, looking at Raven.

"Gathering up my books as you speak," she said, doing just that.

When both girls were upstairs, Daisy looked at Blade. "Oh, my God. I couldn't even look at you. You don't think they have any idea what their parents were just doing?"

"No," he said. "They're high on school play buzz. Nothing else is registering."

Daisy rolled her eyes, but she smiled. "They're both really sharp. We're going to have to be on our toes."

"You want to do it on your toes?" he asked suggestively.

"Stop," she said, holding up a hand.

"Just don't lock the bedroom door tonight," he said.

* * *

She did not lock the door.

He did not turn on a light.

The bed did not squeak, thankfully.

He had the foresight to have a hand ready to clap over her mouth when she came.

And afterward, he held her for a nice long time before he pulled on his pajama pants and quietly slipped from the room.

Chapter 17

They left midmorning for Seattle. Blade drove, and Daisy enjoyed the opportunity to see some of the countryside without having to worry about the road. The girls sat in the back seat, sometimes chatting, sometimes quiet while they looked at their respective phones.

Daisy had looked up stores online the night before and identified a few possibilities that were all in the same mall. The address was already in Blade's GPS. When he pulled into the crowded parking lot, Raven let out a squeal. "Dad, you hate shopping. I can't believe we're doing this."

Daisy turned to him. "I'll make you a deal. You take them to lunch, and I'll shop while the three of you are doing that. Once you're done, I'll take over and go to a few stores with them while you head that direction." She pointed toward a sign for a Pratt Sports Spot store. "Fair?"

"You're trying to make this absolutely painless for me, aren't you?" he asked.

"I appreciate the ride here. It was fun to just look around, see more of the countryside. I just want to repay the favor."

"Mom hates to shop with other people," Sophie offered from the back. "She would never go with her friends in Denver."

"What, is this true?" he asked.

"I am better on my own," Daisy admitted.

He shook his head at her in mock sadness. "You have no shame. You were letting me think that it was all for me. Just for that, we're having dessert with lunch and there will be none for you."

They separated inside the big mall, making a plan to meet in ninety minutes. Daisy practically ran to the first store. Ninety minutes was not a very long time to find a perfect dress.

She found it at the third store, after trying on six other dresses at the previous two stores. She walked in, saw it on the rack and knew. She looked at the price and decided it would be worth packing her lunch for a month.

She tried it on and studied herself in the three-way mirror.

The dress really was pretty great. She paid for it and left the store, her purchase carefully wrapped in tissue paper and folded in a pretty shopping bag. She bought herself a cup of coffee on the way back to the meeting spot. She was there exactly six minutes before they showed up.

"Have you been waiting long?" Blade asked.

"Nope." She smiled. "What's that?" she asked, looking at a familiar box.

"Your cheesecake. Sophie said the French vanilla was your favorite." He handed her the container.

"I thought I didn't get dessert," she reminded him.

"Cruel and unusual punishment has never been my style," he said. "So you got a dress?"

"I did."

"Show us," Raven and Sophie clamored.

No way. Then Blade would see. "Later," she said. "Don't you guys want to see a few stores?"

"Yes, yes," they said, her dress forgotten.

"I gave her money," Blade said, looking at Raven. "She knows her limits."

"Okay. We'll meet you back here in an hour," she said. "Let's go, girls."

He watched the three of them walk off. Daisy in the middle, Raven on the right, Sophie on the left. They were laughing and talking and he felt a sense of peace.

He and Daisy could make this work. He just needed to convince her. She was worried right now about introducing more change into Sophie's life. What he had to do was make her see that it really wouldn't be that big of a deal.

He was outside Pratt Sports Spot when his cell rang. Marcus returning his call. "Hey," he said.

"Sorry it took us so long to connect," Marcus said.

"How was the wedding?" The previous evening, Marcus had been attending a wedding with his latest female friend who had been a bridesmaid.

"There was an open bar."

"That made it worthwhile," Blade said.

"That and a few other things. But Darcy kept saying don't you just love weddings, and finally I had to tell her that I really didn't."

"Buzzkill. You could have lied."

"Nope. Not starting that. Tell me what you found out about the car?"

"Well, oddly enough when my dad got there to tow it, it started right up, as if there had never been a problem. He wanted my mom to look at it. She thinks somebody might have removed and then replaced two of the spark plugs."

There was silence on the other end. "Gutsy to do that on Main Street. I mean, I realize it was an ugly night but still."

"Kind of like it is sort of gutsy to break into one business by kicking in the back door and then do it again just a few nights later to a store two doors down."

"Yeah," Marcus said. "But nobody, not one person, recalled seeing Posse."

"Maybe somebody doing his dirty work for him. Daisy said he was a leader of some type of commune."

"It's possible. You're still keeping a close eye on Daisy?"

"Yeah. We're in Seattle shopping for a dress for the Spring Spectacular."

There was silence on the other end. "I think we might have a bad connection," Marcus said finally. "I thought you said shopping."

"She wanted a dress."

"And you wanted to make her smile?"

"Yeah, pretty much," Blade admitted.

Marcus sighed. "I like her. I really do. But I'm not confident that she's not going to bring trouble into your life."

"Me, either," Blade said. "But if she does, it will be worth it."

"You took her to bed, didn't you?" Marcus said.

"I really like this woman," Blade said. He'd almost said love, but he wasn't ready to have those confessions over the phone with his friend. Certainly not before he'd told Daisy.

"She's got a crazy ex-fiancé," Marcus reminded him. "Now you're mixed up in that."

"You and I both work in jobs where we see people in all kinds of situations. Lives are complicated. I don't know why I'd expect mine to be different."

"Complicated and dangerous have two different definitions," Marcus said. "But if you're happy, then I'm happy for you. I've been telling you to date more. You just took my advice a step further."

A step further. Hell, more like he'd run real fast and leaped off the rim of Headstone Canyon. "We're not telling our daughters or anyone else."

"Jamie?" he asked.

"Not yet. If I get a chance, I will."

"I'm playing handball with him tonight. I could always mention it."

"You'd do it just to throw him off his game."

"Got to have something up my sleeve. Why does the guy have to be good at everything?"

Once they got home from shopping, Blade had only an hour before he needed to be at work. He was covering for a coworker who needed some time off to attend his mother's eightieth birthday party. Daisy sat at the table, going through her mail that they'd picked up at the post office in Seattle on their way out of town. There was nothing of great importance and nothing that suggested Jacob.

Blade intended to drop Raven off at her mom's house on his way to work, leaving Daisy and Sophie alone in his house. She could tell that bothered him. He had already reminded her to lock the bolt locks about five times.

"We've got this," she said. Both girls were still in Raven's bedroom, so she felt safe to lean in and kiss him soundly. "Think about that instead," she said.

"I think too hard about it, and it might make for some embarrassing situations at work. I'm perpetually turned on."

"That's nice," she said.

"Easy for you to say. But seriously, I need to know that you're safe."

"Sophie and I have no plans to leave here today." Her rental car had been dropped off that morning and was sitting in Blade's driveway. But she didn't feel the need to go anywhere. "I'm going to post more photos, highlighting the hazardous materials training. I got a couple of great ones of the firefighters in full gear as they were practicing escaping from an enclosed space. And I know Sophie has a ton of homework."

"You have Marcus's number in case something happens. And 911, of course. And if you change your mind and go anywhere, you need to be very careful that you're not being followed."

"I know. Now, go. By the time you drop Raven off, you'll be late. By the way, have you told Sheila yet that Sophie and I are staying here?"

"Yeah, I called her yesterday morning before we went shopping. I think you were in the shower."

"You didn't want me to hear."

"I… Yeah, not really. I was pretty sure she'd be cool

about it, but sometimes I don't guess right. But she was really sweet. When I told her that someone had broken into your house, she said that you definitely shouldn't be staying there."

"She didn't say I should definitely be staying with you?"

He smiled. "Uh…no. But she didn't say that you shouldn't."

Her phone buzzed. She picked it up. Read the message. "Oh, my God."

"What?" he asked, clearly concerned.

"You're not going to believe this. That was Hosea. He's giving a ten-day all-expense-paid trip to Paris as his silent auction item."

"Wow. That beats the week at baseball spring training I got from the emergency room docs."

"It beats everything. Paris. Oh, I'm going to be so jealous of the winner."

"You want to go to Paris?" he asked.

"You *don't* want to go to Paris?" she asked incredulously.

"I never thought about it. I guess it would be okay."

She held up a finger. "I'll get there someday. I may be old and gray and part of a senior citizen tour, but I'll get there."

They heard the girls come from their room. "I'll see you later," she said.

Once Blade and Raven were out of the house, she looked at Sophie. "How you doing?" she asked.

"Okay. I mean, this is kind of weird, us being here. But I'm not sure I want to be at our house until they figure out who kicked the door in. Do you think it was Jacob, Mom?"

"I don't know. I don't have any reason to. But I don't want to be foolish with our safety. I don't trust him. You should not trust him."

"Do you think everybody lies?"

That was a philosophical question that she wasn't sure she was prepared to answer. "I think there are degrees of lying. If your best friend gets her hair cut and wants to know if you like it and you don't, I think it's okay if you fudge the truth a little. But I choose to believe that most people are truthful when it comes to bigger things."

"How do you tell?"

"Well, I didn't do a good job with Jacob," Daisy said. "I'm sorry about that. I put us in a bad position."

"He fooled everybody. He should be an actor. He'd probably win an Emmy or an Oscar."

Daisy leaned over and hugged her daughter. "*You* are going to win an Emmy or an Oscar. Wait, you're going to win both of them. Maybe a Tony, too."

"That would be so cool," Sophie said. She did a little dance around the kitchen. But then stopped, her face somber. "I don't think Blade lies. I don't think he's pretending to be something that he's not."

Daisy could feel her throat close. Her daughter was very young at times but at other times, so mature. "Do you like him?"

"Yeah. We had fun at lunch. I thought it would be weird without you, but it was a good time. He told us how he and his friends Marcus and Jamie put goats on the high school roof. And that they used to go sledding on refrigerator doors that they pulled behind pickup trucks. Then he said that if either one of us did anything remotely similar, there would be big trouble."

"Do as I say, not as I do," Daisy said.

"Yeah. I think it's pretty cool that he's stayed so close with his friends. I think that says something about a person."

Daisy nodded. "It says a lot."

"Once we move out of here and the Spring Spectacular is over, do you think that you and Blade will still hang out?"

"I don't know," Daisy said honestly. "We sort of got thrown together. We'll just have to see how it works out."

Sophie picked up her backpack, which was on one of the kitchen chairs. "Raven says that Blade works out every day. He has to because of his job. He's really strong. If Jacob came around, maybe it wouldn't be such a bad thing."

The idea of Blade and Jacob getting into a physical altercation made her feel queasy. Would there be no end to the people who would be hurt over her inability to see Jacob's evilness? "I don't want that to happen," she said.

"Just saying, I think Blade could take him."

On Monday, Daisy took a late lunch and drove her rental car to Gertie's Café. As Blade had requested, she watched the other vehicles around her carefully. But nothing seemed out of place. When she got inside, she saw Cheryl.

"By yourself?" Cheryl asked.

"Yes. Maybe I'll just sit at the counter."

"Okay. Coffee?"

"Yes. And I'll have your soup and a side salad. Can

you let Gertie know that I'm here? I just want to touch base about the Spring Spectacular."

"Will do. I voted for the pot roast with potatoes and carrots. It's to die for."

Daisy smiled. "Lots of people are weighing in on their favorites. Voting will get cut off in just a couple days, which will allow Gertie time to order the necessary food and supplies from her vendors."

"Don't worry about Gertie."

Daisy was halfway done with her soup and salad when Gertie took the empty stool next to her. "Feels good to sit," she said. She had a cup of coffee in her hand.

"Lunch is delicious," Daisy said. "I came for that and also to tell you that tickets for the Spring Spectacular are going fast. We're at three hundred and eighty-two guests."

"Wow. I'm glad to hear it, but I think I may need some more help. I've got my regular team, but for big events, I supplement with some high school students. They can do everything but pour the wine. I think I'm going to need a few more."

"I could ask my daughter, Sophie, to help. And maybe Blade's daughter, Raven, too. They might have some friends who are interested."

"Perfect. Tell them it's fifteen bucks an hour and all the food they want."

"What do they wear?"

"Black pants and a white shirt. And a smile. That's the most important thing."

"I'll see what I can do. I feel sort of responsible for creating this monster."

"It'll work out. Have a good day, Daisy," Gertie said, sliding off her stool.

* * *

She called Jane on her way back to the office. "Are you busy?" Daisy asked.

"No, just eating a late lunch at my desk. What's going on?"

Daisy told her about the car, about finding her front door kicked in, about Blade offering a place to stay."

"You could have stayed with me," Jane said.

"I slept with Blade," Daisy said.

"Oh." Then silence. "Well, that wouldn't have happened at my house."

Daisy laughed and laughed. "Thank you," she said, when she got her breath back. "That's exactly the response I needed."

"Did you think I would lecture you?" Jane asked.

"I don't know. You know me. You know it's out of character for me to do something rash. But I wanted to have sex with him. I really wanted it, and I didn't take very much time to think of consequences."

"Consequences as in birth control?"

"No, he took care of that. Consequences in that I would want to do it again."

Now it was Jane's turn to laugh. "Oh, honey. If that is the worst thing that comes from it, I think you should count yourself lucky. I told you once that he was hot. I'll bet he's on fire, get it, in bed."

"Got it," she said. He had certainly sparked a flame in her.

"Are you telling Sophie and his daughter?"

"No. And no one but our most trusted confidants."

"My lips are sealed. But seriously, Daisy. You're a young woman. You should want to have sex with a gorgeous guy. It's normal. Now quit worrying. I have to go. I'll talk to you later."

Daisy went back to work. Jane had been her friend for many years. She'd always trusted her advice and counsel.

Jane didn't think she'd made a mistake.

Jane thought she should enjoy the ride.

She was going to try.

The next few days flew by. The social media traffic was brisk, with lots of people weighing in on the menu. More photos came in. Daisy glanced at most of them quickly and moved on. And she was just about to do just that when one caught her eye. Blade was in the background, unaware that the photo was being shot, and he was dancing with a very pretty blonde in a long lavender dress. It was not Sheila.

"This is you," she said, looking up from her computer. They were sitting in his family room. He was in the chair, watching a basketball game on mute, likely so that it wouldn't bother her. "Someone sent in a photo of you. Raven said you didn't dance."

"I dance," he said, getting up from his chair. "I mean, I sort of shuffle my feet around." He leaned over her shoulder. "Oh, yeah. That was last year. I told you that I'd attended before."

He had. At the time, she just hadn't given any thought to who he might have attended with. Now she found herself intensely curious. "Who is your date?"

"Ashlee with two e's."

"Is that how she introduced herself?"

"More often than not."

"Did you date for a long time?"

"A couple months."

She had a thousand questions. "Who broke it off?"

"I guess I did. It wasn't a big deal. We dated for a while, and then we both got busy with other things and I just didn't call her again."

"She might still be waiting for your call," Daisy said.

"Oh, I hope not. A few weeks ago, I heard she was engaged. She was a pharmaceutical representative who called on Bigelow Memorial. Jamie introduced us."

She sat quietly for a minute. He went back to his chair. "You know," she said, "I haven't given much thought to what your life was before Sophie and I overtook it. That's probably pretty rude of me."

"You didn't interrupt anything of importance," he said. "I had a life. A regular life. Luckier than most. I had a job I liked, a good kid, a relatively friendly ex-wife, good buddies, nice parents. If there had been a Labrador retriever in the picture, it might have been a Norman Rockwell painting."

"You didn't want a dog?" she asked, deliberately focusing on the irrelevant.

He smiled. "We *both* had lives. You've told me about Jacob, but I can't believe he was the only person who has been important to you."

"I was pregnant at seventeen. I liked Sophie's father, but I certainly didn't love him. I didn't know what adult love was. We were kids messing around in the back of his pickup truck." She rolled her eyes. "In our defense, there was an air mattress."

"Your reputation for preferring a bed is intact," he said.

She could feel her cheeks get hot. She'd been bolder the afternoon she'd taken his hand and led him to the bedroom than perhaps any other time of her life. "I was kind of a lost teenager. After my mother died, my life took a substantial turn for the better." She paused. "It took me a lot of years and a little bit of therapy to be able to say that last sentence."

"Want to say it again?"

"Not necessary. I loved my mother. But she was a child in an adult body. I never knew what I was coming home to. Sad Mommy. Drunk Mommy. Absent Mommy. Superhappy Mommy. Some variation of the above."

"Exhausting for a child," he said.

"Very. But Nana Jo was absolutely the opposite. Always there, willing to listen. Considerate with her words. Confident in my abilities. Safe. And I decided that was the kind of Mom that I was going to be."

"Odd how your mom turned out, isn't it, given your grandmother," he said.

"I have racked my brain trying to figure it out. I can't. And I know it bothered Nana Jo that the two of them were estranged. What I didn't realize was how much it bothered Nana Jo that my mom kept me away from her. I didn't realize how much she loved me."

"You and Sophie probably brought a great deal of joy to her life."

"I think we did. We were happy. That's a roundabout way of answering your question. Once I had Sophie and Nana Jo, I didn't really feel the need to date much. I was too busy. Going to school, working a job, trying to be the right kind of parent to Sophie."

"And then you met Jacob Posse?"

"Yes, about two years ago, I met Jacob at a fundraiser."

"Please tell me he wasn't your cochair?" Blade asked dully.

"No. He was a guest. But he made a sizable donation to the cause, and I wanted to thank him in person. He was charming. Polite. He had a very deliberate way of talking that I liked—it was as if he was considering every word. Now, in retrospect, I think he *was* considering every word. He was acting a part, and he was watching to make sure he never strayed from character."

"In kindergarten, he was probably conning the other little kids out of their lunch money," Blade said.

"No doubt. He told me all about his family. His two sisters. His parents who were both attorneys. He had great stories about family vacations and Christmas rituals. I'm pretty sure it was all a lie. When my friend the cop went to Cedar Rapids to investigate him, he couldn't find any evidence that these people existed. So I don't really know if anything he said was true. He told me he'd never been married. It doesn't matter now, of course, but I can't help but wonder if there's a wife somewhere. Maybe another commune member. Or was I the only one stupid enough to fall for his lines."

He reached for her hand. "People intent upon deception don't generally have that tough of a time. The rest of us trust easily."

"I console myself with the knowledge that at least I was smart enough not to marry him. One of the things that bothered me along the way was that he basically ignored Sophie. I mean, he was pleasant to her if she was around when he came over. Several times we took her to dinner with us and that always went okay. But I couldn't shake the feeling that he wasn't the least bit interested in her as a person. When he asked me to marry him, I made a point of saying that Sophie and I were a package deal. I flat out asked him if he wanted to be a stepfather to a then fifteen-year-old girl. He said of course he did. And when we'd go look for houses, he'd say, 'This will be Sophie's room.' But I really think it was just more of reading off a script. It was what he was supposed to say so he said it."

He stared at her. "I know that you and Sophie are a package deal. I'm not scared of having another sixteen-year-old around. Raven and I do pretty well."

She held up a hand. "Whoa. It's way too early for us to be having this kind of conversation."

"Is it?" he challenged her. "I know things have moved fast with us, but sometimes I think that's how it works. I don't want to lose what we have between us just because we're scared. Scared of introducing more change to Sophie. Scared of committing to something as big as marriage."

Marriage? The two of them? That was way too big to address directly. "Did you like being married, Blade?" she asked instead.

"I did. I liked coming home to my wife and my child. They gave me a greater purpose. And it was a bad time for me when it became apparent that Sheila and I weren't going to make it. I'd like to have a wife again. A family. But having had the experience of one marriage failing, I know how important it is that the union be right, that it be strong." He paused. "I think what we have is right. And strong. And that we could make each other very happy."

He'd brought it right back to the two of them. And she had to admit, her heart was bursting. She'd found a brave and wonderful man who wanted to risk it all for her. She wanted to throw herself into his arms. It almost hurt to slowly shake her head. "I have too much baggage right now. We can't have this discussion."

"I'm not afraid of baggage."

"I am," she said. "Terribly afraid."

Chapter 18

On the day of the Spring Spectacular, Daisy woke up to sunshine and a temperature of forty-five degrees. The high was predicted to hit fifty. It was lovely that the weather was cooperating. On her way to the kitchen, she peeked in at Sophie who was still sleeping. Raven's bed was empty as this was her weekend at her mom's.

It was amazing how easily Sophie had adapted to the relocation to Blade's duplex. She supposed it was because they'd been in their house for such a short time that it had never really seemed like home to the teenager—more like a brief bed-and-breakfast stay.

But it was time. There'd been no sign of Jacob for two weeks. No burglaries in the downtown, no other unexplained crime. Marcus thought that if he'd been here, he'd decided not to stay. Had given up.

She supposed it was possible. Better yet, she supposed

it was possible that it never was Jacob in the first place. Maybe she'd left her vehicle unlocked? Maybe the person who'd removed her spark plugs and the person who'd kicked in her front door were two different people, committing two random acts.

Had she made a connection where there was none? Could she simply dismiss those things as bad luck? But what about the gift basket and Morgan Tiddle's description of the sender that could easily have been Jacob? It was maddening.

All she knew for sure was that she wasn't going to be able to hide out at Blade's forever. It had been wonderful. He'd been fun and attentive and the sex, even when they had to be superquiet, had been really, really good.

Blade was working, but would be home by 9:30 a.m. She'd be gone by then. Gertie was meeting her at the community center. Someone from the center would be there to set up tables and chairs, and then Daisy intended to help Gertie and her team with the linens and the flowers. Tables would be set with plates and silverware and glassware. Two portable bars that would be set up in opposite corners of the room had been donated by the wine store at the edge of Knoware, and the owners, twin brothers, had agreed to play bartender. It would be a cash bar, and all proceeds above their costs would be donated to the fire department. In addition, they'd already donated a wine tasting for fifteen as a silent auction item.

They'd stopped selling tickets at noon the day before. The number was 424 or as Gertie said, fifty-three tables of eight. At fifty bucks a head, sales would be over $21,000. That combined with the silent auction bidding and the liquor sales almost certainly guaranteed that even after they paid the photographer and the DJ, the fire department would still net $30,000.

Best year ever. It was exhilarating and certainly not shabby, considering that they'd pulled the whole thing together in a matter of weeks. But she certainly hadn't done it alone. It was a community accomplishment. Such a different experience than when she'd lived in a bigger town.

She didn't want to leave Knoware. And if Jacob was truly not hanging around at the edges, there would be no reason to.

Blade had said he wanted more. She'd been the one pulling back, as if the M-word was a hot potato.

They were having great sex and fun conversation. It was nothing to sneer at. Lots of people might be very happy with the status quo.

But her heart yearned for permanency. In retrospect, it was probably why she'd said yes to Jacob's proposal. He'd offered marriage and said that he wanted children.

And she desperately wanted that. Yes, she had a sixteen-year-old daughter. And others might consider her an idiot for wanting to grow her family. But she was only thirty-four. She could see her life down the road and there were babies. Beautiful chubby-cheeked babies. And while some people might be content to go that way on their own, she didn't want that. She wanted these children to have both a mom and a dad, living together, a family unit.

She drank her coffee and ate a piece of toast. Then she quietly walked back down the hall. After showering and getting dressed, she fingered the navy blue silk dress hanging at the back of the closet. Blade hadn't asked to see the dress, and she hadn't offered. She hoped he liked it. She knew what he was wearing. A black suit, white shirt and dark tie. He would be the most handsome guy there, no doubt.

Before she left, she walked into Sophie's room. "Morning," she said softly.

Sophie opened one eye, then the other. "Good morning," she mumbled.

"I'm leaving. I'll see you tonight. Remember, black pants and a white shirt. Comfortable shoes or you'll regret it."

"Raven and I are planning on drinking the leftover wine," she said.

Daisy smiled. "We'll see about that. I'm off to the community center to help with setup and then I'm stopping at the salon." The woman at the dress store had convinced her to get an updo. Said that her strapless gown practically begged for one. "Blade should be home in less than an hour. I'll lock the door. Don't answer it."

"I'm going to have to answer it when Raven comes to pick me up for play practice."

"Fine. But make sure it's her first."

Sophie sat up in bed. "Are you still worried, Mom? About Jacob?"

"I am encouraged by the fact that nothing else has happened and that nobody has seen him. But I'm not letting my guard down, and you shouldn't, either."

"I know. I guess it's been nice being here. I felt safe."

"I know. Me, too. But we'll feel safe again in our own home."

"We're leaving?" Sophie asked.

"Well, we can't stay forever."

"That's what I told Raven. She said that she thinks her dad really likes you."

"I really like him, too, Sophie. But sometimes it takes more than that."

"I know," she said. "But it's still good, right?"

"Really good, darling. I'll see you later."

The community center, which had seemed vast and empty the last time she'd seen it, was bustling with activity. There were at least ten people setting up tables and chairs. Gertie was in the corner, sorting through table-cloths and coordinating napkins. There was a whole table of vases with fresh flowers. Daisy didn't bother to count them. She knew there'd be at least fifty-three.

"Good morning, Gertie," Daisy said. "How's it going?"

"The chicken is prepped and the lemon bars are already cooling. We'll work on the appetizers and the sides this afternoon. Don't worry, it will all get done."

A week ago, the votes for the menu had been counted. Winner winner chicken dinner. In specific, chicken cordon blue, wild rice with almonds, green beans, Caesar salad, and lemon bars for dessert. The lemon bars had surprised her. "I've got a bit of a reputation for them," Gertie had admitted.

"I have no doubt. I have to tell you that having you be a part of this event has made it possible for me to sleep well."

Gertie looked over both shoulders, as if making sure that no one was close. "I thought that was Blade's job."

Daisy could feel her cheeks get hot. "Uh…"

Gertie held up a hand. "You don't owe this old woman any explanations. All I would ask is that you treat his very kind heart with care."

"I wouldn't ever want to hurt Blade," she said.

"I'm happy to hear that. And by the way, he seems

happier than I've seen him in years. Maybe ever." Gertie turned away, waved at three people who were standing near the kitchen. "Time for the elves to dress the tables," she said.

Daisy fell in line with the rest of the group. Tablecloths first. Then napkins. Silverware. A knife, two forks and a spoon. Then a dinner plate. The salads would be served on a smaller plate, once everyone was sitting. The final touch was a flower vase. It took more than two hours before everything was finished, but it looked stunning. They really had created a bit of magic.

By then, the DJ had arrived and was setting up his equipment. The bars were getting stocked, and twinkle lights were getting strung on the ceiling.

She wandered back into the kitchen where salad dressing was getting made and cheese was getting sliced. Gertie was directing the efforts while she and another woman snapped the ends off a mountain of fresh green beans. "Can I do anything to help?" Daisy asked.

"I think we're in good shape. I've got your cell phone in case we encounter any disasters."

"Don't hesitate to call," Daisy said. "Although I can't imagine being able to solve any problem that you can't. I'm headed to the printers to pick up the menu cards that will be at each place setting and will be back early tonight to get them on the table." In addition to listing the menu, she'd included an acknowledgment of Gertie's donation as well as those of the wine store and the other silent auction contributors. At the very bottom, she encouraged attendees to post pictures of the night on social media. It was never too early to start whipping up interest in next year's event. She likely wouldn't be a cochair, but if the event provided necessary equipment and training that might someday help or protect Blade, then she was all for it.

She left the community center and drove to the printer. There she inspected the printed cards. They were perfect. She paid for them and watched while the clerk placed them in a box.

She had a couple hours before her hair appointment. There was no sense going back to Blade's apartment. He'd be sleeping and Sophie would be at play practice. She drove to Pratt Sports Spot. There were art proofs on her desk for new store signage that needed to be approved, and she needed to write a press release about several new product lines that the store was taking on.

When she got to her desk, the light on her phone was blinking, telling her that she had voice mail. She entered her password. Sixteen messages. What the heck? That was a lot considering there hadn't been any when she'd left the previous night at five o'clock. She pressed 1 to listen to the first message. All she heard after several seconds of nothing was a hang up. She deleted it. She went on to the next message. Same thing. Nothing for several seconds, and then the call ended. She went on to the third message, but did not delete the second message.

Every remaining message was just the same. Sixteen hang-up calls.

What the hell?

Now all thoughts of actually accomplishing something were out of her head. She was consumed with this. She wanted to talk to Blade, to get his read. He was a good thinker. But he'd worked all night. He needed his sleep.

Maybe Marcus. Yes. That was probably the right thing to do.

She found his card in her purse. Punched in his number.

"Marcus Price," he answered.

"Marcus, it's Daisy."

"Are you okay?"

"Yes, I'm fine. I… I'm at work and something odd has happened that I wanted you to be aware of. I had sixteen hang-up calls on my voice mail. They came in sometime after five o'clock."

"Do you have any way of seeing the number they came from?"

"I don't know," she admitted. "I could probably ask someone in the Information Services department. They handle our phones. We have someone in our data center 24/7."

"Call them. I'm ten minutes away."

"I'm not sure you need to come," she said. She was getting really tired of being a bother.

"I'd like to have a listen. Don't delete them."

"I have fifteen of the sixteen," she said. "I'll watch for you. The corporate offices are locked on Saturday."

She was walking down the last flight of stairs when she saw his SUV pull up out front. She unlocked the door, let him in and locked the door behind him. "Thanks for coming," she said.

"Of course. Blade on his way?"

"I didn't want to bother him. I'm sure he's sleeping. I'll fill him in later." After the dance.

Marcus followed her upstairs to her office. There he listened to three of the saved voice mail messages. "What did your IS department say about the number?"

"I left a message with a call center tech. She said that she'd have an analyst look at it, but right now he was focused on our Tacoma store where all the cash registers are off-line for some reason."

"They'll call you?"

"I gave them my number and your number," she said. "I don't think there is much else we can do here now."

"Nothing else unusual has happened?" Marcus asked.

"No. You'll be at the dance later, right?"

"Yes."

"I'll see you there."

She tried to put the calls out of her mind as she drove to the salon. Once in the chair, she was finally able to because she had cold feet. Maybe an up-do was too much. It was really just an after-hours work event.

"You have beautiful hair," the stylist said. Her name was Dee-Dee and her short hair was a lovely red. "Really healthy. Thick. It's a good thing you're a few minutes early. This is going to take a while."

A while was forty-five minutes, but when it was done, Daisy was confident her hair wasn't going anywhere. How was it that a good stylist could pin it and spray it as if preparing for battle but manage to make it look effortless and rather whimsical. It was magic. And she was glad she'd done it.

"Thank you," she said, giving the stylist a generous tip. Then, as her stomach loudly rumbled, she pressed her hand against it. "Excuse me," she said with a smile. "I didn't have any lunch."

"There's a sub place around the corner that's really good," the stylist said.

"I may just do that." If she planned on having a glass of wine before dinner tonight, she better eat a little something now or she might be facedown on the floor.

There'd be a very sexy paramedic nearby, however. Might make it worth it. He could do some mouth-to-mouth. Might be her only chance to get close to him. They'd still not told Sophie or Raven that there was something romantic between them. They would have to keep up that pretense tonight, regardless of how difficult it might be. Hosea would be there. Charlie. All the bosses who might have a legitimate right to be concerned that she and Blade had mixed business with pleasure. She was so new at her job that she couldn't take the chance on *that* becoming her reputation.

"Use the back door. It's closer," the stylist said.

Daisy checked her cell phone as she made the short walk. There was text from Blade. I'm awake, almost functional. How is your day going?

Great. Be back to your house in a half hour to change, she texted.

He was likely to be irritated once she told him about the sixteen hang-up calls. But she wasn't going to let that ruin the night. They'd both worked hard to make this a success.

She walked into the sub shop. She wasn't surprised that it wasn't busy; it was late for lunch and early for dinner. There was one other customer who had his back to her. He was staring out at the parking lot. She could see her rental and maybe fifteen other vehicles. Perhaps he was waiting for someone.

She ordered a small turkey sandwich and a soda to drink from the young girl behind the counter. She waited while her sandwich was prepared, paid for her meal and carried it to a table. When she pulled out her chair to sit, the legs scrapped on the tile floor. The customer turned in his seat to look.

And she almost spilled her soda when the two of them made eye contact.

Chapter 19

The man visibly jerked, his eyes flaring with what might have been panic. But then he quickly looked down at the remains of his lunch. Then he was up and out the door, leaving his trash on the table.

Some people were good with faces. Some were good with names. Daisy had always been good with both. Especially if she'd had conversation with them. It was helpful in her line of work. She was confident that she'd never spoken to the man, but she'd definitely seen him before. She closed her eyes and tried to place where.

Was it the communication conference in Chicago? Or was he a parent at Sophie's school in Denver? Maybe it had been the airport? Damn. She just couldn't put her finger on it. But it seemed as if he'd recognized her, too. Or was it possible that he'd simply been startled by the screech of the chair's legs on the floor?

He was crossing the parking lot, headed toward a beige sedan. She did not recognize the car and couldn't see the plates. Was he one of Jacob's posse? She'd never met them, but the police had described a cult-like atmosphere in the Denver dwelling where Jacob's followers had viewed him as their spiritual leader.

Should she call Marcus?

She was just about to pull out her phone, after all, better safe than sorry, when she saw a woman crossing the lot, also headed to the car. The two of them got there at almost exactly the same time. He drove, she sat shotgun.

Oh, good grief. The man had simply been watching the parking lot, waiting for his wife. For all Daisy knew, the woman might have been in the salon.

She was dreaming that she'd seen him before. Seeing monsters in the corners when there were none. She was grateful she hadn't called. Marcus was going to start to think she was a nut. Or worse, the girl who cried wolf. Then, when she really did need help, nobody was going to believe her.

She finished her sandwich, drank half her soda and threw her garbage in the trash. Then she walked back to her car. She took the long way back to Blade's house, which allowed her to drive past her little Cape Cod. She slowed. The house looked good. She didn't stop. She'd promised Blade that she wouldn't go back unless he or Marcus was with her.

But that arrangement couldn't go on forever. It was time to go home. Sophie needed her own space, not to be living in some other girl's bedroom. And Blade would probably be grateful to have his bed back. He was too tall for the couch. Although he was getting a break from it for several hours every night.

She finished the drive to Blade's duplex, filled with a resolve to move forward with her life after the dance. She'd been in limbo, a sexually-satisfying limbo for sure, for the past two weeks.

She was surprised that the apartment was empty. She had expected Blade to be there. She checked her phone to see if there was a text she might have missed and sure enough, there was a brief message. My mom called. My dad is pretty sick. I'll meet you at the dance. Will try not to be late.

The entire Savick family was going to have really tough days ahead of them. But perhaps this was evidence that Larkin, Gemma and Blade would be there to support each other.

She got ready. It didn't take long. She couldn't shower and risk getting her hair wet so she took a nice warm bath instead. Then she dried off and added a quick spray of her favorite perfume. She pulled on panties but no bra; it was built into the dress.

She stepped into the dress and pulled it up. The strapless satin bodice was tight to the waist, and then it flowed in layers of chiffon. She felt like a princess. She slipped her feet into black sandals with a two-inch heel and added some pearl studs to her ears.

She walked quickly to the car. While it was a lovely early spring evening, it was definitely too cold to be outside wearing only a strapless gown. She got in her rental and turned the heat on high. It was a short drive to the community center. There were already cars in the parking lot, and she assumed it was mostly kitchen and serving staff.

Sure enough, she saw both Raven and Sophie once she got inside. They were in the kitchen, on either side of a butcher-block table, an immense bowl of salad between them. Both were holding tongs.

"Hey, girls," she said, catching their attention.

"Oh, my God," Sophie said. "You look amazing, Mom. No wonder you didn't let us see it early. It's totally awesome."

It was one of the nicest compliments she'd ever gotten. She twirled in her pretty dress. "Thank you."

"Can I have it when you're done with it?" Raven asked.

"She's my mother. I get the dress," Sophie said quickly, her tone teasing.

"Neither of you is getting it," Daisy said. "What are you doing?"

"Plating 424 salads," Sophie said. "They all have to be identical, or as close as we can get them. I put the salad on the plate and then Raven adds three beet slices, six walnuts and a tablespoon of cheese. It's a little ridiculous. I mean, it's just salad."

It was just evidence of Gertie's commitment to consistency and style. "They're going to be beautiful," she said.

"I might do five walnuts or maybe seven on a couple, just to see if anyone notices," Raven said.

"You'll have to live with yourself," Daisy said.

Gertie came around the corner of the table. She stopped short when she saw Daisy. "That is a beautiful dress," she said. "Now get the heck out of my kitchen before you spill something on it."

"What can I do to help?" Daisy asked.

"We're in pretty good shape. They just set up the sound system. Maybe you'll want to check that."

She'd volunteered to write Hosea Pratt's speech, but he'd told her that he was comfortable making his own remarks. She'd delicately reminded him that both he and the fire chief should keep their comments to under five minutes in length. That was long enough. Nobody came to these events to hear someone drone on.

She left the kitchen. When she stepped into the large meeting room, she was amazed at the transformation. It was really lovely. The tables were all beautifully set. The flameless candles on each of the tables had been turned on, and light was flickering through the room. The DJ had turned on the music and soft instrumental filled the room.

She tested the microphones. "Raise your hands in the back of the room if you can hear me," she said. And the three young women who were arranging the silent auction items raised their hands. Excellent.

She turned off the microphone and wandered back to see if they needed any help. "This looks great," she said. For every item, there was a bidding sheet, with a minimum bid already listed. They had also included the detailed information that she'd written about each prize. If she didn't say so herself, it was some persuasive writing. Everything sounded wonderful.

Hopefully the bidding would be fierce.

She glanced at her watch. The event would start in less than a half hour. The first forty-five minutes would be cocktails and appetizers, then speeches. Dinner would be served, then dessert and coffee, and then the dancing and silent auction bidding. By eleven, it would be done. The fat lady would have sung.

And the way it looked right now, her first big event was going to be a rip-roaring success. It was gratifying. And she knew that she owed Blade a great debt. The photos that she'd been able to get had been spectacular.

She turned. Speaking of spectacular. Blade had arrived and was chatting with Cheryl, who was setting up the appetizer table. He looked tall and elegant in his black suit and white shirt. She watched him for a minute, just enjoying the view. He started to cross the room, heading toward the kitchen. But he wasn't making much progress—every two or three feet he'd get stopped by somebody. They probably wanted to comment on some of the photos, maybe thank him for his work. He was such a nice guy, always making time for people, that he would never blow them off.

Finally, she got close enough that when he glanced forward, he saw her.

And if there had been any doubt that the price of the dress had been worth it, they vanished. His eyes told her everything.

"Strapless. You should have warned me," he said, when he got close enough not to be overheard. His hands were at his side, but she could see the tension and knew that he wanted to touch her. "You're beautiful."

He said it with reverence. And her body responded, getting very warm in all the right places.

"You're pretty debonair yourself," she said.

"This old thing," he mocked, motioning to his suit. "I like your hair." He leaned even closer. "I'm going to enjoy taking out every pin," he whispered in her ear.

She couldn't wait.

She stepped away. She really couldn't trust herself. "Do you like the room?"

He turned to look. "It's amazing. All those weeks ago, when they told me that I was the cochair, I couldn't have imagined this. You did it. You made it happen."

"I had good material," she said. "All I did was find an audience."

"I tried to call you earlier," he said. "You didn't answer."

"I'm sorry," she said. "My phone is in my purse. I tossed it under our table." She and Blade would join Hosea and his wife and the fire chief and his wife. "I hope you weren't worried."

"I called Gertie. She said that you were in the building, making last-minute inspections. I just wanted to make sure that your day had gone well, that there wasn't anything unusual."

She thought about the man in the sub shop and her over-the-top reaction. About the hang-up calls. That was a conversation for another time. "No, it was fine. The hair took a little longer than expected."

He glanced at her bare shoulders. "I'm not going to be able to keep my hands off you. We should have told the girls. We should have told everybody."

She smiled. "Maybe that's what makes it exciting. That it's our secret."

He shook his head, his eyes serious. "*That's* not what makes this exciting or different."

Again, a conversation for another time. "Let's check with Gertie one last time," she said. She led the way to the kitchen.

"I've never been in the military," Daisy whispered as they entered the kitchen, "but I kind of think this is what someone means when they say it was a precise military operation. Nothing left for chance."

They watched for a few minutes. "Let's get out of here," Blade said finally. "We'll only mess it up."

It was time for them to be out front, anyway. Guests were starting to arrive. Blade went to the right, Daisy to the left. Each took a spot by the door and welcomed guests as they arrived. They pointed them toward the cash bars and to the complimentary cheese and relish tray in the middle of the room. And they encouraged everyone to closely examine the silent auction items and bid on their favorites.

It was a steady stream of people. Daisy could tell that Blade knew most of the people. Most were strangers to her, but they stopped to introduce themselves and tell her how much they'd enjoyed the Remember This campaign. She saw Marcus and his date, who was a stunning black-haired beauty, arrive. He was followed by Jamie Weathers and his date, a pretty woman who looked good in her red dress. Blade had told her that she was also a physician at the hospital.

Hosea, using a walker, arrived. His wife was a lovely woman who shook Daisy's hand. "Thank you for the work on this fundraiser. It is something that Pratt Sports Spot can be very proud of," she said.

"It was a great introduction to the community," Daisy replied. *And to a certain sexy firefighter.* That she kept to herself.

When it was time for the speeches to start, she and Blade made their way to the table. There, he introduced her to the fire chief and his wife, who both also had nice things to say about the event. Then it was time for the chief to say a few words. He thanked people for coming and thanked Blade and Daisy for their efforts. He introduced Hosea.

Daisy held her breath, wishing that she'd gotten a preview of his speech. But a minute into it, she realized that her fears were misplaced. And knew that she'd never have been able to do the topic justice. Hosea gave a first-person account of what it had been like to be in a serious situation and need the assistance of the brave men and women of the Knoware Fire Department. He talked of the sudden fear of falling, the dawning awareness of waking up flat on his back, unable to move. He talked about the worry of wondering whether this might be it. The end.

And then he talked about the competence of everyone who responded and what a terrific relief it had been to know that these professionals were going to be the difference between a life well lived or a life still worth living.

Daisy could feel her eyes moisten. Hosea was being so open, and it was compelling.

"The two people who made tonight possible, Ms. Daisy Rambler and Mr. Blade Savick, were with me in Myrtle Canyon," Hosea said. "They made a difference that day, and they're making a difference tonight. The rest of us can do the same. I'm begging you, get out your checkbooks. Bid up your neighbor on a silent auction item. There is no better place that your money could go. Thank you and have a good evening. I won't be on the dance floor tonight, but I expect to see all of you."

The crowd gave him a standing ovation.

And then Gertie started putting on her show. At least fifteen teenagers, dressed in black pants and white shirts, carried salads and bread baskets to the tables. Wine bottles, both red and white, were already open and in the middle of the table. Guests wasted no time passing them. As glasses started to fill, there was laughter and conversation and by anyone's assessment, it appeared to be a success. The DJ was continuing to play background music.

Daisy smiled at Blade. "I'm so relieved," she said in a voice that only he could hear.

"Never had a doubt," he replied, handing her the bread basket.

When the salad plates were cleared, dinners started to arrive table by table. Within fifteen minutes, all of the tables had been served. Daisy took a bite. It was delicious.

She could go home happy now, knowing that people got a good meal for their fifty-dollar ticket. But she knew that she would stay until the bitter end. She would see this through.

And she intended to dance with Blade. They'd keep it G-rated. Even if it killed them. The payoff later, when he sneaked into her room, would be worth it.

Once the dinner dishes were cleared, the DJ moved to his podium. "Let's get this party started," he said. And then he played "Ring of Fire" by Johnny Cash. It was the perfect start for a firefighters' fundraiser.

"I'm going to go thank Gertie," Daisy said to Blade. She'd seen several of Gertie's elves setting up the dessert and coffee table that people could help themselves to at their leisure. The kitchen's work was done. With the exception that there was probably a huge pile of dishes. Thankfully the community center had invested in a commercial dishwasher that would make the job less painful.

"I'll go with—"

"Blade," the fire chief interrupted. "There's somebody I'd like you to meet."

"Go," Daisy said. "I've got this."

"I'll find you," he said, giving her a quick wink that only she could see.

In the kitchen, there were kids everywhere, lounging on chairs, chest freezers, countertops. Some were sitting on the floor. A handful of adults, most of whom she recognized as employees of Gertie's Café, were also there. Everyone seemed very relaxed and very happy.

The dishwasher was running. Two high school boys were stacking more dishes in green carts, getting them ready for the wash cycle. She looked around, but did not see Raven, Sophie or Gertie. She did see Cheryl, so she made her way toward the woman.

"You all did wonderful tonight," Daisy said. "The room was full of compliments."

"It was fun. My feet hurt, though," Cheryl said. "I brought a dress to change into because my husband is here, but I'm not sure how much I'm going to dance. It might be fun to sit in the corner with a piece of dessert, however. And have none of my four children clamoring for a bite."

"Totally get that," Daisy said. "Speaking of children, I was looking for Sophie. And Raven Savick, too."

Cheryl looked around the room. "Hmm, I'm not sure." She turned to one of the boys sprawled on the chest freezer. "Have you seen Sophie and Raven?"

He nodded. "Some guy came to the back door. Wanted to talk to Sophie. She told Raven to come with her."

Daisy felt the ground sway. Knew it really hadn't, but the kid's words literally made her head feel disconnected from her body. A guy. Came to the back door. Sophie had needed reinforcements to talk to him.

"Gertie wanted them to take the lemon bars out," the kid on the freezer continued. "When I told her about the guy and that they'd gone outside to talk to him, she asked somebody else to do it, and then she went looking for them."

Should she get Blade? Or Marcus? But Blade was getting face time with the chief. She didn't want to interrupt that if it wasn't necessary. And Gertie could be outside with the girls right now, just chatting. Her work was done.

"I'll just poke my head outside," she said to Cheryl. She walked past the big stainless-steel refrigerators and the six-burner stove. She opened the back door. She knew an alley ran behind the community center, but it was too dark to see it well now; there wasn't even a light above the door. Wait. There was a light. She reached back inside to flip the switch. Did it twice. Nothing happened. Thank goodness there was a full moon.

A streetlight a half block away also helped but not much. "Sophie," she said, her voice loud in the quiet night.

No answer. She took a couple more steps. "Sophie. Raven."

She heard a moan. There were garbage cans to her right. She moved toward them and almost stumbled over the body on the ground. She knelt. "Oh, Gertie," she said.

"Daisy," the woman moaned. "Be care—"

"Hello, Daisy."

Chapter 20

Daisy froze. She knew that voice. She turned her head. Jacob Posse. And behind him, just walking into view, were the man and woman she'd seen get into the car at the sub shop. She spared them barely a glance, because it was who they were hanging on to that she was interested in.

The man had Sophie. The woman had Raven. Both of them had guns.

"No, Jacob," she cried. "No."

"You shouldn't have left me, Daisy. I need you."

Oh, God. "I'll do whatever you want. Whatever. Just let them go."

"You for them. That's what I want. You come with me. You're going to have to be punished for the effort you've caused me, Daisy. But once we're past that, you and I'll be happy. I know we will."

"Yes, yes." It didn't matter what happened to her. "Let them go."

Jacob wrapped his hand tight around her bare arm. He yanked her to her feet. "Now," he said.

He turned to the man and woman. "Take care of them."

"What does that mean?" Daisy demanded.

Jacob held up a finger in her direction, to silence her. "They'll be detained for a bit, allowing us time to escape."

She saw the man and woman exchange a glance. "What about the old lady?" the woman asked.

"She's already pretty close to dead," Jacob said. "Leave her."

"You bastard," Daisy hissed.

He twisted her arm, high behind her back, causing her to cry out in pain. "I warned you to be quiet. That will cost you, Daisy," he said.

She wanted to scratch Jacob's eyes from his head. But she needed to make sure that Sophie was safe. She did not resist when Jacob pulled her down the alley.

"Mom, don't—"

Her daughter's plea was stifled.

"You or them," Jacob said.

Daisy didn't look back. "Just do what they say," she said, loud enough that Sophie would hear. "I love you. Never forget that."

Blade saw Marcus and Jamie chatting near the bar. He walked up, clapping them both on the back. "Your dates already go home?" he asked.

"They're together, checking out the possibility of a week in Paris," Marcus said, nodding in the direction of the silent auction table.

"That one is mine," Blade said.

Jamie narrowed his eyes. "What are you going to do in Paris?"

"A gentleman never kisses and tells," Blade said easily. Then he looked over both shoulders to make sure he could not be overheard. "Daisy wants to go to Paris. I'm going to take her there for our honeymoon."

Marcus bobbled his drink, saving it at the last second before some spilled on the floor. "For the love of God, give me some warning before you say things like that," he said.

"Have you asked her to marry you?" Jamie asked.

"Not in so many words. We still haven't even told Raven or Sophie that we're together. But that's going to change. I'm done hiding it."

"You look happy," Jamie said.

"I am."

"Where is the bride-to-be?" Marcus asked.

"She…" Blade looked around the room. "She went to the kitchen to thank Gertie, but that was a while ago. I need to check," he said, already moving away from his friends.

He opened the kitchen door just as he heard someone yell, "Go get Blade Savick."

It was Cheryl. She was standing by the back door, flashlight in hand. And when she saw him, she motioned with her arm for him to follow her outside. Once the door was shut behind them, she said, "It's Gertie. She's badly hurt. Over there," she added, shining her light.

"Where's Daisy?" he asked. And why was it so dark? He looked up and saw that there was no bulb in the light by the door.

"I don't know," Cheryl said. "I can't find Sophie or Raven, either."

No. No. There was screaming inside his head. But he saw Gertie's body on the ground, and years of training kicked in. Blade grabbed the flashlight from Cheryl's hand. He ran to her side and fell to his knees. "Gertie, we've got you now. It's going to be okay. Can you hear me, Gertie?"

"Blade," the woman said, her voice soft.

Gertie's eyes were closed. He used the light to inspect her for injuries. The right side of her once-white chef's jacket was drenched in blood. He put the flashlight in his mouth and used both hands to rip open the buttons. Saw that she'd been shot in the far right side of the chest. If it had missed a lung or another major organ, it would be a miracle.

"Get Jamie Weathers," he said to Cheryl. "And Marcus Price."

"Already here," he heard Marcus say. "Step back, Blade. Give Jamie some space."

Thank God. They either had followed him to the kitchen or one of the teenagers in the kitchen had been smart enough to go get help. He shifted, making room. "How did you know?" he asked Marcus.

"Spidey sense," Marcus said.

Blade understood. Sometimes you just *knew* that something wasn't right.

"Plus I had overheard Daisy ask the DJ to play Jimmy Buffet's 'Delaney Talks to Statues.' When it started and neither of you were back, I figured something was wrong."

A song about fathers and daughters. Oh, God, where was Raven?

Marcus turned to look at Cheryl. "Go back inside. Keep the workers in the kitchen. I may need to talk to them. Everybody else needs to keep dancing. We're going to need to keep this alley clear."

"Blade." Gertie opened her eyes.

He grabbed for her hand and leaned close. "Help is here. Hang on."

"Dumpster."

"What?"

"Dumpster." Then she closed her eyes.

Down the alley, maybe fifty feet was a large commercial dumpster. He was suddenly too frightened to move. Was she telling him that Raven and Sophie and Daisy were in the dumpster? That they were dead?

He stood up, his legs feeling hollow. Took two steps. The alley in this direction was brighter.

"Blade, what did she say?" Marcus demanded, catching up with him and grabbing his arm.

He shook his friend off. "Dumpster."

Blade got there a step ahead of Marcus. He lifted the lid of the big commercial dumpster, fearing the worst And then he saw his daughter. Whole. Alive. Her eyes more scared than he'd ever seen. There was a gag in her mouth and her wrists and ankles were tied. She was lying on top of bags of rotten-smelling garbage. Next to her was Sophie, looking much the same. "It's okay, girls, we've got you. We're going to get you out of there. He reached in and pulled out Raven. He ripped the gag out of her mouth.

"Daddy," she said.

He wrapped his arms around her tight. "You're okay. You're okay."

Maybe he was reassuring her. Maybe himself. Someone had seen fit to toss his beautiful child into the garbage like a sack of rotten vegetables. He saw Marcus pulling Sophie out.

He ran his hands down Raven's arms and undid the knot in the rope around her wrists. Did the same with her legs. She was whole, and he didn't see any injuries. "Did they hurt you?" he asked.

She shook her head. "Sophie," she said, turning her head.

Marcus had the girl out of the dumpster. Raven reached over and grabbed Sophie's gag and tossed it aside.

"He has my mom," Sophie said, looking at Blade. "You have to find them."

Daisy was still alive. Hope surged. He would hang on to that. "We will, honey," he said.

"Tell us what happened," Marcus said, quickly getting rid of Sophie's bindings.

"A guy came to the back door of the kitchen. He asked for me. When I got to the door, he said that he had information about Jacob Posse that my mom was going to want. I looked outside. I didn't see anybody but him. I asked Raven to go with me. I figured two against one that we were safe." She looked at Raven. "I'm so sorry."

It had been a dumb thing to do, but she was just sixteen. She'd done it for her mom. "Then what happened?" Blade asked. From the corner of his eye, he saw that an ambulance had arrived for Gertie. She was on a gurney, and Jamie was getting in the back to ride with her. That meant that she was still alive.

More police were also in the alley. Squad cars with their lights flashing blocked both ends.

"We got outside, and suddenly, there was a woman. And they both had guns. They told us that they would shoot us if we didn't do exactly what they said. Then

Jacob Posse came walking down the alley. He told me to call my mom on my cell phone and to have her come out the back door. He said to tell her not to tell anyone or that I would die. He said he just wanted to talk to her, but I knew better than that."

"What did you do?"

"I thought if I called my mom that she would tell you, even if I told her not to. She trusts you."

Blade thought his heart might break. Daisy had trusted him, but he hadn't kept her safe.

"I was just about to call her when Gertie came out the back door. I think she was looking for us. She saw what was going on, and she told Posse and the other two to let us go. Posse had a gun, I hadn't seen it until he raised it and he shot her." Tears were running down Sophie's face. "Gertie is dead and it's our fault."

"She's not dead," Blade said. "She's on her way to the hospital, and the best trauma doctor on the West Coast is right next to her. She's not going to die. Tell me about your mom, Sophie. I need you to be very clear. Tell me everything."

"Mom came out. I don't know if she heard the gunshot or she was just looking for us, but whatever the reason, she came out the back door. The man and the woman yanked Raven and I into those doorways down there," Sophie said, pointing. "I don't know where Posse went. It happened so fast. They put their hands over our mouths so we couldn't scream."

"It's okay. What happened next?"

"I'm not exactly sure, because we couldn't see. But I think Mom somehow found Gertie. I heard her say "'Oh, Gertie.' And then I hear Posse say, "'Hello, Daisy.'" Sophie's voice cracked at the end, and she let out a ragged sob.

Raven stepped forward. "That's when the man and the woman dragged us back into the alley, and we saw Posse standing over Daisy and Gertie. Then he said that he would trade us for her. Then something about him punishing her for leaving him and they belonged together. It was hard to keep it straight. Daisy went with him, Dad. She did it to save us."

Of course she had. And Posse intended to punish her. The vision of him hitting her so hard that he knocked her out of her chair almost took him down. He fought to stay focused.

"Did you see any vehicles?" Marcus asked. "Do you have any idea what Posse was driving?"

Raven shook her head. "Posse told them to take care of us. After he left, the two of them started arguing. The man said that Posse meant that they should kill us, that *take care of them* was his code for kill them. The woman said that she wasn't killing any kids. I think the man just wanted to get away as fast as possible. He gave in. They gagged us and tied our wrists and ankles. Then they tossed us in the garbage. We tried kicking the sides, but there was too much garbage."

"You did fine," Marcus said. "It sounds as if you kept a really good head on your shoulders. And you've given us plenty of good information." He looked at Blade. "We're going to lock this county down."

Blade watched his friend walk over to an officer who was standing by the back door. He used the woman's radio. Blade could hear him telling somebody on the other end of the line about Posse, and he heard him requesting assistance from the state police.

"Mom!"

Blade turned. Sheila had gotten past the cops blocking access to the alley and was running toward Raven. He watched the two of them hug.

"She's okay," he said, wrapping his arms around the both of them. "She's okay."

Sheila turned to look at him. "Daisy?"

"Gone. A man named Jacob Posse took her."

"What are you going to do?" she asked, her eyes kind.

"I'm going to find her. I need you to take both Raven and Sophie back to your house."

"Of course."

"The police will need them to make statements. I'll let Marcus know that they'll be with you."

He leaned in and kissed his daughter's forehead. "I love you, Raven."

"I love you, Daddy." She wrapped her arms around him and hugged him tight. "I'm going to be fine. Don't worry about me."

He could not have been more proud of his girl. He turned to Sophie. "You'll be safe at Sheila's house."

"I'm not going," Sophie said. "I'm going to find my mom. I want my mom."

He looked the girl in the eyes. "You said that your mom trusted me. I think that's true. Now I need you to trust me. I'm going to find your mom. And I'm going to bring her home safe." *Please let him not be a liar. Please let him not let Daisy and her daughter down. Please let him not lose Daisy now.* "The best way you can help me be able to focus on finding your mom is for me to know that you and Raven are safe. Please, Sophie. Do this for me. For your mom."

She threw herself into his arms. "Find her. And make sure Posse never hurts her again."

"I intend to." He gave Raven one more hug and handed both girls off to Sheila. "Thank you," he said.

"I'll take good care of them." Sheila had an arm around each girl.

Blade watched the three of them walk off. *Think. Think.* Where would Posse take Daisy? Someplace where he would feel safe. Back to Denver? Blade didn't think so. Too obvious. Posse had thought he wasn't leaving any witnesses behind, but it still felt too risky for him to go back to Denver.

Iowa. Daisy had said that the police had discovered more commune members near Cedar Rapids. It was a long way. Far enough that Posse might feel safe there.

He wouldn't be able to get Daisy onto a commercial aircraft. He could hire a private plane. Marcus and his resources could check for that. If Posse and his accomplices were traveling together, they could drive and spell each other at the wheel. But he didn't think that was likely. They'd split up in the alley and Blade thought Posse would want to keep it that way in order to have Daisy alone. And Posse would have to sleep at some point. A hotel was risky because people might see Daisy or she might figure out a way to signal her distress. Maybe he'd just pull off the road or use a highway rest stop. But that presented a visibility problem. People walking by the car would be able to see into the vehicle.

Not if he was in a truck. A big truck. A semitruck. They could eat, sleep, hell, as disgusting as it was, if Posse had a bucket, he wouldn't even have to let Daisy out to use the restroom.

Daisy had said that Posse drove a semi. That he didn't own one, but rather picked up jobs along the way. That meant he would have been able to get access to one. Blade ran over to where Marcus was talking to a group of police officers. He grabbed his arm. "Posse knows how to drive a semi. Focus on trucks headed east."

Marcus stared at him for just a second. "You're thinking Iowa?"

"Yes."

Marcus nodded, then turned back to the group of cops. Blade didn't wait to hear him pass on the information. He was already running toward his own vehicle.

Marcus caught up to him when he was six feet from his SUV. "What the hell are you doing?" Marcus asked.

"Going after them," Blade said.

"You don't have any authority to stop another vehicle. And if you try to force a truck off the road, you're likely to get shot."

Blade shook his head. "On the interstate, where is every truck required to stop?"

"At the open weigh stations. The state cops will be all over that. Every truck will get searched."

"He won't stop. Not if he has Daisy with him."

"If he blows past, they'll catch him."

"I can't take the chance that they'll let him slip through. I need to be there."

"He's got at least a half hour's head start," Marcus said.

Blade pulled his phone. Pressed a key. "How's Gertie?" he asked when it was answered.

"In surgery. I got her stabilized on the ride to Bigelow Memorial. She's lost a lot of blood, but I'm cautiously optimistic."

Relief flooded Blade's body. He knew Jamie had likely fought like hell to save the woman. "Does she need you tonight?"

"Nope. Out of my hands."

"Then I need you."

"Of course," Jamie said.

"I'll meet you at Rainbow Field. I'll explain everything there."

"On my way. ETA fifteen minutes."

"Thank you," Blade said and hung up.

"You're going to do what you did when you chased Sophie cross-country," Marcus said.

"It worked once," Blade said. And then he told him his plan. What he needed Marcus to do.

"I can make all that happen," Marcus said when he finished. "But I'm also going with you."

"No. I want you here. I could be wrong. Maybe he's not going to Iowa. I need you here to make sure that nothing gets missed here. I need you here to be close if there should be any more trouble for Raven or Sophie. They're at Sheila's. I want somebody parked outside, watching the house."

"Consider it done." Marcus paused. "You don't want me there because you think I'll try to stop you."

Blade looked him in the eye. "I think you'd try. It likely wouldn't end well for one of us."

Marcus gave Blade a rough hug. "Just don't be an idiot, okay?"

Chapter 21

Daisy was freezing. And her head was pounding. For the last forty minutes, Jacob had lectured her nonstop on her many mistakes, starting with her not being appreciative enough of him while she lived in Denver and ending with all the inconvenience she'd caused him when he'd had to chase her to Knoware. She huddled against the door of the truck cab and stared at the inside temperature indicator, which said fifty-six.

He was wearing a flannel shirt and an insulated vest. Certainly more than a strapless gown. But she wasn't asking him for heat. She wasn't asking him for anything.

Not that he seemed to care. And not that it seemed to slow his diatribe down.

"You didn't really think I'd let you leave me, did you? Nobody leaves Jacob Posse. I leave people. Not the other way around."

How could she have ever thought this man was sane? Because he was a consummate actor. But now the play had closed, and backstage, he was letting it all hang out.

"You know technology is a wonderful thing," he said. "Your daughter sends a message to her friend. We hack into that kid's computer, gets your kid's IP address, and in seconds, we've got you within a fifteen-mile radius. From there, it wasn't hard to find you. Everybody was talking about the woman who started the Remember This campaign."

She had known it would be hard to disappear. Had hoped that he'd just forget about her once she wasn't so easily within reach.

"Where we're going, there aren't any computers, no technology inviting Big Brother in to snoop on our lives. Off. The. Grid." He turned to look at her. "I want sons. Three of them. You're going to give me sons. I've always thought you were an excellent mother. I want that for my children."

She would die first. She would not be able to bear having any responsibility for bringing more of his madness into the world.

Maybe it showed on her face because the next thing she knew, he was lunging across the cab and grabbing her by the throat. He choked her. She clawed at his hand, trying to push him away. But he was enraged, and her strength was no match for his.

It was only when the truck's tires hit the shoulder rumble strips that he let go and focused on bringing the truck back onto the road. She sucked in air. He was going to kill her. Maybe not today or tomorrow, but at some point, she wouldn't be able to hide her disgust with him and he would kill her in response.

He'd been an actor and fooled her. Maybe it was time to reverse the roles. Sophie was a heck of an actress. Maybe she'd gotten some of that talent from her. She licked her lips.

"I want your children, Jacob. That would be my privilege."

He turned his head so fast she was surprised he didn't hurt himself. "Do you mean that, Daisy?"

Stay in character. Be a simpering fool. Feed his ego. "I do. I've missed you since I left Denver. I was going to call you, but I've been so busy at work."

"You made a fool out of me," he said. "My friends laughed at me."

"I'm sorry. Were those people with you tonight your friends?"

"Followers. My stepsister, Michelle, and her husband, Trevor."

"I saw them today. Watching me."

"They've been watching you for weeks. Ever since I figured out you were in that little hole of a town."

"Did you do something to my car, that night I was at the ice cream shop? Did you break into my house?"

"That was Trevor. I told him to shake you up a little."

"Did he break into those businesses? Did he steal from them?"

"I don't know what you're talking about."

Maybe it had been Trevor. Maybe someone else. None of that mattered now.

"He made a mistake today when you saw him," Jacob said. "I wondered if you'd recognized him. That's when we decided it had to be tonight."

"Where would I have seen him before?"

"When we went to the theater in Denver. They were

there that night, too. They had tickets just down the aisle from us."

If only she'd have figured that out earlier. She'd have known it was too much of a coincidence. She could have been watching for Jacob. Could have warned Sophie. Dear sweet Sophie. "My daughter is safe, right?" He'd said she was just going to be detained, but how could she trust that he'd told her the truth. "I'm going to need proof." Sophie had to be scared to death to see her mom taken that way.

"I don't have to give you proof of anything," Jacob said.

"I could never raise another child if I didn't know that Sophie was safe."

Jacob sighed. "Fine. I'll get you your proof."

It didn't mean he hadn't lied. But she had to stay hopeful, had to believe that Sophie and Raven were both okay. "Where are we headed?" she asked. It was time to start figuring a way out of this.

"You don't need to know. Just settle in."

"I'm going to need to stop soon to use the restroom."

"I'll tell you when we're going to stop." Then he reached for the radio and turned it up.

She closed her eyes. She just had to outlast him. He'd get tired eventually.

Blade stopped at his apartment on his way to Rainbow Field. He quickly took off his suit and pulled on jeans and a sweater. Dress shoes were replaced with work boots. He grabbed a heavy coat and gloves. Then he unlocked the gun safe that he kept on the top shelf of his closest and removed the weapon. He wasn't as good with a gun as Marcus, but he regularly went to the shooting range with his friend.

He wouldn't shoot his foot off and, if necessary, he wouldn't hesitate to use it on Posse. The man had intended for his daughter and Sophie to be killed. He'd taken Daisy.

Marcus had warned him not to be an idiot. He wouldn't be. But he also wouldn't be a fool. He was going to take Posse down, one way or another.

Posse would not kill Daisy. That thought was the only thing keeping him from losing his mind right now. But he could hurt her, scare her, maybe even successfully hide her for a period of time. Blade had waited his whole life for someone like Daisy. He wasn't going to lose her now or let her suffer in any way if he could help it.

He left his apartment less than five minutes after arriving. Still, by the time he got to Rainbow Field, he saw that Jamie's vehicle was parked in the dimly lit lot and that his friend was already getting the plane ready for flight. Before he got out of his SUV, he leaned over to reach his glove compartment. He pulled out a map of Washington State and stuffed it into his coat pocket. Cell phones and GPS were great, but sometimes an old-fashioned paper map was really helpful.

"How you holding up?" Jamie asked as Blade approached.

"I'm okay," he said. "Any change on Gertie?"

"I got a report from the operating room. The surgeon was about to close. Everything looks good. She needed four units of blood. She'll be monitored closely for the next twenty-four hours. If she makes it through that, the chances of recovery are excellent."

One thing was going right. Actually, two things.

Gertie would make it and the girls were safe at Sheila's house. Now all he had to do was find Daisy. "I think Posse might be driving a semitruck, headed east toward the Midwest. I think he'll stay off the main highway if he can, but through this stretch," Blade said, holding up his phone where he'd pulled up a map of the State of Washington, "there really isn't a good choice. There's a weigh station right there. Marcus will make contact and let them know that every truck needs to be carefully searched. If any truck blows through, the police will run them down. When they do, I want to be there. That's where you come in. I need you to get me to the closest airfield to that weigh station. Marcus is going to get me a ride from there."

"You're putting an awful lot of stock into a handful of assumptions. That they're headed east. That they'll be in a truck. That this is the route." Jamie ticked the list off on his fingers.

"Everything that Daisy told me about Posse leads me down this path. I know I could be wrong. But I have to do something."

Jamie took out his own phone and pushed keys. Finally, he looked up. "The closest airfield, a small one, is thirty minutes north."

"I guess that will have to do," Blade said.

They had been driving for almost two hours. Daisy did not know this part of the country well enough to know what road they were on, and if there had been a sign, she'd missed it. It was impossible to tell the direction they were traveling. The only thing she was confident of was that it wasn't west—they'd have been in the ocean by now. Guessed it was north or east, given that they'd been in the mountains now for at least forty minutes. They'd met just a handful of cars coming from the other direction. No one had passed them.

She felt very alone.

Jacob showed no signs of tiring. He had, fortunately, stopped talking.

She was so cold that her teeth were chattering. She had her jaw clenched, trying to make them stop, not wanting Jacob to hear, not wanting to give him the satisfaction of knowing that she was cold. He was keeping the heat down on purpose, she decided, after she'd seen him put on his gloves about halfway through the trip. She suspected the steering wheel was cold—everything else in the truck was.

They'd be looking for her. But the farther she got from Knoware, the less hopeful she felt. She had no cell phone for them to track. Jacob did. Twenty minutes into the trip, he'd pulled a cell phone from his pocket and dialed a number. He said two words. "Well?" at the beginning and "Later," at the end.

But he'd seemed satisfied.

She was less so. His phone was no doubt a burner, certainly not purchased under his real name. If Jacob Posse even was his real name. She wasn't sure about anything anymore.

Except that her heart was breaking over losing Blade. She loved him. Had been afraid to say it because it would lead them down a path to a conversation that she hadn't been ready to have.

Stupid, stupid, stupid. She'd wasted precious time.

Her excuse that she couldn't throw one more change at Sophie had been just that—an excuse. Because she'd been frightened that maybe she was making a mistake again, that Blade wasn't as wonderful as she thought.

And now he was out there in the dark somewhere, worrying about her, looking for her. And it felt terrible to admit, but she had a sinking feeling that it wasn't going to work. Jacob would take her somewhere and make her his prisoner. It could be years before she finally escaped.

Blade would have moved on. The world would have changed.

Sophie would grow up. How could one simple sentence bring such immense sadness and joy? Yes, she would miss seeing it. But Sophie would have a life. Daisy would never regret trading herself for Sophie and Raven. She'd brought Jacob into their lives. She should pay the price for that, not her daughter.

Blade got out of the plane. There was a state police car waiting two hundred yards from them, and he hurried toward it.

"Blade Savick," he said, from thirty feet.

"Trooper Hogan." The man, maybe just a few years older than Blade, extended a hand. "How was the flight?"

"Fine." Blade didn't want to be rude, but he wasn't interested in small talk. "Any feedback from the weigh station?" he asked.

"No unusual incidences. Every truck has pulled over as required. Every vehicle has been searched. Every driver has been compared against the photo of Jacob Posse that was circulated to me and all other law-enforcement personnel in six states."

"No trucks have circumvented the stop?" Blade asked.

"None," the trooper said.

The thought that he'd been wrong was heavy on his

heart. It had now been almost two hours since Daisy had been taken from the alley. She could be anywhere.

His cell vibrated in his pocket. When he looked at the number, he saw that it was Marcus. He immediately thought of Raven and Sophie. "Everything okay?" he answered.

"We've picked up Posse's two accomplices," Marcus said.

The ones who had thrown his daughter away like a sack of garbage. "Tell me they resisted arrest."

"No. We got a lucky break. Did Daisy tell you about the hang-up calls on her work phone?"

"No."

"No matter. Suffice it to say that she had a bunch of hang-up calls. We discussed it, and she asked her tech people to find the number. She gave them my name to contact if they couldn't reach her. They called with a number. We were able to locate the phone. It belonged to the man, who was with his wife at a motel outside of Knoware, laying low."

"Did they tell you where Posse is headed?"

"Claim they don't know. But they really wanted to make sure that they weren't taking the fall for shooting Gertie. They confirmed the girls' statements that it was Posse."

"Okay." He supposed it was good news, but Marcus seemed overexcited about it. "Anything else?"

"Yeah. We saw an incoming call that came in about an hour ago on the guy's phone. He said it was from Posse. We've successfully traced the location of Posse's phone."

Blade could feel his heart start to beat faster. "Tell me."

"He's on Blue Turtle Pass, headed east."

"Hang on." Blade yanked the map from his coat pocket and spread it out across the hood of the police car. Trooper Hogan handed him a flashlight off his utility belt. Posse was either crazier or more cunning than Blade had anticipated. He was traveling back roads through the mountains, roads that were certainly not built for semi-truck traffic. Roads that weren't guaranteed to be plowed. But if he had chains on his truck and he was damn lucky, he might make it.

It took him less than a minute to figure it out. Damn. Posse had already passed their location. "I've got the location," he told Marcus.

"We're scrambling some resources right now to have our folks available to meet him when he crosses Interstate 90."

It made sense. But that left Daisy in a dangerous situation longer. If Posse didn't hurt her intentionally, he might just send her sliding over a mountain pass to her death.

"What's going on?" Jamie asked from behind him.

Blade brought him up-to-date and gave him a chance to study the map. Then he said, "I'm thinking of the summer after high school graduation. Travis Ridge."

Trooper Hogan frowned at him, clearly puzzled. But Jamie smiled. Looked at the map again. "Okay," he said.

Blade folded his map and stepped away from the car. "We're sorry to have wasted your time. We'll just be getting back now."

He and Blade wasted no time in getting back to the plane. Jamie had it in the air in less than five minutes. Neither of them spoke.

Finally, Blade said, "I don't want you to take any chances. This isn't your fight."

"He shot Gertie, left her for dead," Jamie said, not

looking at Blade. He was focused on flying. "Scared the hell out of two teenage girls. Abducted a woman that my friend intends to marry. It is definitely my fight. It's everybody's fight."

Blade swallowed hard. "How much farther?"

"Five minutes, tops. It's going to get a little dicey now."

Chapter 22

Dicey, as in they were going to have to get low enough to see the lights on the road, but avoid clipping their wings on the surrounding mountains. Blade studied the ground below them.

"There," he said, pointing at the lone set of lights.

Jamie said nothing, just took the plane a little lower. He was cutting way back on speed. The bright moonlight and the white snow helped visibility, but a mountain was a dark place.

Lower. Lower.

Looking. Judging.

Finally, he turned to Blade. "Hang on."

And less than a minute later, the wheels touched down on the highway that thankfully had been plowed since the last snowstorm. It was hard and rough and by the time the plane skidded to a stop crossways on the highway, with its nose and front wheels encased in the packed snow alongside the road, Blade thought some of the fillings in his teeth had shaken loose.

He sucked in a breath. He'd been holding his. "Amazing," he said.

"Better than Travis Ridge?" Jamie asked, as if it had been no big deal.

They'd been eighteen and fearless then. And there hadn't been any snow on that highway. "Good thing Marcus isn't here," Blade said. That night, their friend, who'd been in the back seat while Jamie flew and Blade rode shotgun, had thrown up twice once they were on the ground.

"Good thing," Jamie agreed. "We're about five miles down the road. I want to give him a nice long time to put on the brakes so I'm going to jog up ahead and light some flares."

That was a good idea, assuming Posse wasn't truly a crazy bastard and rather than stopping, would try to plow through the plane parked in the middle of the road.

"The man probably doesn't have a death wish," Jamie said, proving that he was tracking with what Blade was thinking.

"He's a con artist. He'll think he can talk his way out of most anything," Blade said. "I think we have to assume that if he's been watching Daisy, he might recognize me. You should stand by the plane. Make him get out of the truck. I'm going to be over there," Blade said, pointing to some tree cover. "I'll make sure it's him."

"Then what?"

"Then I'm going to take him out."

Daisy saw the lights of the low-flying plane, and it made her think of how she and Blade had chased after

Sophie. Flashes of the day came back to her. Blade silently warning his friend not to push her into conversation. Him buying her a candy bar when he could see that she was just about to fall over. His face when he came to find her to tell her that Sophie was outside pumping gas.

From the beginning, he'd been a rock.

Exactly what his coworkers counted on him being. Cool. Calm. Focused.

Exactly what she counted on him being. Kind. Caring. Loving.

She would hold on to those memories and hope that they got her through the long days ahead. And she would look for her chance to escape. Always look.

She jumped when Jacob uttered a curse under his breath. Then saw the flare. What the heck. Jacob was slowing down. They rounded the next curve. Another flare. And then a hundred yards out, she saw it.

A plane. A man standing in front of it, waving his arms.

It was Jamie Weathers.

Her heart was beating so hard and so fast that it would be a miracle if Jacob didn't hear it. But she didn't move a muscle. Stayed curled up next to the door, as if she was half-asleep.

If Jamie was here, then Blade was nearby. He'd come. He'd found a way.

Jacob brought the truck to a stop. They were now less than fifty yards, half a football field away. He turned to her. "Stay in the truck. If you don't, I'll find you and I'll kill you."

"I don't think I'd get very far dressed like this," she said.

"You always were a sensible woman." Jacob reached

down toward his right ankle. From inside his work boot, he pulled out a gun. He slipped it into his coat pocket. "Remember," he said, "if you make any noise, this guy dies and that'll be on your conscience."

Right. It certainly wouldn't be Jacob's fault.

He got out of the truck and walked toward Jamie. He had one hand in his pocket. Daisy wanted to scream out a warning, but she was afraid that might spook Jacob and he would shoot. She thought about what Blade had said about Jamie. That he was supersmart. Surely he was anticipating that Jacob would be armed.

Blade lay on his stomach in the trees and waited for Posse to make his move. From his vantage, he could not see into the cab of the truck. But he knew Daisy was in there. He could just feel that she was close.

Finally, he saw the door of the truck open and a man step down. It was Posse. Blade had studied that face over the last week. He walked toward Jamie with one hand in his pocket. Blade resisted the urge to run over to the truck, to pull Daisy to safety. He would take care of Posse first.

"Boy, am I glad to see you, mister," Jamie said, his voice carrying in the still night. "I had engine trouble and had to ditch my plane."

"That's too bad," Posse said. "But unfortunately, I'm in a bit of a hurry and you're going to need to move it to the side so that I can pass."

"If only I could," Jamie said. "The damn thing is stuck."

"You either get it out of my way or I will," Posse said.

"I'm not sure—"

"Shut up," Posse said. "And move over there," he said,

pointing toward the side. "If you're lucky, somebody will come along and pick you up."

Posse intended to push the plane out of his way, literally off the mountain. Blade sure as hell wasn't going to let that happen.

"Listen, man. There's no need to do something crazy," Jamie said.

"Move or I'm going to use the gun I have in my pocket, and your biggest worry is not going to be about your plane."

Jamie stepped to the side, his hands in the air.

Posse took four steps. Then turned. Pulled the gun. Aimed it at Jamie. "Can't leave any witnesses. You under—"

Blade charged him. Leading with his shoulder, he hit him with a flying tackle that would have made his high school football coach proud. The two of them rolled, landing, unfortunately, with Posse on top. He got in two good punches before Blade managed to scramble free. Blade hit him hard. Once. Twice. Posse fell to his knees. Blade yanked him up and hit him again.

"That's for knocking Daisy out of her chair," he said.

He hit him again. "That's for our daughters."

He pulled his fist back, but didn't land the punch because Jamie was pulling him back. "That's enough."

"He was going to shoot you," sputtered Blade. Damn, his nose was bleeding.

"But he didn't. You saved me, like I knew you would. Somebody here wants to say thank you, as well." Jamie stepped aside. "I've already assured her the girls are just fine."

Daisy, beautiful Daisy, wearing Jamie's big coat, was standing fifteen feet away. "Watch him," Blade mumbled.

He withdrew his own weapon from the waistband of his jeans and handed it to Jamie.

Then he ran and scooped Daisy up. He held her tight and kissed her hard. "Did he hurt you?"

"No," she said. She held his face in her hands. "Your poor face. You're bleeding."

"The bastard landed a couple. No worries. You're safe. That's all that matters." And then, on a moonlit night on a mountain pass, he fell to one knee. "Daisy Rambler, will you marry me?"

She knelt. "Sophie said that she thought you could take Jacob. She was right. And she was also right when she told me that I could trust you. I love you, Blade. I'm sorry for the trouble I've brought to your life, but if you still want me after all that, then yes, yes, I will marry you. Tomorrow, next week, any day you pick."

He stood and pulled her up with him. "We have to make sure it's a day that Gertie's free to cater the reception."

"Is she..." Her voice trailed off.

"She's going to be okay. It's all going to be okay." He turned.

Jamie had the gun aimed at Posse and was holding his cell phone up to his ear. He finished the call. "That was Marcus. He's already on his way. After he talked to Trooper Hogan who told him we were talking about Travis Ridge, he knew what we were up to."

"I want to go home," Daisy said. "I need to see Sophie. See for myself that she's safe."

He handed her his cell phone. "I'll get you there, I promise. For now, call her."

"Can I tell her our news?" she asked. "She'll want to tell Raven, and you probably want a chance to do that."

He smiled. "That's okay. She'll understand and she'll be superhappy. Go make your call."

It took time for everything to get sorted out. Daisy didn't really mind the wait. Her conversation with Sophie had given her peace. Both girls were doing fine at Sheila's and Sophie had said she was thrilled about the proposal.

She, Blade and Jamie sat in the cab of the truck, where they turned the heater on nice and high. From that vantage, they had a clear view of Jacob who had been secured to a tree.

It made Daisy happy to think that he was probably a little chilled.

At one point, Jamie turned to Blade, studied his bruised hand. "You could have just shot him."

He shook his head. "Nope. I wanted him to know what it felt like to have somebody hit you so hard that you fell down. I wanted it to hurt. I want him to rot in jail and maybe get his ass kicked there a few times, too."

She reached over and stroked his battered hand. "My hero," she said, her voice cracking.

"Nobody pushes my girl around," he teased. "This should get me out of dishes for, what, maybe a week or two?"

"For sure," she said. She settled back to wait. Everyone she loved was safe. The rest would work out.

Once Marcus arrived and arrested Jacob, it didn't take long to get him bundled into the back seat of the police vehicle and headed on down the mountain. The three of them had to continue to wait. For two tow trucks. One to tow the semi and one to tow the plane. When the vehicles finally arrived, Daisy was relieved to see that they'd brought a black SUV with them. It would make for a more comfortable ride home.

Once they were on their way, Jamie drove and Blade sat in the back with her. There were some jokes about him feeling like he was their dad and chaperoning them on their first date. Blade didn't seem to mind. It was as if both could not bear to be separated. She thought it was especially nice when she curled up with her head on Blade's shoulder and closed her eyes.

She woke up when they arrived at Rainbow Field. "I'm going to go check on Gertie," Jamie said, letting them off at Blade's SUV.

Even though she still had on Jaime's jacket, she shivered when she got into Blade's cold vehicle. "I am never wearing a strapless gown again. They are useless."

"Oh, I disagree," he said. "I really like that dress. You were the most beautiful woman there tonight." He paused. "I planned on bidding on the Paris trip. I wanted to win it and surprise you."

He knew how to warm her up. "I don't need Paris." If she had Blade and Sophie, that was more than enough.

"We'll see," he said. "Let's go get your daughter."

"It's late."

"They'll be up," he said.

He was right. Every light in Sheila's house was on. Sheila opened the door at their knock. She hugged Blade first, then Daisy. "I hear congratulations are in order. Very happy for the both of you."

Then Sophie was in Daisy's arms and all was right with the world. "Let's go home, honey," Daisy said. She turned to Sheila. "Thank you for watching over her. I'm grateful."

"We're in this together now," Sheila said, giving Daisy

another quick hug. Then the two moms stood there and watched their daughters hug so tight it was lucky that no one broke a rib.

"Your house?" Blade asked once they were in the car.

There was no reason they couldn't go back home. "I think Sophie should get to sleep in her own bed."

"Fair enough," he said.

"Is it really over, Mom?" Sophie asked as they pulled into their driveway.

"Yes. Marcus said that he's confident that Jacob will spend a long time in prison. Attempted murder. Kidnapping. Assorted other charges. We don't have to worry about him."

Blade walked them to the door, but he didn't step inside.

"What's wrong?" Daisy asked.

"I just figured the two of you might need a night to yourselves."

"I was really hoping you'd stay," Daisy said.

"Yes," Sophie said, and did a fist pump in the air. Then she kissed her mother good-night and gave Blade a quick hug before almost running up the stairs to her room.

"You have to be tired," he said.

"Not that tired. Come on." She took his hand. "You know my preference for beds."

* * * * *

Look for more books in Beverly Long's
Heroes of the Pacific Northwest series
coming soon from Harlequin Romantic Suspense!

WE HOPE YOU ENJOYED
THIS BOOK FROM

⬡ HARLEQUIN
ROMANTIC
SUSPENSE

Danger. Passion. Drama

These heart-racing page-turners will keep you guessing to the very end. Experience the thrill of unexpected plot twists and irresistible chemistry.

4 NEW BOOKS AVAILABLE EVERY MONTH!

#2151 COLTON 911: FORGED IN FIRE
Colton 911: Chicago
by Linda Warren

While Carter Finch is trying to investigate a potential forgery, Lila Colton's art gallery is set on fire. As a result, Lila becomes the main suspect. Carter stays by her side and they're drawn into multiple mysteries that threaten a possible future they could have together...

#2152 A COLTON INTERNAL AFFAIR
The Coltons of Grave Gulch
by Jennifer D. Bokal

Police officer Grace Colton is being investigated for unlawful use of force. Internal Affairs Investigator Camden Kingsley is charged with finding out what happened—but there's more to this case than meets the eye...and romance is the last thing either of them expected.

#2153 STALKED IN SILVER VALLEY
Silver Valley P.D.
by Geri Krotow

Former FBI and current undercover agent Luther Darby needs linguist Kit Danilenko's talents to bring down Russian Organized Crime in Silver Valley, and Kit needs Luther's law enforcement expertise. Neither wants any part of their sizzling attraction, especially when it becomes a liability against the two most powerful ROC operatives.

#2154 COLD CASE WITNESS
by Melinda Di Lorenzo

When Warren Wright is caught witnessing several armed men unearthing a body, he has no choice but to run or be killed. His flight leads him to seek cover, and he inadvertently draws Jeannette Renfrew into his escape plan. The two of them must work together to solve a mystery with connections to Warren's past.

"Kit, you misunderstood me. Let me try again."

He saw her shake her head vigorously in his peripheral
vision. If he could grab her hand, look her in the eyes, he
would. So that she'd see his sincerity. But they'd started
to climb and the highway had gone down to two lanes,
winding around the first cluster of mountain foothills.

"No need. Just take me back home." This version of
Kit was not the woman who'd greeted him this morning.
Great, just great. It'd taken him, what, fifteen minutes to
make mincemeat of her self-confidence? He felt like the
lowest bird on the food chain, unable to escape the raptor
that was his big mouth.

"I'm not taking you home, Kit. We're going on this mission, together. I'm sorry if I pushed too hard on your history—it's none of my business. None of it." He needed to hear the words as much as say them. The reminder that she was a mob operative's spouse, albeit an ex, would keep him from seeing her as anything but his work colleague.

She was nothing like Evalina.

The memory of how the ROC mob honcho's wife had used him, how stupidly he'd fallen for her charms, made his self-disgust all the greater. It was one thing that he'd allowed himself to be duped and his heart dragged through the ROC crap. It was another to cause Kit, a true victim of her circumstances, any pain.

"Are you sure you can trust me, Luther?"

Don't miss
Stalked in Silver Valley *by Geri Krotow,*
available October 2021 wherever
Harlequin Romantic Suspense
books and ebooks are sold.

Harlequin.com